A Merry
MONTGOMERY
Christmas

Cover Design: Kari March Designs

Edits: Jillian Rivera

## PRAISE FOR SAMANTHA CHASE

"If you can't get enough of stories that get inside your heart and soul and stay there long after you've read the last page, then Samantha Chase is for you!"

-*NY Times & USA Today Bestselling Author* **Melanie Shawn**

"A fun, flirty, sweet romance filled with romance and character growth and a perfect happily ever after."

-*NY Times & USA Today Bestselling Author* **Carly Phillips**

"Samantha Chase writes my kind of happily ever after!"

-*NY Times & USA Today Bestselling Author* **Erin Nicholas**

"The openness between the lovers is refreshing, and their interactions are a balanced blend of sweet and spice. The planets may not have aligned, but the elements of this winning romance are definitely in sync."

- ***Publishers Weekly, STARRED review***

"A true romantic delight, *A Sky Full of Stars* is one of the top gems of romance this year."

- ***Night Owl Reviews, TOP PICK***

"Great writing, a winsome ensemble, and the perfect blend of heart and sass."

# PROLOGUE

## THE DAY BEFORE THANKSGIVING...

"I HATE TO SAY IT, but it looks like we just guaranteed that we won't be home for the holidays."

William Montgomery frowned at his eldest son, Mac. "That's not necessarily true. There's still a chance..."

"Dad, please," Mac quietly interrupted while rubbing his temple. "J.F. Matheson has been courting this merger for the last nine months and you decided last week to go ahead with it. You had to realize this wasn't going to happen overnight."

"Well...I knew it wouldn't happen quickly, but I don't believe we need to throw in the towel on the holidays just yet," William argued lightly. Only...he wasn't quite sure he believed his own words. "Let's just say—worst case scenario —we put in seven-day weeks from now through Christmas Eve. It's possible that..."

"No," his middle son Jason chimed in. "No way. Maggie and I are committed to several holiday parties and events, we've got kids coming home from college, and Nicholas and Carson are both performing in the holiday concert at school.

No can do, Dad. We have a lot to do before we all head to the retreat."

"Same here," Mac agreed. "Gina's been talking a lot about me cutting back now that the kids are older so we can travel. She has a show at the Charlotte gallery that's going to be at least three nights, and I'm not missing it. Her mother's coming in for it and joining us all at the retreat for Christmas, so..."

The groan was out before William could stop it. "The holidays are supposed to be a joyous time. You know that there is nothing *joyous* about spending time with Barb."

Fortunately, Mac snickered. "Still, Gina's been very patient with the extra hours I put in over the summer while handling the Whitley account. The holidays are important to her—to us—and I'm not going to tell her they're canceled because of poor timing on your part."

"I wouldn't say it was poor timing..."

But it was.

"Lucas," he said to his youngest son. "Back me up here. Can we pull this off before Christmas with only a handful of weekends or not?"

The weary sigh Lucas began with wasn't a good sign. "Honestly? I don't think it's possible even if we went 24/7 from now through Christmas Eve to get it all done. Sorry."

Leaning back in his chair, William closed his eyes and fought the urge to sigh as well. There was a time when decisions like this came easily to him. He ran this company like a well-oiled machine and never missed a birthday, an anniversary, a school play, and certainly not a major holiday.

Until now.

No doubt everyone was going to be upset with him, but what choice did he have?

"Is Lily going to make it home this year?" Jason asked his brother.

Lucas' smile said it all. "She's surprising Emma, and honestly, I can't wait to see her."

"She's been away for almost a year," William said with a small laugh. "Of course you miss her! We all do! That's my first grandchild and as proud as I am of her, I'm going to have to talk to her about staying away for so long!"

"Dad..."

"I know, I know...I'll say it with love," he promised. "We all know she loves dancing and she's incredibly talented, but she still needs to come home and see her family. I'll bet Emma's going to burst into tears when she sees her."

"Last night I caught her crying while holding Lily's first recital portrait," Lucas told them. "I'm telling you; it nearly broke my heart. I almost caved and told her."

"When exactly is she coming home?" Mac asked.

"The eighteenth," Lucas replied. "And I want to be there to greet her too."

"You will," William said firmly. "You will. We'll just have to come up with a plan for a new timeline and how we'll get it all done."

There was a knock on the office door and William smiled warmly when Noah Wylder—one of their up-and-coming junior executives—tentatively stepped into the room.

"Noah! What can I do for you?" William asked.

"Sorry to interrupt, but I have those breakdowns you asked for on the Mathesons branches." Handing William several folders, Noah nodded before taking a step back. "They have double the locations that Montgomerys does, but they're not all particularly profitable. Several of them are being mismanaged and could really benefit from having members of our team go in and restructure things."

The four Montgomerys simply stared at him for a moment before he continued.

"If I may," he went on, "I would recommend bringing in the heads of all the locations—Mathesons and Montgomerys—and taking several days to feel things out and discuss a strategy so everyone knows where they stand and what's going to be expected moving forward. We'll want to reassure them we're looking to work with them, not remove them."

William was beyond impressed. There were several members of his executive team that never took this kind of initiative, but he knew Noah was young and hungry. There wasn't a doubt in his mind that one day Noah would be sitting at the conference table with the other top-tier people; this project would simply be a launching board for him.

"And when do you think we should do this?" William asked out of sheer curiosity.

"With Thanksgiving being tomorrow and then the long holiday weekend, there isn't time to start putting a plan into action. However, maybe getting our people together and having a tentative agenda in place that we can share with Matheson about how exciting things are coming after the new year. No need to put anyone on the defensive or make them feel like we're pressuring them right before the holidays."

William nodded. "Go on."

"Then, come January, we could possibly rent one of those corporate retreat places," Noah went on. "Of course it's hard to say if they'd be available on such short notice, but if you can find a place that offers privacy, comfort, and enough rooms for two dozen or so people, I'd say to aim for maybe the first week of January so there's still a sense of festiveness in the air. If what we're doing is positive, it kicks off the year on a high note."

Looking at his sons, William could tell they were all impressed as well.

"Thank you, Noah. I'll take all of this into consideration," William said and then waited until Noah was gone and the door was closed before he said anything. "Well? What do you think? Do you think we can realistically get away with working for a few days while everyone's together at the retreat to put into this and then we can start fresh in the new year?"

His sons all looked at one another before responding.

Mac spoke first.

"Dad, as good as this all sounds, I don't see Mom agreeing to this. Or Aunt Janice. Or Aunt Eliza. Or..."

William held up a hand to stop him. "I get it. You think there's going to be some pushback, but just leave that to me. It's not often that we get all of the Montgomerys together and not work. This time we'll at least all be together under one roof. Besides, a few hours a day where we're working is completely doable."

Not one of his sons looked convinced.

That was okay, though. William was used to smoothing things over and making sure everything worked out when no one else thought they would.

And not just in business.

It had been many years since his matchmaking days, but he wasn't opposed to reminding his family of it if he got any pushback about work. After all, most of them owed their years of wedded bliss to him and his uncanny ability to find them all their perfect match. So, if he had to boldly reminisce about how crafty he was and how lucky they all were to be married to such wonderful people, he'd do it.

Hell, he'd enjoy reminding them!

And that suddenly gave him an idea...

Standing, he smiled at his sons. "Boys, if you'll excuse me, I need to get my assistant in the loop on what needs to happen starting next week."

"But...wait," Jason began, "are we really planning on working while at the retreat?"

"I think if we put all our focus on this merger leading up to the holiday trip, we can get away with maybe working two hours a day tops while we're all together. I'll have Rose get in touch with all your cousins so we're all on the same page."

"Dad..."

"Christmas is going to be a massive celebration this year!" he announced with a broad smile. "Every Montgomery will be under the same roof—aunts, uncles, cousins, siblings, grandchildren—fifty-four of us! Believe me, we'll all be looking for a little peace and quiet away from the festivities. You'll be thanking me when all is said and done!"

"Somehow I doubt that," Mac murmured, but William didn't let it deter him.

"Keep working on what you're doing and I'll see you all tomorrow for Thanksgiving!"

And with a bit of pep in his step, William strode out of the office and straight to his assistant. "Rose, I've got a top-secret project for you!"

# ONE
## WILLIAM & MONICA
### "IT'S NICE TO SEE I HAVEN'T LOST MY TOUCH."

"THERE'S MY BEAUTIFUL BRIDE," William announced as he walked in the door carrying a bouquet of purple irises. He knew they were his wife's favorite and considering he was about to put a monkey wrench in her well-planned holiday retreat, he knew he was going to have to do his best to dazzle her a bit. Kissing her on the cheek, he handed her the bouquet. "Beautiful flowers for a beautiful woman."

"Oh, aren't you sweet," Monica said before kissing him in return. "Although...I'm not sure I can still be called a bride after almost fifty years of marriage."

"Nonsense," he told her. "You'll always be my bride and you're certainly always beautiful."

"Such a way with words, you wonderful man," she cooed. "And look how lovely these are! I need to get them in water right away." She turned and walked toward the kitchen, and William followed. For several minutes, she fussed with the flowers and hummed appreciatively until they were perfect. Then she turned and gave him a knowing smile. "Now why don't you tell me what you're buttering me up for?"

"Me?" he asked incredulously. "Why would you even say that?"

With a soft sigh, she shook her head, making her silver hair swing slightly. "William, the only time you get me purple irises is when there's something you know is going to upset me. It's the night before Thanksgiving and I have a ton of work to do before everyone gets here tomorrow, so please, spare me the dramatics and just tell me what's going on."

After so many years of marriage, it would be crazy to think his wife didn't know all his secrets, so even as his shoulders sagged slightly, he said, "Fine. We've hit a snag with the merger, and it means we may have to spend some of the time at the retreat working."

Then he waited for the fallout.

"Is that all?" Monica asked as she waved him off. "Honestly, William, everyone knew that was going to happen anyway. But thank you for being willing to admit to it beforehand."

"Wait, so you..."

She stepped in close and gently patted his cheek. "If there are more than two Montgomerys together anywhere, work is going to be discussed. That's a given. Considering there are going to be over fifty of us at the retreat house, I knew it was definitely going to happen."

"Well...just because you knew it and are seemingly okay with it doesn't mean everyone else is going to be," he argued lightly.

"Janice and I talked about it already and neither of us minds. We're going to have such a wonderful time with all the grandkids that we probably wouldn't have even noticed if all of you locked yourselves away in..." She paused. "Hmm...I don't believe there's a spot that is going to be particularly conducive to what you're looking to do, William."

"How is that even possible?" he let out a small laugh. "That place can sleep 80 people, Monica! Surely there's a spot where a dozen of us can sit and talk without interruptions!"

She made a non-committal sound. "I booked the house as a place where everyone could stay under one roof as a family. There are no conference rooms or boardrooms, dear. You're going to have to be flexible."

"I knew I should have paid more attention to the brochure you were waving around..."

"If you time it right, you might get time in the dining room. I'm sure Janice, Eliza, and I can keep the kids occupied in the pool or the game room or even the theater room each morning to give you the time you need." Another pause. "Who is going to be sitting in on these meetings?"

Walking over to their kitchen table, William sat. "Obviously myself, Mac, Jason, and Lucas."

"Naturally," she said as she sat down beside him.

"Robert will—undoubtedly—try to take the lead on this, but I'm not going to let him."

All his wife did was nod.

"Then there's Zach, Ryder, Summer, and Ethan," he went on. "Gabriella may want to sit in out of curiosity, but I'm sure Zach can fill her in if she really wants to know."

"And what about James?"

"James isn't involved in this part of the business. He's amazing with designing the grounds at all our locations, but he won't need to sit in on these meetings."

"Oh? You're not going to go to all these Mathesons locations and freshen things up?" Monica asked.

"Um..."

She smiled and preened a little. "I do love that I can stump you once in a while. It's nice to see I haven't lost my touch."

"Monica..."

"Oh, stop. I'm just teasing." She reached over and squeezed his hand. "So...about James?"

"I suppose he can sit in on some of this if he really wants to, but we'll leave it up to him."

She nodded.

"Then it's Christian and Megan. That's everyone. My plan is to have everyone working on specific things leading up to the trip, then having the time to work things out face to face should give us everything we need for a smooth transition."

"Good for you, dear. Just remember that we're all there to celebrate the holidays. We haven't done anything like this in years and I want it to be fun and not a chore."

"Did you hear that Gina invited Barb to join us?" William murmured. "You know she's going to suck some of the joy out of this."

Frowning, she swatted his hand. "Be nice. It's going to be loud and festive and wonderful. Even Barb will have no choice but to have fun. After all, how can you be miserable when you're surrounded by a group of people who are all in healthy and happy relationships?"

That made William smile. "Yeah...and I'm responsible for that."

"We," she corrected him. "*We're* responsible for that. You didn't act alone on all those matches."

"Yes, yes, yes...you did your share as well." He let out a long breath. "We had a lot of fun doing it too, didn't we?"

"Definitely. I couldn't believe how much I enjoyed being a little devious," she said with a giggle.

"I still remember when I orchestrated getting Lucas and Emma together. No one understood what I was trying to do, but getting them snowed in together was a stroke of genius!"

She frowned again. "I think you're forgetting how your little plan caused Emma to crash her car. Lucas was furious with you over the entire thing."

"Lucas was furious at everyone back then," he reminded her. "But it turned out to be the best thing for him."

"Mmm...I have to agree. He never saw that coming."

"And neither did Jason with Maggie."

"Poor Maggie didn't see that coming either. I still don't know how you pulled that whole thing off and had it work as brilliantly as it did."

"I'm a people watcher, Monica. You know that. And while it wasn't an obvious situation like we had with Lucas and Emma, I knew Jason and Maggie had the potential to be a good match both in the office and out of it."

"Still...Jason still brings up how guilty he felt about getting involved with Maggie in the beginning."

"Because he's an honorable man," he said proudly. "But they owe their happiness to me and my craftiness."

"And apparently the Rock and Roll Hall of Fame," Monica replied cheekily. "After all, it was a slow dance during that gala that led to their first kiss."

"Hmph. I suppose I can share credit." Then he paused as a familiar pang of sorrow hit. "Just like I would have shared credit with Art for matching Mac and Gina."

"You still should. After all, Arthur was the reason Gina came back to North Carolina."

His best friend had been dying of cancer and he and his daughter had been estranged for many years. She came to visit him in his final days and spent a lot of time with Mac, which led to them falling in love.

"I hate that it happened that way," William murmured. "I wish Arthur could have lived to see how happy they are together."

"He would have been thrilled," Monica said quietly as she squeezed his hand again. "You were a good friend to him. Always. And you know he's looking down, pleased as can be that you're still watching out for Gina."

"I adore her as if she were my own daughter," he said gruffly. "Hell, I love all our girls as if they were our own instead of just related through marriage."

Relaxing a bit, Monica smiled serenely. "It's wonderful to finally have more females around here. After raising three boys, I wasn't sure I'd ever get the chance to buy dresses or do anything girly."

He couldn't help but laugh. She'd been saying the same thing for years. "I think you got more than you bargained for with all our granddaughters. I know we're an equal lot now, but our granddaughters are far more outgoing than our grandsons. It's been fascinating to watch all these years."

"That it has. Janice says the same thing about all of their grandkids."

"Which...not to toot my own horn, but..."

"Yes, yes, yes, William, we know. You helped that all happen too. First with James and Selena..."

"You're forgetting Casey and Ryder!"

"Sorry, but you really can't claim their match. They reconnected all on their own."

It was an argument they'd been having within the family for years—all in good fun, of course. "If it weren't for me needing Ryder to help stand in with the wedding planner..."

"He had already sought out Casey. You need to let this go."

"I made it possible for them to spend more time together," he grumbled.

"Fine. But paying for an entire high school's reunion was a little over the top for James and Selena."

"That boy was the most stubborn of the lot! The universe wanted the two of them to be together, I just had to..."

"Give the universe a nudge?"

"Exactly!"

"Summer and Ethan weren't really your doing either," she went on. "Those were special circumstances."

Sadly, he had to agree. "Still, I could see what was happening and just...guided where I could."

"It's big of you to admit that," she said with a wink. "Same with Zach and Gabriella. That was already in motion."

"No. Absolutely not. I am taking full credit for that match! I made sure that Gabriella was right there so that Zach had no choice but to finally notice her! And when things got rocky, I knew when to help her. It was a little like playing chess—very challenging, but very rewarding."

Monica's only response was a loud sigh.

"But you saw how much fun I was having and decided to give it a shot," he said. "Admit it. Getting Megan and Alex together was fun."

"Oh, I'm not denying that for even a minute! After seeing them at Zach and Gabriella's wedding, we were certain they were going to get together."

"And they did."

"Yes, but only briefly. Getting them *back* together was a little harder. Fortunately, Megan was agreeable to moving."

"It all fell into place beautifully. Just like Christian and Sophie! You were on a roll!"

She beamed at the compliment. "As soon as Eliza and I met Sophie, we knew she would be perfect for Christian."

"But how? She was such a free spirit and he was... well...not."

"That's why she was perfect. We knew she'd bring him out of his shell and she did!"

"Well, I was seriously impressed," he told her. "But what you and Eliza did with Carter and Emery? That was... that was a thing of beauty!"

Now she grinned like the Cheshire Cat. "Wasn't it? As much as I hated that poor Emery had to be in hiding to get away from that creep of an ex-fiancé, I was thrilled that Eliza was able to help her."

"And throw the poor girl right into Carter's path! They had been enemies since grade school! Why on earth would you think they were right for each other?" He already knew the answer, but this was one of his favorite topics to discuss.

"There's a thin line between love and hate, William. And Eliza swore she knew Emery was the girl for Carter since they were kids. Turns out she was right."

"It was a wild ride there for years," he said and heard the wistfulness in his own voice. "It made me feel more alive than any business deal ever did."

"It makes me wish all the grandkids were a little older," Monica replied with that same wistfulness.

"I fully agree. Although, I'm not sure we're as involved with their lives as we should be in order to make a good match."

"It doesn't matter, William. They're not old enough to be thinking about finding their forever people. The only one even remotely possible is Lily, and she's too focused on her dance career to have an interest in settling down." She glanced at him and her gaze narrowed. "And we need to respect that. Dancing isn't the kind of career that one can have forever. She needs to embrace it while she's young and her body is in its prime."

"Why are you looking at me like that? I didn't say a word!"

"Because I can practically hear the gears in your head working."

"Darling, this is a family vacation. There's not going to be anyone around to even casually try to fix our grand-daughter up with. Maybe in another year or two…but not now. Not this trip. This is all about Christmas with the family."

She didn't look fully convinced. "Yes. Christmas with the family, with just a hint of work thrown in."

"I promise it will all be done the day before Christmas Eve. You have my word."

"Perfect." Standing, she kissed him softly on the lips. "Now if you'll excuse me, I need to see what time Gina and Emma are coming over tomorrow to start cooking with me. I'll see you at dinner." And she gave him another kiss before walking out of the room.

"Sometimes it's almost too easy," he whispered once she was out of earshot.

Of course, he was referring to making sure his wife was comfortable with his work plans during their trip, but now that he was thinking about his oldest grandchild, he knew he was going to be on the lookout for the perfect man for her.

Just because she might not be ready to settle down just yet, didn't mean he couldn't be scoping out some candidates for when she was ready, right?

# TWO

# LUCAS & EMMA

## "WHAT'S ANOTHER SNOWSTORM?"

THE ALARM WENT OFF JUST like it did every morning, and Lucas took a moment to savor the warmth of having his wife in his arms. In a few hours, things were going to get chaotic—in the best possible way, of course—but he knew Emma's attention would be elsewhere. Fortunately, they spent the previous night getting everything packed so they could get on the road to Asheville and head to the house his parents rented for the holidays.

House? More like a hotel, he thought to himself. Logistically, it made total sense, but every time his mother talked about their family retreat, it just seemed crazy that they required a space that large.

Emma hummed softly in her sleep as she snuggled closer, and Lucas couldn't help but place a soft kiss on her shoulder. This was one of his favorite times of the day—the early morning where the sun wasn't fully up, everything was peaceful, and the two of them were cocooned in their own little world.

In a few hours, peace would be a distant memory.

When their oldest daughter came walking through the

door, Emma was going to burst into tears, and his other daughters—Becca and Sloane—would definitely let out their own ear-splitting screeches too. If he was lucky, he'd get all of five seconds with Lily before she was whisked away for some girl time before they hit the road.

*I'm so outnumbered...*

Yeah, that was a common thought in his mind, but the truth was that Lucas wouldn't want it any other way. His daughters and Emma were his whole world and even though no one seemed to share any of his interests, they had given him more joy than he ever thought he'd have in this life. After a career-ending injury in the NFL, he had resigned himself to a solitary life in his cabin up in Asheville. Then, one day Emma literally came crashing into that solitude and changed everything.

For the better.

"Mmm...did the alarm go off already?" Emma sleepily murmured.

Lucas kissed her bare shoulder again. "It did."

Slowly, she rolled over in his arms and placed a kiss of her own on his chest. "What time do we need to leave today?"

He hugged her close. "If we're on the road by two, we'll be to the house before it gets dark."

"Have you looked at the forecast?"

The low chuckle was out before he could stop it. "There's a slight chance of snow."

Squirming against him, Emma pulled back slightly. "You know how I feel about that sort of thing. Maybe we should leave sooner? The car is packed, you have the day off, and there's no reason for us to just sit around and wait. Your parents are already there."

"Em, come on. You know that Becca and Sloane aren't

even going to be awake for another couple of hours and then they'll take their time getting ready." He fought the urge to roll his eyes. Honestly, why did they have to spend so much time in the bathroom? "Everything's going to be fine."

She snorted. "Please, I've heard that one before."

"That was over twenty years ago. And it never happened again after that one trip. Besides, what's another snowstorm?" Leaning in, Lucas kissed her soundly. "And, if memory serves, everything worked out pretty damn great for us."

She hummed softly, smoothing her hand over his chest. "If you don't count wrecking my car, spraining my ankle, and a potential concussion, then sure. It was great."

The slight twitch of her lips told him she was teasing. Carefully, he rolled her beneath him. "Maybe I should remind you of some of the highlights of that snowstorm."

Her arms slowly wound around him, and then her legs. "I think a refresher is definitely necessary."

Morning sex was something they both loved, and right now, he couldn't think of a better way to start the day. "I totally agree," he said before kissing her soundly and reminding her of all the highlights of their getting stranded together all those years ago.

The doorbell rang and Emma sighed wearily. No one was even attempting to answer it. As much as she wanted to remind everyone that she was busy too, she knew it would fall on deaf ears as her daughters were running around getting ready for their trip.

Honestly, she loved spending the holidays with her in-laws, but this whole retreat house with over fifty Montgomerys was threatening to overwhelm her.

Or maybe it was just the fact that she was overly emotional around the holidays.

Especially this one.

Lily wasn't coming home because she had been working as a dancer on a cruise ship and couldn't get the time off. As much as Emma wanted to be supportive, it was a daily struggle not to buy a ticket for the cruise and skip the whole Montgomery hoopla.

The doorbell rang again and she did her best to force a smile as she opened the door.

"Surprise!"

"Oh my God! Lily!" she cried excitedly, unsure if she was truly seeing her baby girl standing there in front of her. "Lucas! Lucas! Lily's home! Girls! Your sister's home!" Then she hauled Lily into her arms and hugged her fiercely. "Why didn't you call and tell me? How did you get here? Are you staying through the holidays? Are you coming home for good?"

In her arms, her daughter laughed softly. "Um, Mom? You're going to need to stop asking questions and maybe loosen your hold on me so I can breathe and answer."

"I will in a minute. I just can't believe you're really here!" Tears stung her eyes and before she knew it, she was full-on crying.

"Mom..."

"I knew you were going to cry," Lucas said as he joined them by the front door. He wrapped his arms around them in a mini-group hug before adding. "And you owe me five bucks."

Lily laughed as she tried to break free. "I really thought she'd hold it together a little longer."

"Wait..." Emma said and was surprised that she was the one to actually break the hug. Turning to her husband, she frowned. "You knew she was coming home?"

"Um..."

"We wanted to surprise you!" Lily said as she reached up and wiped Emma's tears away. "I thought you'd be excited and all giddy and whatnot. I really didn't think you'd cry."

"Oh, well..."

"But Dad made this happen, so really, you should be thanking him. I couldn't get the time off and then Dad just sort of swooped in and made things happen!"

Closing her eyes, Emma shook her head. "Lucas, what on earth did you do?"

He at least had the good sense to look a little guilty. "I made some calls to their...um...legal department and mentioned how there are labor laws against keeping someone working an extensive number of consecutive days without a break."

"Oh, good grief...it wasn't like she was forced to dance 24/7!"

"She was on a cruise ship and couldn't leave!" he countered. "It had been a year and we only saw her twice because of the schedule! She was exhausted and no one was listening to her, so I stepped in!"

Before Emma could argue, their daughter chimed in.

"It's true, Mom. I was the one who called Dad and asked for help," Lily said solemnly. And again, before Emma could respond, she was talking again. "And I'm not just home for the holidays. It looks like I'm on an extended break."

The gasp was out before she could stop it. "You mean..."

Lily nodded. "But it's all good. I'm okay. Really. It was a

fun job and I made some great friends, but I'm ready to move on to something else."

Then no one could say anything because Becca and Sloane came running down the stairs, screaming with excitement. Both Emma and Lucas took a step back and watched as their girls were hugging and jumping around together before running off to the kitchen. It wasn't until things grew slightly quieter that Emma faced him.

"You know she's a grown woman, right?"

He nodded.

"You know that she could have worked this out on her own."

Another nod. "I know."

Then she threw herself into his arms and hugged him tight. "Thank you. This is seriously the best gift you could have given me."

He chuckled softly in her ear. "Does that mean I should take back the other gifts I bought you?"

Pulling back, she pouted. "You wouldn't dare."

His grin was a little cocky and the exact look that made her fall in love with him all those years ago. "You're right. I wouldn't."

"Good." Kissing him soundly, she cupped his face and simply enjoyed the moment. "You know these next two weeks are going to be pure chaos, right? I mean...your family is..."

"We're a lot. I know. But this is something my folks have wanted to do for years and I think it's going to be great. The house is large enough for twice the amount of people we have, so it won't feel overly crowded."

"Still hard to believe such a place exists and that it's not an over-the-top mansion."

"More like a private hotel-slash-corporate retreat," he explained.

"Oh my God, Lily! That's *amazing!*" Sloane cried out from the kitchen.

"What do you say we join our girls for breakfast so we can get on the road?" Lucas suggested.

Emma couldn't help but smile. "That sounds perfect."

# THREE
## JASON & MAGGIE
### "WE CAN STILL PRETEND, RIGHT?"

"LAPTOP, charger, tablet, backup tablet, phone charger..." Jason straightened and looked around his home office and frowned. Was it possible he had everything he was going to need for this two-week family retreat? He was about to sit when his wife rushed into the room, shut the door, and breathlessly leaned against it. "Um...Mags? Are you okay?"

"I don't know what we were thinking by agreeing to this trip," she mumbled, more to herself than to him. Then she looked up and met his gaze. "Our children have been giving me nothing but grief all morning while you've conveniently chosen to hide out in here."

"Grief? Over what? They love spending time with their cousins!"

She slowly pushed away from the door before walking over and collapsing on his sofa. "That was before Logan found out all his friends were going skiing in Vale and Mila had to turn down a trip to New York City to see the tree in Rockefeller Center."

"Okay, but..."

"And Nicholas and Carson just stomped into the

kitchen to tell me how they wanted to be back home the day after Christmas because they're too old to play with their younger cousins. Too old!" She snorted with disgust. "I'm telling you, Jace, it's like they waited for the last possible minute to throw this nonsense at me just to make me crazy!"

With a low chuckle, he walked over and sat down beside her before pulling her into his arms and kissing her. "I don't see why they would do something like that. I mean...what's the purpose? To get you all riled up and then pile into the car and making everyone miserable for two hours?" He shook his head. "That just doesn't make sense."

"Nothing teenagers do make sense," she murmured as she pressed her face against his shoulder. "All I know is that I'm already exhausted and we haven't even loaded the car yet."

"I was just packing up my office and..."

"And avoiding the chaos. Trust me, if I could have done that, I would have."

He laughed softly again. "They're not that bad."

She moved out of his embrace and collapsed back against the cushions. "Do you remember what it was like when it was just the two of us? Like when we first met?"

"You mean when you pretended to be married to someone else so no one would hit on you?" he teased. It was a memory they talked about every now and again—mainly because he still felt guilty about kissing her when he thought she was a married woman. Obviously, she wasn't and there was nothing to truly feel guilty about, but for some reason, he did.

"How about we lock the door and pretend that we're those carefree single people again?" Her sultry smile was slowly winning him over. "We'd have to be fast and quiet, and it can be like the days we used to fool around in the office when one of us felt tense. We can still pretend, right?"

It was beyond tempting. Ever since Logan came home from college for winter break, and Mila and the twins' vacation started, it had been a little loud and hectic around here. He glanced toward the door and noticed it was locked.

"Did you have this planned?" he asked gruffly, as he moved closer. "I see you already took care of the door."

Biting her lip, Maggie nodded. "I have no idea how much privacy we're going to have with fifty Montgomerys all under one roof. I thought we could be naughty for a few minutes before going back to being responsible adults with demanding children."

It was probably the best suggestion he'd heard in a long time.

"Sweetheart, I love the way you think."

"I hope no one expects me to babysit," Mila grumbled as she handed her father her suitcase. "Because this is my vacation too." Then she spun away and climbed into their family's SUV.

Maggie stood back and sighed. "You want to know something funny?"

Jason nodded even as he tried rearranging all their luggage. "Sure."

"On an average day, this SUV feels fairly massive. Some days, I wonder why we have it." Pausing, she watched as he began pulling all their suitcases out again. "Now it suddenly feels too small. Maybe we need to take two cars?"

Without even looking at her, he shook his head. "Absolutely not. We're driving up to Asheville as a family. We don't get a lot of time where it's just the six of us since Logan started college a few months ago. I was really looking forward to having a little quiet time where we could all just talk and joke around like we used to do on family trips."

It didn't seem possible that she could love this man more than she already did, but listening to him talk about how much he loved their family just made all she felt for him feel like...more.

"I would love that too, but I don't think we can honestly fit six people and a dozen suitcases in here comfortably or safely."

He was shaking his head again. "The manual says you can fit ten pieces of luggage back here and I'm going to make that happen, dammit!"

It would be wrong to point out how that still left two suitcases out, so instead, Maggie took it upon herself to grab the two smallest bags and strategically placed them inside the car. Naturally, there was some complaining and that's when she finally lost her patience.

"I have had *enough!*" she shouted and then watched as all four of her kids stared at her in wide-eyed silence. "All morning you've done nothing but walk around complaining and I am *not* going to listen to it anymore!" Pushing her hair away from her face, she let out a small huff. "Your father and I have been looking forward to having this time together —this *fun* drive that was like the road trips we used to take when you were kids—and you are ruining it!"

"Mom, no one's ruining it," her daughter responded. "But judging from some previous holidays, we're just saying..."

"No," Maggie interrupted. "No one's saying anything, okay? You're upset because your friends are going to New York. I get it. But you never thought to mention that until today." Then she turned to Logan. "Just like you never said a word about Vale. And for the record, we spend this holiday together as a family. Always!" she added for emphasis. "Until you're married with families of your own, *this* is the group of people you're going to be with. Got it?"

She was primed to stomp away and go see how Jason was managing with the luggage, but obviously the twins felt like they had to get their say in.

"Everyone's younger than us," Carson whined. "And it's totally lame to have to play with all the babies."

"Yeah," Nicholas chimed in. "I'm sick of being told that we have to watch out for the younger kids and keep them entertained."

Maggie pinched the bridge of her nose as she silently counted to ten. "Okay, here's the deal—no one's asking any of you to babysit. There are going to be twenty-five adults there. If someone needs to be watched, you can guarantee there will be an extra parent or two who can handle it. This house your grandmother rented has a game room, an indoor pool, and a movie theater. Outside, there is a full playground, a tennis court, basketball hoops, and there are trails to ride ATVs. Believe me when I tell you, everyone's going to be busy."

"Who would play basketball in the snow?" Mila asked, but she was staring at her phone and not looking at anyone.

Before Maggie could respond, Jason closed the hatch—loudly—and then came to join her on the side of the vehicle.

"For all you know, snow-basketball could be the next great sport and we'll be the ones who invented it," Jason said with a big grin as he wrapped his arm around her waist. "Now, if you're all done complaining, I'd love it if you could apologize to your mother while I go and lock up." He kissed the top of her head and was about to turn and walk away when he leaned slightly into the SUV. "And if you don't apologize, then I'm confiscating everyone's phones for the duration of the trip. Then I'll take the long way while listening to music your grandparents listened to in high school. Loudly." His smile grew. "Are we all on the same page? Because I have the fifties station programmed on the radio and you know it's commercial free, so..."

"We're sorry, Mom!" Logan called out.

"Me too!" Mila said as she leaned forward and reached for Maggie's hand. "I love you!"

"Sorry, Mom!" Nicholas added. "And you look so pretty! Did I mention that today?"

"I'm sorry too, Mom!" Carson said loudly. "You're the best mom in the whole wide world and...we promise not to complain until after the new year!"

Beside her, Jason laughed softly before whispering in her ear, "My work here is done." Then he kissed her again and strolled off to lock up the house.

# FOUR
## MAC & GINA
### "THERE WILL BE NO JOY SUCKING!"

"ALL I'M SAYING IS that we need to stop and think about this," Mac said calmly, even though he was screaming on the inside.

"I *have* thought about it," his wife countered with more than a little heat. "And you would have too if you spent a little more time at home while this was all going on."

Yeah, he'd been a little MIA in the last few months because he had been trying to close a deal and now he was paying the price. He and Gina had talked about him cutting back his hours now—especially since their kids were all in high school—so they could do things as a family while they were all under one roof.

And now she wanted to add her mother to the mix.

*Ugh...*

"Can't we wait and talk about this after the holidays?" he suggested. "I realize this is a big decision, and I think we need to think it through from every angle."

"Mac..."

But before he could plead his case more, their daughter

Brianna walked in. "Hey, is it alright if I bring my guitar with me? Is there going to be room in the car?"

"Of course you can," Gina said with a smile. "You can lead us all in Christmas carols around the tree!"

"That was part of the plan!" she replied excitedly before walking out of the room.

"As I was saying," Mac began, but...

"Dad, my tablet just crapped out. Do we have time to stop somewhere along the way so I can get a new one?" their middle child, Harry, asked with a face full of worry.

"Actually, I have a new one I haven't even opened yet," Mac told him. "It's in my office in the far-left cabinet. Help yourself."

"Thanks, Dad!" and then he ran off.

"Again, I was saying..."

"You're always just saying," Gina said stiffly. "You're always talking and rarely listening."

"We said we wanted this time for us as a family," he reminded her. "The five of us. Time for us to have with the kids before everyone is too old to want to travel with us or off at college. If we move your mother in with us, that time is gone, Gina! You know she always manages to suck the joy out of everything!"

"There will be no joy sucking!" she replied hotly. "And I don't really believe she does that."

"That's debatable," he countered. "All your time and energy will have to be on her." He paused and let out a long breath. "Can we please just put a pin in this until after the holidays?"

Those big, beautiful eyes narrowed at him. "You don't get to always have your way, Mac. I've been patient through all your overtime hours at work—time you didn't seem to worry about being away from us. So, you better be damn sure that you're serious about cutting back your hours if you want to continue arguing about this into the new year. Our kids are only going to be at home with us for a few more years. Do you really want to keep missing out?"

He leaned in and murmured, "That was a low blow. I have never missed any of the important stuff!"

"No, but you missed some of the quiet moments that were actually milestones and big to them," she said quietly, taking some of the wind out of his sails.

"What do you want me to say here? Your mother's going to be with us for the holidays. Let's see where we're at when that's all said and done, okay?"

By the way she was still glaring at him, he could tell she wasn't fully convinced. There was a time he didn't have to work so hard to get Gina to see his side of things. She always understood him, even when she didn't agree with him. But lately it seemed like things were just getting...harder for them.

And that bothered him.

A lot.

"Can I just ask one thing?"

She nodded.

"Do you honestly believe we're going to have this idyllic family life if Barb moves in with us and I..." Pausing, he swallowed hard. "I semi-retire?"

Now her eyes went wide. "Semi-retire? I thought you'd just cut back a bit...like working a normal week."

Mac shook his head. "If I do this, I need to do it right because I love you and I love our family. That's what's most important. And with the way this merger is going, I think I can make that transition without too many obstacles. Hell, I probably won't even be missed." Carefully, he moved in close and wrapped his arms around her waist. "Just...think about it, okay?"

Another nod.

"Thank you." He kissed her soundly, but knew this discussion was far from over.

It didn't matter how many times they had gone away on vacation, Gina always felt like she was forgetting something. Now, as Mac was loading their luggage into their SUV, she did a final walk around the house to make sure everything was as it should be and that she hadn't forgotten anything.

She heard someone running down the stairs and knew it had to be Tanner. He was always the one they were waiting for, and she watched in fascination as he wandered around a bit as if searching for something. "Everything okay, Tanner?"

"What? Huh?" He looked up at her and she smiled. Tanner favored her looks more than Brianna and Harry, and in that moment, she wanted to reach out and smooth his dark, unruly hair.

"Are you looking for something?"

"I know it's gonna be snowing and all that up in the mountains, but I was trying to find something we can play with Matt, Brayden, Jamie, and Jensen. You know, some kind of ball game."

"I think Grandma said there were basketball hoops..."

"Perfect!" Fortunately, they had a lot of his sports equipment in the mudroom, so he was able to run off and grab the ball without it turning into a long search. He ran from the room and then came right back to her. "Hey, Mom, can I talk to you about something?"

"Absolutely," she told him. "What's up?"

"Well…I kind of heard you and Dad arguing earlier."

Crap.

"You should know that Dad's around a lot more than most of my friends' dads. I mean…he never misses one of my games or one of Brianna's concerts," he explained. "And remember when he flew home because Harry was in the spelling bee?"

Gina couldn't help but smile at the memory because Mac had left a meeting on the West Coast just so he could make it back to Charlotte in time to see Harry hit the stage. "I do remember that."

"So…maybe don't be so hard on him," he said carefully, doing his best not to make direct eye contact. "I know it upsets you when he works a lot, but that doesn't mean Grandma Barb has to move in with us."

*Say what now?*

"Um…"

"I mean…I love her—we all do—but…she's a lot of work, Mom," he went on. "Like…a lot. I know I'm only fourteen and probably shouldn't be saying this, but…you get totally weird when she's around for too long."

"Weird?" she repeated. "I do *not* get weird."

"Mom, trust me. You get weird and tense and we all dread it." His shoulders sagged slightly. "I'm only saying this because I don't like it when you and Dad fight. It makes me sad." Then he shrugged. "Am I gonna be grounded for saying all of this?"

She laughed softly before pulling him close and hugging him. "No, you're not going to be grounded. I think it was very mature of you to come and talk to me like this, so…

thank you." She gave him one more squeeze before giving him a nudge toward the door. "Go and see if your father needs help loading everything and I'll be out in a minute."

"Cool! Thanks, Mom!" And then he took off out the door, leaving Gina a little dazed and confused by their conversation.

Well, maybe not confused, but...sad.

*Do I really get weird when Mom's here?*

She knew if she brought that up to Mac, he'd jump all over it. He had a lot of issues with her mother—and with good reason—but...what was she supposed to do? She was an only child and that meant caring for her aging mother was her responsibility.

Before she could explore that thought further, Mac came strolling into the room. "Car's loaded," he said with an easy grin. "Doing your final walk-through?"

He knew her so well. "Just finishing up. Did you pack the cooler I had in the kitchen?"

"I put it in the back next to Harry like we always do," he said with a hint of amusement. This was the conversation they had every time they went on a road trip. "Tanner's already annoying Brianna by attempting to spin his basketball on his finger. I think we're going to have to put it in the back in order to keep the peace."

She nodded. "Then I guess we should hit the road. Your mother texted to let me know they're expecting snow tonight, so the sooner we leave, the better chance we have of not having to drive in it."

"Sounds good." Mac turned to walk back outside when Gina called his name and stopped him. He looked at her oddly. "Everything okay?"

"Do I get weird when my mother's around?" she blurted out.

Instead of giving her an answer, he simply reached for her hand and gently tugged her along behind him. "Sweetheart, I wouldn't touch that question with a ten-foot pole. Now let's get on the road and start celebrating the holiday!"

She knew a distraction when she heard one.

*Yup. I get weird.*

# FIVE

# RYDER & CASEY

"AND THEN, they want me to have one of my staff come running in all frantic and everything, saying that they hit the guy's Ferrari with the catering van!" Casey said with a laugh. "Of course we didn't, but it's all for the dramatic effect. Isn't that hysterical?"

Ryder looked at his wife as if she'd lost her mind. "Um..."

"I was talking to the producer, and she said I should come running outside in my stilettos and wearing one of my fancier dresses and be really over the top!" She sighed happily. "I think I can totally pull that off, don't you?"

They were in the car, halfway to Asheville to spend the holidays with his extended family, and with their three kids in the back seats, he knew he needed to tread carefully.

"I don't think I understand what's happening," he began. "I thought this was a reality show and you were doing the wedding for some actress or something." Then he paused. "It was an actress, right?"

She nodded enthusiastically. "Yes, Dana St. Ivy. She's like...the queen of those time-travel dramas. Doing her wedding was already going to be a huge deal for the business. But getting to be part of the reality show they're filming around it? Ryder, this is going to be huge for me!"

"I get that, but..."

"I've been doing this for over twenty years and, honestly, I was feeling a little burned out. But this has breathed new life into the business and how I look at it! I'm completely dazzled by all the possibilities!"

And that right there was a huge red flag for him.

"Have you talked to Julie and Selena about this?" he asked. "Are they all on board with it?"

Her hesitation spoke volumes. "Well, Julie's not big on any of it because she hates reality TV. Mostly because it's all scripted."

"Correct me if I'm wrong, but...why does reality need to be scripted?"

The huff of annoyance she gave him also spoke volumes. "Ryder, that's just the way it's done. Most people don't have an excessive amount of drama in their lives, and in order to have a show be something that people need to watch, you have to orchestrate the drama sometimes. Oh! That reminds me, they wanted me to ask if you'd be a part of it."

"Me? Why?" And yeah, he was instantly suspicious.

"I told them what you and your family do—because they asked. I didn't just openly share it—and they thought it would be funny to have you be on camera rolling your eyes at my antics and all that. So what do you think?"

"I think I want to know what Selena thinks of this and if she mentioned it to my brother," he murmured.

"Most of this just happened yesterday and we said we'd talk about it once we got to Asheville. I mean, we're all going to be together for the next two weeks, and we don't have to meet with the production team until the second week of January, so...we have time." Turning her head, she smiled at him. "I'm really excited about this, Ryder. I just can't believe this opportunity landed in my lap like this. We're going to be a huge success once this show airs."

Reaching over, he took one of her hands in his. "Sweetheart, you're already a success. You and Julie were already successful when you and I got together all those years ago. When Selena joined you and the two of you merged your businesses, you became the premiere event planners on the Carolina coast. Technically, you don't need this show."

Her smile faded slightly. "Wait...you don't want me to do the show? Because if I don't do the show, I'm not going to be able to do the wedding. It's a package deal."

That's what he was afraid of.

"I know it all sounds exciting, but...it also sounds like they might not paint you in the most flattering light, Case. I mean, who is going to want to hire you if they think your staff is so incompetent that they'd crash your catering van into a Ferrari?"

"It was just a suggestion," she argued. "And I'd make sure they cleared things up so we're not responsible. Easy fix."

"Somehow, I doubt that," he mumbled.

"Excuse me?"

"Nothing, let's just..." He paused and let out a long breath. "Can we please just wait until we can sit and talk with James and Selena about this? I mean, if Julie's not on board, and Selena's not on board..."

"I never said Selena wasn't on board," she corrected. "She's just as excited as I am. And if she's excited, then James will be too. I can guarantee that you're going to be the odd man out."

"Are you just meeting my brother? Do you think for a minute that he's going to want to be on camera at all? He's the most private guy I've ever known in my entire life!"

She didn't comment.

He squeezed her hand before bringing it to his lips and kissing it. "Casey, I love you and I have always supported whatever you do with your business, but...this might not be the right thing for you and you need to keep an open mind."

"Hmph..."

"Dad," his son Brayden called from the third seat. "Are we almost there yet?"

Ryder looked at the GPS screen and groaned. "Two more hours. But we're going to stop soon to grab some lunch, okay?"

All three kids groaned.

"This trip is taking forever," his daughter Emily moaned.

Same, he thought. I feel exactly the same way.

They were back in the car after stopping for lunch at a Cracker Barrel restaurant. It was loud and noisy and not someplace they would normally eat, but the food was delicious and Casey was pleasantly full. It was a nice distraction to be off the road for a little while, and it helped to make her forget how annoyed she was with her husband.

Casually, Casey gave Ryder the side-eye as they pulled back onto the interstate. How could he not see how exciting this opportunity was for her? Not only was the wedding a massive coup, but she was going to be on TV! The wedding planner is always behind the scenes and normally it's a good thing not to be seen. For years she thrived on that sort of thing. But...sometimes it left her feeling...invisible. Sure, her brides and grooms were always gushing over the work she did, but didn't she deserve her moment in the spotlight just once?

Her phone vibrated in her hand and she glanced down to see an incoming text from her sister-in-law.

**Selena: Hey! Just giving you a heads up, James is NOT happy about the show**

**Casey: Neither is Ryder**

**Casey: Must be a brother thing**

**Selena: Damn. I was hoping Ryder would convince him how awesome this is going to be**

**Casey: So what do we do?**

**Casey: Can we just pretend they're happy and just do it?**

**Selena: You know that producer chick was excited about having them on the show**

**Casey: I mentioned that part to Ryder and he wasn't impressed**

**Selena: James was adamant that he wouldn't do it**

*That's not surprising...*

Casey: What if we got the rest of the family on our side?

Selena: What do you mean?

Casey: We know most Montgomerys are going to be working during this first week, right?

Selena: Right

Casey: So we take that time to talk to everyone else

Casey: And once we get everyone psyched about it, we bring James and Ryder back in for the discussion

Casey: Thoughts?

Selena: Ooh...that could definitely work

Selena: You know how we have the group text about The Bachelor?

Selena: So you know we already have a group that loves reality TV

Casey: Exactly!

Casey: We just have to get them on board with OUR reality TV

**Selena: Shouldn't be that hard to do**

**Casey: That's what I'm thinking.**

**Casey: We'll wait until that first business meeting they have and then we'll start our little campaign**

**Selena: Lol! I kind of love that we have a plan**

**Selena: I was almost afraid we were going to have to just give up**

**Casey: Nonsense. This is our business and we're good at it.**

**Selena: This is going to be awesome! Can't wait to see you!**

**Casey: Same! We should be at the retreat in a little under two hours. You?**

**Selena: We're an hour out. See you soon! Love you!**

**Casey: Love you too! And we've got this!**

Smiling, she slid her phone back into her purse.

"Everything okay?" Ryder asked.

"What? Oh, that was just Julie letting me know how today's event is going," she lied.

"It was really nice of her to take all the holiday parties so you and Selena could be out of town."

"Julie's the best. And she wanted the time off in January, so it all worked out."

"You've created something great, Casey," Ryder said as he smiled at her.

"Definitely," she agreed.

And by New Year's Eve, he'd see just how much greater they were going to be.

# SIX

# JAMES & SELENA

## "ARE WE HAVING FUN YET?"

"I AM SO excited to see the snow! Do you think it's going to keep snowing? Is it really going to be a white Christmas?"

James smiled as he listened to his daughter excitedly go on and on about the wonders of snow. Living on the coast of North Carolina, she'd never seen it. Every once in a while, he thought about taking her up to New York in the winter-time to see it, but the thought of potentially getting stuck up there always stopped him. But listening to her now, he felt a little guilty.

"I checked the forecast," he told her. "It looks like we're definitely going to have snow on both Christmas Eve and Christmas Day."

"This is amazing!" she cried before reaching over and playfully shaking her older brother. "Don't you think this is amazing? We can build snowmen and have snowball fights and build forts!"

Jamie was staring down at his phone and simply said, "Uh-huh."

Yeah. His son was a man—well, not technically a man yet, but close—of few words.

Like father, like son.

"Are you excited about the snow, Mom?" Isabella asked.

Beside him, his wife finished typing a text before sliding her phone into her purse and smiling at their daughter. "I am! It's been a long time since I've seen snow, so I'm looking forward to going out and playing in it for sure."

"What about you, Dad? What's your favorite thing to do in the snow?"

"Hmm...I used to love to go sledding down this massive hill in my cousin Kent's neighborhood. We used to spend hours doing that."

"Wow! Do you think there are any hills near the house we're staying in?"

"I know Aunt Monica mentions trails for ATV riding and I know there's a ski resort not too far away, but I don't think she mentioned hills specifically," Selena replied. "But it's a mountain town. I'm sure there are parks for that sort of thing."

"I'm going to look it up on my phone," Isabella said cheerily, and James knew that meant she was going to research the hell out of the topic. She thoroughly enjoyed looking things up and learning all kinds of random trivia. He had no doubt they were going to see her on *Jeopardy!* one day.

James smiled at his wife. "What do you think? Would you go sledding with me down a hill?"

"That depends," she said with a sassy grin. "How big of a hill are we talking?"

"I can't say with any great certainty, but..."

"There are parks!" Isabella called out. "Like five of them, and they're all close to where we're staying! You ride tubes instead of sleds! This is going to be so cool!"

Chuckling softly, James shook his head. "So...would you go tubing down a hill with me?"

Selena was laughing too. "I think that sounds like a lot of fun and I would definitely share a tube with you if it's allowed."

"I'm sure they have tubes built for two," he assured her. They drove in silence for a few minutes. "So, who were you texting with? Is Julie okay with today's party?"

"Julie could handle ten parties on her own and be fine, but that was Casey I was texting with."

"Oh?"

He had no doubt they were talking about this ridiculous reality TV wedding and how to convince him it was a great idea. Honestly, he thought it could be a good thing for their business, but there were several things that just didn't sit right with him. He'd already planned on getting his brother alone to talk about it and hopefully they could be on the same page and try to convince their wives not to jump into anything too soon.

"I just wanted to make sure they got on the road okay," she said, shifting slightly in her seat. "I know she was worried about leaving Julie alone with all the upcoming events, and you know how Casey can be. I'm sure she wanted to go to the office and look over everything herself."

He nodded, but he also knew when his wife wasn't being completely truthful with him. She squirmed more and always got restless—exactly what she was doing right now, which completely confirmed what he was thinking—they were talking about the TV show.

"So, did they leave on time?"

"What?" she asked a little too quickly. "I mean...yes. Yes, they're about an hour behind us."

"Excellent! I can't wait to see them. I realize we only

live 90 minutes apart, but we don't spend nearly enough time together. It will be good to see my brother and just hang out."

Selena's gaze narrowed. "Since when do you love to just hang out with anyone? Normally you try to avoid any big get-togethers."

"Pfft...please. Since you and I got back together, we've spent a lot of time with my family. Granted, I don't feel the need to see them every weekend, but it's nice when everyone's around for a holiday or something."

He offered her an endearing smile, but she didn't look like she completely believed him, and that was fine. She wasn't totally wrong, either. He still enjoyed his privacy and, after spending so many years estranged from his family, he found that being around them was fine in small doses.

He just hoped they'd all survive two whole weeks together.

*Look at him, thinking he's so smart. So charming. I know he's probably planning on getting Ryder alone to come up with a plan to stop me and Casey from doing this show. He can try, but Casey and I are going to come out on top and prove to these Montgomery men that we're just as savvy and smart in business as they are.*

"You okay?" he asked, frowning.

"Sure. Why?"

"Because you look like you're mad at the world over there. Your face got all scrunched up." His grin was back. "What were you thinking about to put that look on your face?"

*Wouldn't you like to know?*

"Um...I guess I'm just...uh...fifty people in a house is a lot. I keep trying to figure out how this is all going to work and...I know how much you enjoy your privacy and I'm hoping we can pick a room that's not in the middle of everything, that's all."

He took one of her hands in his. "Well, you are very sweet to be so concerned, but I think it's all going to be just fine. We saw the floor plan and how many rooms there were and we all sent Aunt Monica our requests. I can't imagine that she'd completely disregard everything we asked for."

"For all you know, everyone asked for a corner room," she countered lightly. "I mean...at the end of the day, we all like a little peace and quiet."

He shrugged. "Zach's going to want to be close to the gym, Carter's going to want to be close to the kitchen, Christian's going to want to be close to the bunk room so he can be close to the kids because he's a worrier..."

"You know what I'm saying, James. I guess I just worry about logistics. Actually, I *know* I worry about logistics. It's part of my job as an event planner. I tend do overthink things like this because I want everyone to be happy, even though there's always a chance somebody won't be."

"If we get a crappy room, we can easily switch. I'm not seeing any problems and I hate that you're actively looking for one."

Selena sighed wearily. "I told you; I can't help it. I'm not looking for a problem, I'm just working out potential scenarios so there won't be a problem. There's a difference."

They both grew quiet again.

"I don't have to sleep in the bunk room, do I?" Jamie asked, his focus still firmly on his phone.

"Probably not," Selena assured him. "The bunk room is

really going to be for the younger kids who won't mind sharing a bed, but you might end up sharing a room with one of your cousins. Each of the bedrooms has a bed and a sleeper sofa."

"I'm calling the bed," he said firmly. "I'm one of the oldest, so that means I automatically get dibs."

Both she and James laughed. "I'm not quite sure it works that way, but we'll see what the aunts all came up with. I believe Aunt Monica, Grandma, and Aunt Eliza were working together on the room assignments so…"

"That means no arguing," James said as he glanced in the rearview mirror at their son. "If you have a problem with whoever you're supposed to room with, talk to me or your mother and we'll handle it, okay?"

"Whatever," Jamie mumbled, and that was the end of that discussion.

Letting her head lean back against the seat, she closed her eyes. "Are we having fun yet?"

"This is going to be a great vacation," James assured her. "And if I think it, then you know it has to be true. We all know I'm usually the grumpy one in most situations, so…"

"Welcome to Asheville!" Isabella called out excitedly. "Do you think we'll pass one of those tubing places as we drive through town?"

"Why don't you look on the map and tell me?" James suggested.

"Oh! I should have thought of that! Thanks, Dad!"

More silence.

"So, um…have you decided if you're going to sit in on any of these merger talks your family is planning?" she asked him. Once it was put out there to everyone, she'd been curious, but as of a few days ago, James still hadn't decided.

"Like I've said, I'm not sure I'm really needed. I mean, I'm really just on the fringe with the business. I handle the properties and all that. I don't work for that part of the business."

"Still...it could be interesting to see if you might get this new acquired company's properties to manage. This could actually be something great for you."

"Hmm...maybe."

*And it will keep you busy while I convince your family to see why this TV show is a good thing. Selena—1, James—0.*

# SEVEN

# SUMMER & ETHAN

## "BECAUSE OF COURSE THE PUPPY WOULD PEE ON THE PLANE."

"I REALLY WISH we could have made this a road trip."

They were at the airport and watching as all their luggage was loaded onto the Montgomery corporate jet, and Ethan swore he wasn't going to have this discussion with Summer again.

They'd been having it daily for the last three weeks.

Summer viewed everything as an adventure waiting to happen, while he...did not.

And honestly, driving across the country—from Oregon to North Carolina—with three kids and a puppy was not the adventure he wanted to have.

"Mom! Lulu pooped and I can't find a bag to pick it up!" their daughter, Ariel, called out, and Ethan groaned.

Loudly.

"Oh, hush," Summer murmured before she reached into her massive purse and pulled out a small plastic bag. "I've got one right here, Ariel!"

Ethan watched her walk over to their daughter and couldn't help but shake his head in amusement. Even without hearing the conversation, he knew his wife was explaining to the dog that she was a good girl and precious and wonderful. Then she would praise Ariel for taking her for a walk. After that, the conversation would turn to how important it was to make sure the dog got it all out of her system before they had to get on the plane.

Glancing at his watch, he wondered where Zach, Gabriella, and their kids were. It was rare for them to be late for anything, so he had to stop for a moment and seriously wonder if he should be concerned yet or not.

Summer came strolling back over, looking like she didn't have a care in the world. Her blonde hair was blowing in the wind and her cheeks were a little red and glowing, but considering it was thirty degrees out and they were all standing outside on the tarmac so the dog could do her business, she looked exactly as she should.

Perfect.

Yeah, it didn't matter that they'd known each other for most of their lives or that they'd gotten married and had three beautiful kids together; every time he looked at her, she simply took his breath away.

She was smiling as she approached and then walked right up to him, wrapped her arms around him, and gave him a very thorough kiss. "There. Now you look more relaxed," she said softly, smoothing her hand along his jaw. "You were looking a little fierce there a moment ago."

"I was actually getting a little concerned about Zach and Gabriella."

"Really? Why?"

"When was the last time they weren't the first ones to arrive somewhere?"

Her smile dropped slightly. "Ooh...you're right. Hang on. Let me call her and see where they are." Summer took a step back and pulled her phone out, and Ethan already missed the warmth of her.

"Ugh, Dad, stop looking at Mom with that goofy face," their oldest daughter, Autumn, said as she came to stand beside him. "I swear, you and Mom are the only parents I know who still look at each other like that. It's weird."

Placing his arm around her, he hugged her close. "Or... it's not weird and it's awesome because it means we're still in love."

"Ew...Dad..."

"Oh, stop. It's a good thing. Trust me. We know a lot of divorced couples, and that's just hard on everyone."

"A lot of my friends' folks are divorced," she said quietly. "My best friend Daphne's parents just split up. Like...they told her the day after Thanksgiving. That's just mean. Daphne's a complete mess and I hate this for her."

He heard the sadness and the protectiveness in her voice and he loved that she felt so strongly about a friend's feelings. A few days ago, Summer mentioned to him that this situation was upsetting for Autumn, but this was the first time Autumn was talking to him about it. "I'm sorry for her too. For all of them. It's not easy for anyone."

"It seemed pretty easy for her parents to just give up. Would it have killed them to just...you know...suck it up through the holiday?"

"It might not have killed them, but there was never going to be a good time to break that news. Granted, maybe it would have been kinder to wait, but you don't know what's been going on between them. I'm sure they had their reasons."

"I doubt it," she said stiffly. "All I know is that it makes me sad that I'm not going to be there for her for the next two weeks. This trip is like...this is just the worst timing."

Ethan fought the urge to chuckle and kept his composure by resting his head on top of hers. "Well, you can video chat with her, and if things are really bad, maybe we can see about flying her out after Christmas for the last week. What do you say?"

Autumn turned in his arms and gave him a fierce hug. "Thanks, Dad. You're the best!"

~

"Okay, we'll see you guys in a few minutes, Gabs. Bye!" Hanging up the phone, Summer turned to tell Ethan why Zach and Gabriella were running late, but the sight of him hugging Autumn stopped her.

"Is Autumn gonna be a total downer this whole trip?" their son Jensen quietly asked as he came up behind her. "I thought she'd cheer up once we got Lulu, but she didn't. Then I thought this trip would be exciting because we're gonna get to see everyone, and now she's all weepy over there with Dad." He groaned. "Seriously, why are girls so dramatic?"

Laughing softly, Summer turned and faced him. "She's sad for her friend and that's not a bad thing, okay? I'm sure once we get to North Carolina and she sees everyone, she'll perk up a bit. In the meantime, please don't give her a hard time."

"I won't. I just don't like seeing her like this," he mumbled.

Rather than make a big deal out of the fact that it was incredibly sweet of him to admit that, she simply hugged him. "You're a good brother." One of the flight attendants stepped out of the plane and waved them on. "Now we can finally get out of the cold and get on board!"

"Finally!" he said before jogging toward the plane.

Ariel was about to run after him along with Lulu, but Summer quickly stopped her. "Let's just see if she'll pee one more time, okay?"

"Fine," Ariel huffed before walking away.

Not too far away, she saw Ethan give Autumn another hug before nudging her toward the plane. Then he spotted Summer and walked over to join her.

"Is Autumn okay?" she asked.

"She's really upset about Daphne. I had no idea she'd take it this hard."

"I know. I think because all she knows is how we are with each other, that she just doesn't understand how things like this happen. I hate it for her."

"Well, I told her that maybe we'd see about having Daphne join us in Asheville after Christmas. You know, it would only be for a few days, but..."

Then Summer was hugging him the exact way their daughter did just moments ago. "You, Ethan Reed, are an amazing man. I love you."

He held her tight. "I love you too, sunshine." They stayed like that for several moments before he pulled back. "Did you talk to Gabriella? Are they almost here?"

"Um...they are, but...there is a small complication."

"I don't know what that means," he said. "What kind of complication?"

"Well, remember how Gabriella went to Seattle to see her family last week and how it had been years since she'd spent any real time with them?"

"Yeah..."

Summer paused and wondered how much she should share and if she should just wait until they got there and let Gabriella or Zach explain it for themselves.

"Summer, come on, you're freaking me out. What's going on?"

"Mom! Lulu peed on the plane!" Ariel called out from the airplane door.

*Because of course the puppy would pee on the plane...*

Sighing softly, she shook her head and put her focus back on Ethan. "Okay, just know that I just found this out too, so I don't have a whole lot of information or details."

He nodded.

"When she went to visit, her niece was there and she just had a baby. She's only seventeen. Apparently, she didn't want the baby, the ex-boyfriend didn't want the baby, Gabriella's sister refused to even acknowledge that there *was* a baby, and then her parents were mortified that their granddaughter had a baby at seventeen," she blurted out quickly.

"Holy crap! That's a lot!"

Summer nodded too. "I know, right?"

"So, what does that have to do with them being late?"

"Um, okay, so..." Off in the distance, a car horn sounded, and they both turned to see a large black SUV pulling onto the tarmac. "I think that's them. I'll let Zach explain the rest. It's...it's wild." Ethan frowned, and he was totally cute when he was confused. She instantly reached up and caressed his cheek and then smoothed the crease between his brows until his face relaxed a bit. "Smile. Look relaxed. I think we all need to just..."

"Relax?" he said with a small laugh.

"Exactly. Now let's go and greet them so we can get everyone on the plane and take off on time."

"They're the ones who were late," he murmured.

"Yes, yes, yes, but with good reason."

As they got closer to the vehicle, Summer spotted her

brother Zach getting out, followed by his daughters, Willow and Skylar. They were both the spitting image of Gabriella and she loved them so much!

"Hey!" Zach called out with a wave. "Sorry for the delay!"

"No worries," Ethan told him. "Just glad you're here. Everything okay?"

Just then, Gabriella climbed down from the SUV and stood back as their driver reached in and got something for her.

A baby.

# EIGHT
## ZACH & GABRIELLA
### "SLEEP IS HIGHLY OVERRATED."

THE SHOCKED LOOK on his sister and brother-in-law's faces would be comical if he wasn't so damn tired. There was a time when he didn't need a lot of sleep, when he thrived on the adrenaline of getting through a day when he should be exhausted.

Those days were long gone, as he found out a week ago.

A baby.

He and Gabriella adopted a baby.

Willow and Skylar were hovering over their new brother and quietly arguing over who was going to get to carry him onto the plane.

It was the first time he'd ever been thrilled to hear them fight.

"Girls, why don't you take Cayden's diaper bag and carrier base up to the plane for us? You know he's too heavy with the carrier for either of you to get him up there by yourselves. We'll be up in a minute, okay?"

They nodded and then kissed the baby on the head before grabbing what they needed to and heading toward the jet.

Zach yawned broadly before taking the carrier from Gabriella. "Hey, buddy. You ready for your first flight?"

"Are you sure this is a good idea?" Summer asked as she came over to get a look at the baby. "Is it safe for him to fly? He's so little, but he's so cute!" She leaned down and touched his hand. "Hey, sweetie. I'm your Aunt Summer and I am in love with you already!"

Okay, that was one Montgomery down. He still had no idea how the rest of the family was going to react to the news. Obviously, they were going to be thrilled, but he knew there was also going to be a lot of concern—like what was a couple on the verge of sending their first child off to college doing with a newborn?

Yeah, he was still asking himself that question too.

But when Gabriella had called him from Seattle and told him what was going on, he knew they had to do something. Actually, he could tell by the sound of her voice that she desperately wanted them to adopt Cayden.

"We always said we wished we tried a little longer for another baby," she had reminded him. "And you always wanted a boy..."

"Yeah, but I love our girls," he'd told her. "They are everything to me and I never regretted not having a son instead of our daughters."

"I know, and that's not what I'm saying. I just...I can't explain it, Zach. I saw Cayden and he looked up at me with these big dark eyes, and it was like he was looking into my soul." Her voice shook with quiet emotion and he hated that he hadn't gone on this trip with her. She had sworn it was something she needed to do herself, and he'd foolishly agreed. But once the topic of the baby had come up, he was on the next flight to Seattle.

He arrived and met his wife at her hotel and was

surprised that Cayden was with her. Zach had taken one look at the tiny boy and simply fell in love.

This was their son.

After that, things moved much faster than he thought they would, and the only thing he walked away being absolutely sure of was that Gabriella's family was just as awful as they'd always been. Not one of them showed any emotion or remorse that they were giving Cayden up. And he knew for a fact that they'd never hear from any of them ever again.

Good riddance.

"Zach?" Summer prompted.

"What? Oh, yeah, no, it's fine. We were at the pediatrician's this morning—which is why we were late getting here —and he gave Cayden a clean bill of health and permission for us to fly with him. We had to pick up a few extra things on the way and...here we are!" he said with a near-delirious smile.

"Gabs?" Summer asked. "What about you? How are you doing?"

"I'm tired," she said before yawning. "But in the best way. Sleep is highly overrated when it's for a good cause, right?"

"I guess?" Summer replied, before reaching for Gabriella's hand. "Come on. Let's get you settled on the plane and maybe you can sleep for a few hours. You know there are plenty of extra arms to hold Cayden so you can get some rest."

"Oh, I don't know..."

"You too, Zach," his sister said firmly. "The two of you should go to the back of the plane and rest while you can. Ethan and I have this under control."

"We do?" Ethan asked with a small laugh, but when he

caught Summer's stern look, he instantly sobered. "I mean, we do. Totally."

"I'm sure we'll be fine," Zach countered. "We don't expect any special treatment." But his eyes felt heavy, and the thought of a few hours of uninterrupted sleep sounded too good to be true.

The four of them—well, five with Cayden—made their way to the jet and up the stairs. All the kids were chatting loudly, there was a puppy yipping happily, and it was pure chaos. Zach did his best to get his own family settled before Ethan gave him a gentle shove toward the back of the plane. The sixteen-passenger jet had two sofas in the back of the plane that were slightly separated from the rest of the seats. There was even a small door that you could close for even more privacy. As soon as he and Gabriella got settled back there, he wasn't sure which of them fell asleep first.

Gabriella woke with a start, feeling slightly disoriented. It took a solid minute for her to remember they were on a plane heading to North Carolina to spend the holidays with Zach's family. With her hand resting over her rapidly beating heart, she took a moment to simply catch her breath and relax.

"You okay?" Zach asked sleepily. He was on the sofa opposite hers and looked adorably mussed up.

"Just forgot where we were," she said with a small laugh. "I have no idea how long we've been asleep."

Lifting his hand, he looked at his watch. "About four hours." Then he yawned.

"And it's a six-and-a-half-hour flight, so..."

"So we technically can sleep for another two hours," he said as he got more comfortable.

"Zach..."

Slowly, he sat up. "I know, I know...we really should be out there with everyone and see how Cayden's doing."

"I can't believe they didn't come in to wake us up. He must have needed to be fed and changed."

"Gabs, Ethan and Summer know how to change and feed a baby. Hell, our daughters know how. And I'm guessing Autumn and possibly Jensen could even step in if they needed to. Cayden's probably being spoiled rotten out there."

"Good. He should know what it's like to be surrounded by people who actually love and want him," she said, hating how angry she sounded.

Zach was immediately beside her on her sofa, cupping her face in his strong hands. "Hey, he is always going to know how much he is loved and wanted. We'll make sure of that."

"I just hate to think of what would have happened if I hadn't gone there..." Tears stung her eyes and she hated how emotional this entire situation made her. From the moment she sat down in her sister's living room and heard about Cayden, she'd been on an emotional roller coaster. Hopefully, she'd pull herself together soon.

Like...by the time they got to the retreat house.

"Hey," he said softly, interrupting her thoughts. "We've got this."

Gabriella nodded, but that didn't stop the tears from falling. "It's been so long since we've had a baby in the house. What if...what if we get overwhelmed?"

He chuckled before resting his forehead against hers. "Gabs, we're a team. Always have been, always will be.

There has yet to be any obstacle or situation or anything that we haven't been able to handle." He paused and that's when she saw the sheen of unshed tears in his eyes. "The thought of doing this all again with you is like...the greatest adventure ever."

There was a time when Zach chased after every adventure he could—skydiving, race car driving, triathlons, scuba diving, and mountain climbing. The mountain climbing was the one that nearly killed him and ended his quest for the next adrenaline rush. But he was right about them. In all the years they'd known each other—first as boss and assistant, and then as husband and wife—they'd tackled everything together. And there wasn't anyone else she'd want to tackle this next season of life with.

"I know I kind of threw this at you," she said shakily. "And the girls..."

"The girls are absolutely in love with that boy. I think it's the first time in years they're actually fighting over something good." He placed a kiss on the tip of her nose before pulling back.

"It's just...it's going to change everything. Our entire world is going to be upside down...the dynamic's going to change..."

"For the better," he told her. "It's going to be exciting!"

"Like jumping out of an airplane?" she mocked lightly.

The look he gave her said he caught the reference. "Willow and Skylar have kept you and I on our toes since they were born. We've played sports with them, gone to recitals, danced, sang...every day is like a mini marathon with them, and I love the thought of doing it all with Cayden and seeing what kind of personality he's going to have and what activities he's going to be into..." His bark of laughter startled her before he added, "I can't wait!"

Deep down, she knew Zach was right. There were so many firsts they were going to get to experience and the fact that their daughters were on board with it all meant they'd get to experience it as a family.

"The day I woke up after falling off that mountain, I was mad at the world. And I stayed that way for a long time," he said solemnly. "And when I came home, you marched into my house and took over and put me in my place and..." He squeezed her hand. "You saved me. And now? Now we get to walk in and save that little boy. Together. If you could tackle someone as stubborn as me, raising a baby at our age will feel like a day at the beach."

"I love you so much," she whispered before kissing him, and she knew that no matter what else life threw at them, they'd be just fine.

# NINE

# MEGAN & ALEX

"LADIES AND GENTLEMEN, we have been cleared for takeoff."

Alex reached over and took Megan's hand in his. "Okay, final leg of the trip and then we can finally relax."

Beside him, her eyes were closed and she looked a little tense.

He couldn't blame her; they just took a minor detour on their way from Oregon to North Carolina that could potentially change their lives.

"Dad," his son Daniel whispered from across the aisle. "Since this is first class, can I get a glass of champagne?"

"It wouldn't matter if this were a private jet. The answer is no," Alex told him quietly, but firmly.

"You're asking us to keep a big secret," his son reminded him. "I'm just saying...I do this for you and maybe..."

With Megan's hand still firmly in his, Alex leaned across the aisle and gave Daniel his sternest look. "You're only sixteen. It's illegal for anyone to serve you alcohol, and if you'd like to continue with this line of negotiating, I can guarantee you that I *will* give all of your Christmas presents away."

He chuckled nervously. "To Andrew? *Pfft!* He'd still give them to me."

Alex grinned. "Nope. I'd distribute them all to your cousins. Even the ones you don't get along with."

Daniel's expression fell. "Fine. I was just kidding anyway. Jeez. No need to be a grinch, Dad." Then he promptly shoved his earbuds in and tapped the TV screen in front of him.

"Okay, that's another crisis averted," he mumbled before getting comfortable in his seat. "What about you? Would you like a glass of champagne?"

Megan shook her head. "No, but thank you."

"Are you going to keep giving me the cold shoulder?" he asked softly. "I never said I was going to take the position, but I had to at least go and check everything out for myself."

Alex had his own physical therapy clinic that he started fifteen years ago and it had been very good to him. He made his own hours, made some serious money, and it afforded him and Megan the opportunity to have a good life. She worked with Zach, Summer, and Ethan at Montgomerys and together, they made a very good living. But lately, he was just growing a little disenchanted with...well...a lot.

On a whim, he'd reached out to a couple of headhunters just to see what was available in his field. He'd honestly just thought he'd see what was out there and realize that he had a great setup exactly where he was.

Only...that wasn't quite the way it played out.

Within a week, Alex had over a dozen offers, and one was more dazzling than the last. But the one that intrigued him the most was a position with a massive sports clinic in Boulder, Colorado. The money was almost twice what he was currently making, they would cover all their moving expenses, and pay their rent for up to a year until they found a house to buy. The schools were amazing—both public and private—and there was just something about the facility that genuinely appealed to him.

So...they left for their trip to North Carolina two days early and went to Boulder for an interview and to check out the area as a family. Their three kids weren't thrilled at the thought of leaving their friends, but they were at least open-minded about it. His wife, however, was clearly not on board.

"Megan, come on. Talk to me. Please," he whispered.

She opened her eyes and turned her head to look at him. "I wish you had talked to me before just...jumping in and reaching out to recruiters," she said wearily. "You just dropped this bombshell and made all these plans without saying a word to me. How did you think that was going to make me feel?"

"We've been over this," he replied with equal weariness. "I didn't think it would get to this point. I was just curious."

"You never once mentioned being curious. Ever. I thought you were happy. I thought *we* were happy."

"You know we're happy, Megan. This has nothing to do with you and me. This was about my job and...I don't know...it felt like I lost my joy in doing what I'm doing and I was bringing everyone down with my mood."

"And you think moving us away from everything we've ever known is going to put you in a better mood? Seriously?"

"Um..."

"And now we have to go and spend two weeks with my family with this hanging over our heads," she hissed. "Do you think the kids are really going to keep that to themselves? And am I supposed to lie to my cousins and not give them a heads-up that we may be moving and that I'll have to resign?"

The sigh was out before he could stop it. "No one said any of that is happening. I just thought it was important for us to go and check it out. That's all."

"Hey, Dad?" their daughter Nora asked from the seat behind him.

Twisting around, he looked at her. "What's up, baby girl?"

"Andrew took my earbuds, and the ones the flight attendant gave me hurt my ears. Do you or Mom have an extra pair?"

"Um..."

Beside him, Megan reached down, pulled her purse out, and handed him a small case without a word.

It was going to be a long flight.

It was the worst possible time to be stuck on a plane. All Megan wanted to do was get up and walk away and go somewhere so she could be alone to think.

Or maybe crochet.

Something that was currently impossible and just making her even more angry.

She accepted a cup of tea from the flight attendant and two packages of cookies. When she was stressed, she ate. Junk food of any kind and sweets were her preference and there wasn't a doubt in her mind that she'd be asking for a third snack sooner rather than later. Alex—the jerk—was currently nursing a bottle of water and some healthy granola bar.

Just another reason to be mad at him. He always ate healthy.

Always.

It didn't matter how stressed he was, the man was the epitome of healthy living.

She crammed an entire cookie in her mouth and hoped it bugged him. She was reasonably certain that he was watching her snack choices and judging her. Well...good. Let him. She was sitting here judging him too. How dare he make these life-changing decisions without even consulting her or sharing with her that he was struggling? They were a team and they were always honest with each other. Even when it was something that would cause a fight, they still talked it through. Why did he keep this to himself? And what was she supposed to say to her family?

Looking out the window, she stared at the clouds. It was only a three-hour flight and she knew she was going to have to get herself together. There was no way they could show up for a family reunion with her and Alex not speaking to each other. So, she popped another cookie in her mouth and tried to think of what she needed to say to make things at least a little better.

After a moment, she took a sip of her tea and mentally counted to ten before facing her husband. "I really didn't know you were struggling," she began and then waited for him to look at her. The sorrow and regret were obvious. "Why didn't you talk to me?"

Alex shook his head. "I really thought it wasn't a big deal. That I would get over...whatever it was I was feeling. Every day I'd have to be up and positive for everyone—my staff, my clients—and then I'd go home and feel like I had to be the same way. It was exhausting, but I thought it was normal." He took a sip of water before continuing. "The search was a fluke. I thought it would make me feel better about what I was doing and maybe motivate me again. But..."

"But it confirmed that there's more out there," she said flatly.

He nodded. "I never meant for this to turn into such a mess. Once I heard about the offer, I knew I had to check it out. But I needed you with me because this isn't only about me. I know you believe that I don't see it that way, but it's true. If this isn't good for both of us, then it's not happening."

"Alex, how is that fair? So then...what? We go home and I'm happy and you stay miserable? That's ridiculous."

The huff of frustration told her that this discussion was far from over. "Megan, be realistic. We can't have it both ways. Maybe I just need a break. For all we know, this two-week trip with your family is all I need to clear my head and gain a little perspective. So...let's just...we'll wait until after the holidays to make any decisions."

It would be easy to say yes, but...

"Do you think that's realistic? That the kids aren't going to mention our stopping in Boulder and looking at schools and houses?" she pointed out. "I think we need to be honest and put it out there."

"Why? So your entire family can tell me how I need to suck it up and finish what I started? Or how I owe it to you to let you stay where you are so you can keep working with Zach, Summer, and Ethan?" And yeah, he was heavy on the sarcasm.

"Okay, I didn't think of it like that," she murmured. "I guess I don't know what to do. All I know is keeping things a secret is wrong."

His eyes went a little wide.

"You were wrong, Alex. This was something you should have shared with me."

They sat in silence for so long that Megan just braced herself for the long-winded reprimand at how she was the one who was wrong and that she was just being dramatic.

When he finally spoke, his voice was raw. "You're right. I'm sorry." He hung his head and shook it. "I love you. You taught me a long time ago the importance of talking about my feelings and...I failed you."

"No. You didn't." She cupped his face and kissed his cheek. "And we'll get through this. Somehow."

# TEN

# CHRISTIAN & SOPHIE

## "THE HOLIDAYS JUST SEEM TO HIT HARDER."

"I CAN'T BELIEVE you chartered a jet."

"It was the only way to get everything we needed from California to North Carolina."

"Still...it feels a bit excessive."

Christian gave his wife a patient smile as he walked around and made sure their kids were all settled on the plane. And while Sophie wasn't wrong—this was completely excessive—there was no way to get the two of them, their four kids, and all the presents that were supposed to be shipped out four days ago across the country.

"I know I dropped the ball on the gifts," Sophie said as he sat down beside her. "But in my defense, Lena's holiday recital really did me in. With all the costumes I had to help with and the sets..."

"It's okay, love," he told her, leaning in to kiss her cheek. "In case you've forgotten, I prefer to travel like this. And if Zach and Ethan hadn't reserved the company plane first, I totally would have gotten it for us instead of this." He glanced around again. "I almost wish we had more people traveling with us."

"I had reached out to Megan to see if they wanted us to fly into Portland so they could join us, but she said they already made plans." Then she paused. "And she didn't sound happy about it. Do you think she hates flying commercial like you do? Is that a family thing?"

He couldn't help but laugh. "Soph, are you just meeting us? My sister and I are very much alike and I'm sure she hated the thought of flying during the holidays too. Maybe we'll see if they want to join us on the way home. I know they already booked their tickets, but maybe they can get a credit or a refund or something."

"Hmm...maybe." She nibbled her bottom lip. "I don't know. I feel like there was more to it, but she kind of cut me off and said she had to go."

"Well, let's be honest, it's a good thing they didn't join us for this leg of the trip. With all the presents we're traveling with, there wouldn't be a lot of room for five extra people," he teased.

"Ha, ha. You're hilarious," she deadpanned. "The time just got away from me, and if you were so worried, you could have taken them all to the post office yourself, you know."

"It's really not a big deal. You know I'm just joking."

"Maybe..." she grumbled. "I still can't help but feel bad. Nana would tell me to stop being so scatterbrained and focus. She probably would have smacked my hand too."

Now he felt bad for teasing. Sophie's nana had been gone almost ten years now and she still struggled with the loss. And whenever she started a sentence with "Nana would tell me..." it usually meant she was feeling overwhelmed.

"You know what else your nana would have said?" he asked softly.

She shook her head. "No, what?"

"She would have said how proud she was of you for sewing all those costumes for the girls and how beautiful the sets looked. Then she would have said how she doesn't know how you keep up with four kids and make it all look effortless." He kissed her cheek again. "And then she would've told you how amazing you are and how you got it all from her."

Luckily, that earned him one of her amazing smiles. "Thank you, baby," she cooed before kissing him. "Sometimes I need to remember things like that."

"It's all true. You are amazing and you do more than anyone else I know."

"But the gifts…"

"So what? We're getting them there, aren't we?" he asked with a laugh. "And now we're guaranteed that nothing will happen to them and everything will arrive in one piece. So really, it's a good thing that you didn't get to the post office."

"I know you're just saying that to make me feel better, but thank you."

"I try my best."

The plane took off and it wasn't until they reached their cruising altitude that Christian felt himself relax. He had been working longer hours the last few weeks, putting together reports and projections for this merger. As much as he hated the thought of a working vacation, it wasn't often that all the Montgomerys were together in the same place for an extended period of time, so he knew their time would be productive.

And no one was going to let them work too long.

Still, with the new year starting off with the acquisition of a new company, he wondered if maybe it was the right time to start cutting back and handing off some responsibilities to his own team. Years ago, after the health scare that brought Sophie into his life, he drastically changed his work habits. For the most part, he kept that pace, but every once in a while, the need to prove something hit him and he'd put in far too many hours.

Until Sophie was the one to remind him of what that kind of pace nearly did to him.

He was so thankful for her, and he was desperately looking forward to this time away together.

Even if it came with almost fifty other Montgomerys.

*Oh, Nana...I wish you were here right now. I wish you were on this fancy plane, sipping a mimosa, and telling Christian how much you love to be spoiled. I miss you so much always, but the holidays just seem to hit harder.*

It was crazy how emotional she still got after ten years. Nana had been her whole world and even though she lived long enough to see Sophie and Christian get married and even got to meet their kids, she couldn't help but wish she was still with them.

"Hey, Mom," her youngest daughter Noelle whispered as she climbed into the seat beside her. "Can I ask you something?"

"Of course, baby. What's going on?" Wrapping her arm around her daughter, she hugged her close.

"I wanted to get Dad something special for Christmas," she said quietly as she looked around to make sure Christian wasn't nearby.

"O-kay...but I thought we took care of everything. We bought your father the new Apple Watch he wanted. The four of you decided on it."

She sighed. "I know, but...I really wanted to get him something else just from me. Something special."

"Hmm...I guess we could sneak out one morning while he's working with everyone and do a little shopping," Sophie suggested. "We'll have to see what shops are in the area. Do you know what you want to get him?"

Noelle bit her lip and nodded, but didn't say anything.

"Is it a secret or can you tell me?" she whispered, resting her head against her daughter's.

"Do you promise not to laugh?"

Pulling back slightly, Sophie frowned. "Of course I wouldn't laugh. Why would you even think that?"

Shrugging, Noelle replied, "Because I told Evan and he laughed."

"Okay, well, remind me to talk to him about that." Pausing, she looked around and fought the urge to go and do just that right now. "So, what would you like to get for Dad?"

Noelle glanced around again before moving even closer to Sophie. "Do you remember when we went to the Fun Zone a few weeks ago for my friend Maddie's birthday party?"

Sophie nodded.

"And you know how tense and serious Dad always is?"

The giggle was out before she realized it, but she quickly stopped it and nodded again.

"Well, he was playing the basketball game—you know, the one where you shoot the smaller basketballs and it's got the netting on the side? Do you know what I'm talking about?"

"Um..."

"Can I use your phone?"

"Um...sure." Reaching into her purse, she pulled out her phone and handed it over. A minute later, she was looking at...well...pretty much exactly what her daughter had described to her. "And you want to get this for your father?"

Nodding, Noelle explained. "Mom, he was laughing and smiling and joking around with the other dads and he just looked so relaxed. So I thought maybe if we had that at home, he'd be able to relax like that all the time." Then she frowned. "You think it's stupid too, don't you?"

"Not at all. As a matter of fact, why don't we order it right now and have it delivered to the house? I'll bet we can get it in time for Christmas."

"Really?" Noelle asked excitedly. "And...and you think he'll like it?"

"Sweetie, if it's from you, then I know he'll love it." Leaning over, she kissed her daughter's head and then focused on making the order. It took a little longer because she had to search for the retreat address, but once she got that in, everything else was a breeze. "And...done!"

Noelle launched herself into Sophie's arms. "Thanks, Mom. You're the best!"

"That's what I've been saying for years," Christian said as he walked over and smiled down at them. "What have you two been talking about?"

"It's a secret," Noelle said as she stood up. She gave Christian a fierce hug and said, "I love you, Dad," before walking away.

"Wow, what was that all about?" he asked as he sat back down.

"We were just talking about some stuff to do while we're in the mountains," Sophie said, which wasn't a complete lie. "And remind me to talk to Evan about teasing Noelle."

He frowned. "When was he teasing Noelle?"

"She just mentioned how she went to him with an idea she had for a Christmas present and he laughed at her."

"I'll admit he shouldn't have done that, but...it's kind of what siblings do. I'm sure he wasn't trying to be mean."

"Still...I want him to be a little more aware of how he reacts to things. I want our kids to be close and actually like and respect one another. I was an only child, so...this is all new to me."

"And then you married me and got more siblings and cousins than you ever thought possible. Life's funny, isn't it?"

She nodded. "In the best way possible."

# ELEVEN

# CARTER & EMERY

### "ALL YOUR FANCY CHEESES WILL GET FED TO THE BEARS!"

THERE WERE a million things Carter needed to do in order to get out of the restaurant and to the airport on time, and it looked like things weren't going to go as planned.

"Boss, Chef Maxwell just called from the emergency room. It looks like they're going to have to do surgery. The cut on his hand is too deep and there may be nerve damage."

Carter cursed under his breath and nodded. "It was a freak accident and I hate it for him," he said to his assistant and manager, Rocco. "I hope his wife will keep us posted."

Rocco nodded. "That's what I asked her to do."

Another nod. "Okay, good. Who do we have that can cover for him? Anyone?"

"Um..."

"Rocco, I'm supposed to be on a flight to North Carolina in two hours. Emery's already ticked off at me because she's flying there alone with the kids from New York. If I don't meet them at the airport, I'm going to be sleeping on your couch indefinitely!"

With a small huff and more than a mild look of annoyance, Rocco approached Carter's desk. "Okay, Chef Blake has offered to cover half of Max's shifts."

"Great! That's an excellent start!"

"But he needs tonight and tomorrow off in order to make it work."

"Shit."

"You'll still make it to North Carolina, but..."

"Not in time to meet Emery and the kids at the airport," he murmured. "Who else can we call to help cover Maxwell's hours through the holidays? I can be back right after New Year's Eve..."

"I've put in calls to the managers of all your restaurants to see if they can spare anyone—I figured you wouldn't mind paying to fly someone here to New Orleans and put them up in a hotel..."

"Hell, they can stay at my apartment if they agree to come," Carter added. "Anyone respond yet?"

Rocco shook his head. "But Chef Delia has offered to take on some extra hours..."

But Carter shook his head. "She's too new. I don't think she can handle the holiday crowds we get here, and I'm not willing to take the chance. If we get someone else from one of the other locations and she wants to assist..."

"She may surprise you, Carter. I think she's come a long way."

"No. She does fine with the lunch crowd, but the one dinner shift she had, she got way too frazzled. I can't risk it. Let me make some calls and see what we can figure out." Looking at his watch, he cursed again. "And I need to call Emery."

Rocco chuckled lightly. "Good luck."

Luck wasn't going to do anything for him. What Carter needed was a miracle.

With a weary sigh, he scrubbed a hand over his face and hit Emery's number on his phone.

"Is your flight on time?" Emery said frantically as a way of greeting. "Because our flight is delayed by an hour."

"Um, I'm not sure, Em. Listen, I..."

"Oh, no," she quickly interrupted. "No. No, no, no..."

"You don't even know what I'm gonna say!"

"You're going to say that you're not getting on that flight this afternoon and that there is some restaurant emergency keeping you there."

Damn.

"Max sliced his hand badly—like almost severed a finger. He's in the ER right now awaiting surgery. I know you're upset, but this is a legit emergency."

"This time."

"You know I wouldn't do this if it weren't an emergency, Em."

"The thing is, Carter, everything's an emergency to you. We're going to see *your* family and now you're not going to be there!"

"I will be there, just...not today."

"When then?"

"I'm working on it. I swear. Rocco and I are making calls and I will be there as soon as I possibly can. And you know I will because I wouldn't miss Christmas with you and the kids and I'm the one cooking for everyone!"

She was silent for a moment before saying, "Just know this—if you don't show up, I'm serving everyone Pop Tarts for breakfast, frozen pizza for lunch, and popcorn with ice cream on the side for dinner."

If he didn't think she was serious, he would have laughed.

"And all the fancy cheeses you probably had your aunt

order for you will get tossed in the trash or lit on fire or fed to the bears!"

"Okay, if I'm not there in forty-eight hours, you can do all those things, okay?"

"You better be there, Carter," she said sadly. "I really am sorry about Max and I hope someone's taking care of his wife and kids for him, but you need to be here with *your* wife and kids too. Can't you just...close the restaurant for a few days?"

His head nearly exploded. "Let's call that Plan B, okay?"

"Fine. Just...be there, Carter. Please."

"You have my word, Em. I promise."

It wasn't that Emery didn't believe Carter; it was just that she was a realist.

She was devastated for Chef Maxwell and was actively praying for his full recovery. But she was sad for herself too. The fact was, though, that it was the week before Christmas and it was going to be hard to find someone to fill in for him.

Now, as she sat in the crammed gate area of the airport with their two sons, all she could think about was how she was going to break it to them that Carter wasn't meeting them in North Carolina. They both worshipped him and were looking forward to having him basically to themselves for the next two weeks and now...they weren't.

"He's not coming, is he?" their older son Hunter asked with an angry huff.

"Chef Maxwell got hurt and is going to need surgery. He nearly severed one of his fingers," she explained with a calmness she didn't particularly feel.

"Ew. Gross."

"What's gross?" Austin, their younger son, asked as he pulled one earbud out to join the conversation.

"Chef Maxwell cut his finger off and now Dad's not coming for Christmas," Hunter snapped.

"Okay, that's not what I said," Emery gently reprimanded. "He's going to be there for Christmas. Actually, he's just going to be a few days late. He needs to find someone to take over Maxwell's shift and then he'll meet us in Asheville. Forty-eight hours, tops."

*At least...he better be...*

"This sucks," Austin murmured.

"Typical Dad," Hunter grumbled right after him.

Unfortunately, no matter how disappointed she was with the entire situation, there was no way she was going to let her sons think poorly of Carter.

"Guys, come on. Do you remember the last time we went to New Orleans with your father and Chef Maxwell made the two of you chocolate-filled beignets?" Emery reminded them. "And didn't he teach you how to make his famous gumbo and the best way to make crawfish?"

"Yeah, but..."

Emery immediately cut them off. "The fact is that Chef Maxwell has always been very good to us and if your dad has to step in and take care of things at the restaurant so Chef can heal, then that's what needs to be done. Instead of grumbling about it, we should be proud of your father. He could have just left and made Rocco take care of everything, but he didn't. Why? Because he's an incredible boss."

Neither boy looked fully convinced, but she understood their disappointment.

"Look, I'm not thrilled with the situation, guys. I was

annoyed when he decided to go to New Orleans a week ago, and I've kind of been annoyed every day since."

"You were pissed," Austin said with a snicker.

"But when you're angry with Dad, we get to eat junk food, so..." Hunter said with a laugh of his own.

"Okay, okay...we're getting off topic here," she interjected. "The fact is, we were going to fly to North Carolina without him anyway. Now we'll pick up the car and head to this big family retreat, just the three of us, and it's going to be fine. All your cousins will be there and maybe you'll get to go snowmobiling or skiing or snow tubing."

"Mom, we do that stuff at home. It's not like it's a big deal," Austin said.

"No, but...you don't get to do it with your cousins, aunts, and uncles, so...look at it as an adventure. Maybe you'll get to teach Evan, Brayden, Lena, and Noelle how to do those things. You know they tend to gravitate more toward the beach activities. I'm sure Christian and Sophie have taken them to the mountains once or twice, but they probably aren't as skilled as you guys."

Again, neither looked thrilled, but there were only so many positive scenarios she could put out there when she was feeling this down.

"Can we go grab a snack and something to drink?" Hunter asked.

"Yeah, sure. Go ahead." Then she paused. "And see if they have any cookies or chips or something for me, please."

"You got it!" They were up and running in the blink of an eye and as much as she hated to admit it, she was thankful for a few minutes alone.

She contemplated calling Carter back to see if he had any luck finding coverage, but knew it was probably unlikely in the last ten minutes. Still, she stared at the phone in her hand and basically willed it to ring.

It didn't.

*Please come home for Christmas, Carter. The boys and I need you.*

# TWELVE

# THE GANG'S ALL HERE

IT WASN'T LIKE everyone showed up at the same time, but it certainly seemed that way.

Monica felt like she, Janice, and Eliza were constantly welcoming everyone and then showing everyone to their rooms and around the massive house. None of them were strangers to living in large homes, but this place had her feeling her age.

"Thank God for the elevator," she murmured as she rode up with Lucas, Emma, and their girls.

"This place is massive, Grandma," Lily said with a smile. "And I get my own room, right?"

With a patient smile, Monica took her eldest grandchild's hand in hers. "For now."

"For now? Why for now?"

"Everyone has a bed and some of your cousins are three to a room or sharing a double bed in the bunk room. So you need to be prepared just in case someone has to share your room."

"Grandma..."

"Each room has a king bed and a futon. They can realistically sleep four people. Which means..."

"Which means if someone needs to share your room, you'll gladly do it," Lucas interrupted with just a hint of firmness. "We understand that you're the oldest, but there are a lot of people here, Lily, and it needs to be fair."

She huffed with mild annoyance, but figured she could smooth over any issues her cousins were having and manage to keep the room to herself. "I get it, Dad. No need to get all worked up over something that probably won't even be an issue, right? We all get along great."

But he gave her a look that said he knew exactly what she was thinking and that he was on to her.

"How did you work out all these rooms, Monica?" Emma asked as they stepped out of the elevator onto the upper level.

"It wasn't easy; trust me. Janice, Eliza, and I spent a week working on it and basically we tried to keep the kids in the bunk room and the bedrooms surrounding it. We're all just hoping everyone's going to get along and there won't be any issues with who we paired everyone with."

"We're all just going to be using our rooms to sleep," Emma said. "And I'll bet they're all soundproof, so even if there are kids in them, they won't be disruptive."

"I'll bet most of them will be hanging out and potentially falling asleep down in that game room," Lucas said with a laugh. "I'd be seriously impressed if we got everyone in their beds at the same time each night."

Off in the distance, the doorbell rang and there was a round of loud voices and laughter. Besides Lucas and his family, William and Monica, Eliza, Robert and Janice, Jason and his family, and Mac, Gina, Barb and the kids, no one else had arrived.

Well, and whoever just came in the door.

"Okay, Lucas and Emma, you are in bedroom number seventeen here at the end of the hall. There's a king bed, a futon, a full bathroom, coffeemaker, and a mini fridge. Why don't you get settled and I'll take the girls down to the other end of the hall and show them their rooms?"

"Sounds good. Thanks, Mom," Lucas said, kissing her on the cheek. As soon as they were alone, he closed the door, locked it, and collapsed on the bed. "How long do you think we can stay in here undetected?"

Emma joined him with a laugh. "I'm sure Becca and Sloane are going to want to tell us all about their room, so... maybe five minutes?"

"I'm exhausted already," he groaned. "A five-minute nap will go a long way."

"Right there with ya," she said, snuggling up beside him.

Downstairs, James and Selena, along with Jamie and Isabella, were getting the grand tour from Janice.

"We have the game room, a movie theater that has seating for 55, a small gym, and an indoor pool down here!" she explained. "And outside, there are two hot tubs! I hope you brought your bathing suits!"

Selena chuckled. "Aunt Monica mentioned that in all of her emails about the house. Personally, I'm looking forward to the hot tub."

James wrapped his arm around her waist before kissing her cheek. "Me too."

"Ew, stop," Jamie mumbled before walking over to the elevator. "Can we take this up to our room?"

"Absolutely," Janice told him. "But a few words about the sleeping arrangements..."

Her grandson groaned loudly.

"You're sharing a bunk with Jensen," she told him. "And

Isabella, you're sharing one with Emily."

"Ooh, fun! We've been reading the same books, so we're going to have a lot to talk about!" Emily said.

"The bunk room is huge!" Janice went on. "It sleeps 16, has two massive bathrooms, and each of the bunks has its own charging stations for your phones." They rode the elevator up to the upper level and stopped in the bunkroom first, where she pointed out which bunks they were using. "Why don't you two get your things put away while I show your folks their room?"

"Thanks, Grandma!" Isabella said as she excitedly claimed her bunk.

They walked out of the bunk room and down the hall to the left a bit before they stopped at the first bedroom. "You have bedroom number fourteen. King bed, a futon, full bath, coffeemaker, and mini fridge." Then she laughed.

"What's so funny?" Selena asked.

Waving her off, she chuckled again. "I feel like a broken record. I've been making that speech all day and only half of the group is here so far!"

In the distance, the doorbell rang and while she was certain it was Eliza's turn to answer it, she couldn't be sure.

"You two settle in. We're going to meet down in the kitchen for a little welcome reception at five. Everyone's supposed to be here by then. So, relax and I'll see you later!" She kissed them both on the cheek before she left them and quickly made her way down the stairs.

Over the next two hours, the house filled up. Ryder and Casey arrived, Christian and Sophie and a mountain of gifts showed up looking a little frazzled, Emery and the boys pulled up without Carter, and it was pure chaos.

Or so they all thought.

When Summer and Ethan walked through the door

with warm smiles, huge hugs, and a tiny pug who immediately peed in the entryway, everyone was thrilled to see them. But when Zach, Willow, and Skylar walked in and paused, everyone sensed something big was coming.

That's when Gabriella walked in with a tiny bundle in her arms.

"A baby?" Janice cried, her voice echoing in the large entryway. "How...? When...? Why didn't you say anything?" Then she ran over to Gabriella and instantly fell in love with the tiny face blinking up at her. "Oh, my goodness..."

"Mom," Zach said, wrapping his arm around her. "Meet your newest grandchild—our son, Cayden."

She instantly burst into tears. "I don't...how did this...we just saw you at Labor Day," she said as Gabriella placed the baby in her arms.

"What's all the racket about?" Robert demanded as his voice echoed around the large entryway. "I thought I heard Janice..." He came up short when he spotted his wife holding a baby. He looked around in utter confusion because—while they were quite a large family—news of a baby was always shared long before the child's arrival. "Who...?" Stepping up beside his wife, he stared down at the bundle in her arms.

"Dad," Zach said quietly, "We'd like you to meet your new grandson, Cayden."

"What...? When...?" His eyes instantly went to Gabriella. "We just saw you both for Labor Day. Why didn't you say anything?"

"It's a long story," Zach replied. "And I'd really love it if we only had to tell it one more time, so why don't we wait until everyone's here?"

"That sounds like a good idea," Janice said before

kissing the baby softly on the head. "But I'm not letting him go."

Chuckling, Zach gave her a small squeeze. "Believe me when I say we're not going to argue with you about it, but we'd love to get things settled in our room for him, if that's possible."

"I'll show you the way," Monica said as she came over and hugged both Zach and Gabriella. "And if either of you feels like giving me the abbreviated version of the story while we go..."

"They're the first bedroom on the right, Monica," Janice quietly scolded. "And you'll hear all about it with the rest of us."

Fortunately, her sister-in-law merely shrugged before telling Willow and Skylar that their room was upstairs and also the first room on the right.

Slowly, Janice walked toward the massive living room and sat down. There were so many people who followed and there were so many different conversations going on, but her sole focus was on Cayden. When her husband sat down beside her and reached for the baby's hand, her heart felt incredibly full. "I thought becoming great-grandparents was next for us," she said softly. "Can you believe this little guy?"

"I honestly can't wait to hear all about him, but...even if Zach and Gabriella didn't want to share the story, it wouldn't matter. I'm already crazy about him."

She smiled up at him. "I love you."

He met her gaze with a smile of his own. "Love you too."

Glancing around, Janice tried her best to get some kind of head count, but it was almost impossible. "Is everyone here? Are we missing anyone?"

Eliza walked over and joined them. "We're just waiting for Megan and Alex. She texted to say they landed and were on their way. Apparently, there was some sort of confusion with the rental car, but they finally got it all worked out."

"Oh, that's good. It seems like the travel gods were all on our sides today." Unable to help herself, she stroked a finger along Cayden's cheek. "He's perfect. He's just so perfect."

"It's been a long time since we've had a newborn in the family," Eliza commented before sighing dreamily. "And they never said a word to you about him?"

Janice shook her head. "This was a total surprise—a great one, don't get me wrong—but a complete surprise." Cayden yawned broadly and then his little face scrunched up. "Uh-oh. I know that look." She glanced around frantically. "Is there a diaper bag anywhere? A pacifier? Is he hungry?"

Before she got herself too worked up, Zach appeared and held out his arms. "He probably needs to be changed and then fed."

"Can't I feed him?" she asked as she handed the baby over.

He laughed again. "Absolutely. Why don't you come to our room so we can get him changed and then we'll figure out where to heat up his bottles and all that good stuff."

"Every room has a mini fridge, microwave, and coffeemaker. You should be able to do it all right in the privacy of your room," she told him as she followed him across the massive space.

"Really? I honestly didn't even notice. I simply dropped the bags and took a moment to wash up and then came out to join you."

Patting his arm, she smiled. "This is going to be the best

Christmas ever."

Back in the living room, Eliza stood and frowned. Emery mentioned that Carter was going to be detained, Megan and Alex were late, and she had news of her own to share. Of course, she hadn't planned on making her announcement until after dinner, but she hated how it was always her branch of the family that seemed to come with the most drama.

*This was supposed to be a new beginning...*

"You okay, Eliza?" William asked as he made his way over to her. "You look like you're in a little distress."

William was always one of the good guys. Possibly one of the greatest guys. How many years had she spent wishing her Joseph could have been more like his brother? But sadly, he couldn't and had died far too young and far too angry and left far too many scars on her and their children. Carter, Megan, and Christian were all happy and successful adults, but there were still lingering hurts from their father, even all these years later.

"Eliza?"

"What? Oh, I was just worried about what was keeping Megan and Alex, and I'm sure you heard that Carter was detained."

Nodding, he wrapped an arm around her and led her to the kitchen to pour her something to drink. "Emery assured me it was a genuine emergency," William told her. "One of his chefs nearly severed a finger, so he's staying on until they can cover his shifts through the holidays."

She nodded and silently prayed her son would be able to find coverage. It wouldn't be the first time he'd missed a holiday, but, to be fair, it hadn't happened since he and Emery got married and had their boys.

"I guess I'm a bit pessimistic," she murmured.

"Understandable," William replied before she could explain. "Carter's business doesn't come with normal hours. I remember Joseph telling me about the many years Carter didn't come home for the holidays." He paused and took a sip of water. "We'll just have to think positively that it won't be the case this year. Besides, he wouldn't do that to Emery or his sons."

"I hope you're right."

He nodded confidently. "Eliza, have I ever been wrong?" he asked with a hearty laugh.

She was about to comment when the doorbell rang. "That'll be Megan and Alex!" And she quickly made her way to the door to let them in. Eliza knew she was smiling from ear to ear, but from the look on all the faces greeting her, there wasn't much to smile about. "Um..."

"Hey, Mom," Megan said quietly before stepping in and hugging her.

"Hi, Gram!" Daniel, Andrew, and Nora each called out as they stepped in and gave her a hug too.

Alex was the last one in and his expression was definitely tense—and completely unlike him. Alex was the perpetual optimist and always had a smile on his face. What on earth could possibly be going on?

"This place is massive!" Andrew said as he looked around. "Where's everyone sleeping?"

"Let me take you on a tour and then you can check out your rooms. We're all meeting up for a little welcome reception in around thirty minutes and I'm sure you'll want to freshen up."

Both Megan and Alex nodded silently.

*O-kay...*

Eliza closed the door and started her whole tour dialogue, telling them about the house. "Megan and Alex, your bedroom is here on the main floor. You're in room number six and it's right down this hallway here. Do you want to put your bags in there before we finish walking around?"

"Sure," Alex said with a small smile. "Just give us a minute." He grabbed two large suitcases and Megan followed with two smaller ones.

Turning to her grandchildren, she asked, "Did you have a good flight?"

They looked at each other awkwardly and then simply smiled and nodded.

Yeah, something was definitely going on.

When Alex and Megan rejoined them, Eliza took them down the stairs and showed them all the recreational amenities, and then up in the elevator to show the kids their rooms. The boys were going to be in the bunk room, and Nora was going to share a room with her cousins, Autumn and Ariel.

"Can we stay up here and hang out with everyone?" Andrew asked. "Or do we need to be downstairs?"

"You can certainly stay up here for now, and we'll call up when you need to join everyone. How does that sound?"

"Perfect!" he said before heading back to the bunk room where most of the cousins were all hanging out.

Turning toward her daughter, Eliza eyed her warily. "Would the two of you like some time to freshen up, or are you ready to come down to the living room with everyone?"

Alex said, "Freshen up," at the same time as Megan said, "Ready to see everyone."

Eliza inwardly groaned. "Follow me," she said as she led them to the elevator. They stepped inside, but she didn't press any buttons.

"Um, Mom? You need to..."

"Oh, I know, but I wanted to say something while it's just the three of us." She paused and let out a steadying breath. "There's obviously something going on with the two of you and while I respect your privacy, I'd appreciate it if you could pull it together for now. If you need to go and fight something out, I'd definitely appreciate it if you wouldn't do it here in the house."

"Mom!" Megan cried. "What in the world?"

"I have been looking forward to this trip for months and I was hoping that everyone would show up and be just as happy," she admitted. "I had something important that I wanted to discuss with everyone tonight, and just knowing that the two of you are fighting...it just...it..." Tears stung her eyes and she hated that she was basically manipulating them into making up.

"Eliza," Alex began quietly. "We're fine, okay? We do have some stuff going on, but we're not going to need to drive off anywhere to fight it out. You don't need to worry."

"I don't mean to pry..."

"You're not prying, Mom," Megan assured her. "You're just noticing the obvious. I promise we're fine. But...maybe we will take a few minutes to freshen up before we join everyone. Will that be okay?"

Eliza sniffled. "I feel terrible adding more stress to you both..."

Rather than answer, Megan wrapped her in her arms and hugged her. "You're not adding any stress, believe me. We've both been looking forward to this trip too and you know travel days are always a bit tense."

She nodded. "If you're sure..."

Alex hugged them both. "We're good, Eliza. Don't worry. Let's go down to the main floor and you can rejoin everyone and we'll join you in a little bit."

Stepping out of their embrace, she nodded and pushed the button for them to go down. "Thank you. You're both wonderful and I appreciate you taking the time to calm my nerves."

"Are you sure you're alright?" Megan asked. "And what important thing did you want to discuss with everyone tonight?"

The elevator doors opened and Eliza slipped out first. "You'll just have to wait and hear it with everyone else. Now go and freshen up. We're having cocktails and appetizers at five. Love you!" she called out with a wave as she walked away.

"Okay, that was weird," Megan quietly said as she and Alex stepped out of the elevator.

"It's not like it was hard to figure out that we're fighting," he replied as he turned down the hallway toward their room.

"Can we just...not right now, Alex? Please? It's been a stressful enough day and I really just wanted to get here and relax with my family."

He nodded. "Sure."

In their room, Megan took her turn in the bathroom first and then stepped out so Alex could do the same. She unpacked two of the suitcases and had to admit, the room had a rustic charm to it while offering almost every amenity you could need.

When Alex joined her, he unpacked the last big suitcase before carefully pulling her into his arms. "I'm sorry."

"I know," she whispered. "And I promise I'm going to try to be more open-minded about the whole situation. I'm just..."

"I know," he interrupted. "Let's just forget about the whole thing, okay? I don't need to move or change jobs. I think this trip is going to go a long way in helping me sort of...you know...regroup?"

She wasn't sure she quite believed him, but...it was exactly what she had been hoping for. "I love you and I just want you to be happy."

"Your happiness makes me happy," he told her, resting his forehead against hers. "C'mon. Let's go join everyone and see what it is your mom has to share with all of us." He kissed her softly. "What do you think it is? A boyfriend?" Then he laughed and fortunately, Megan laughed with him.

"Oh my goodness! Could you imagine!" Then she laughed harder. "I highly doubt that's her news, but I'm hoping it's something good and nothing sad or..." She gasped.

"What? What is it?"

"Do you think it's her health? Do you think she's going to tell us she's dying?" Her knees buckled, but Alex held her tight. "Oh God! Why would she wait for the holidays to do that?"

"Okay, okay...I think you're getting a little ahead of yourself. Let's think positively." He hugged her close before leading her to the door. "Positive. Good news. It's all going to be okay." He opened the door and they both stepped out into the hallway and froze.

"Do you...do you hear that?" Megan asked. "Is that...?"

"That's a baby crying," Alex said, looking around in confusion. "Who had a baby?"

"I have no idea..."

Taking her hand in his, he started walking down the hall. "It looks like this is going to be one hell of a Christmas retreat."

# THIRTEEN

# ARRIVAL DAY DINNER

## "I'D HONESTLY KILL FOR PIZZA RIGHT NOW."

IN THEORY, it sounded great to gather everyone on the main level for a bit of a welcome reception. They were going to serve snacks and drinks and essentially toast the start of their holiday retreat.

The reality was that if it weren't for the catering staff they'd hired for the evening, nothing would have gotten accomplished.

Monica breathed a sigh of relief when she noticed the staff working hard in the kitchen and placing out platters of food and lining up piles of plates and utensils and napkins along with tubs filled with ice and drinks. William stepped up beside her, wrapping his arm around her waist, and whispered, "You ready?"

She nodded. "If you can bring order to this chaos, then I say go for it." Then she reached for a glass of champagne and handed it to William before taking one for herself. Behind her, their servers were waiting with trays of drinks to hand out once everyone was ready.

"May I have everyone's attention?" William called out and surprisingly, the room grew quiet quickly. "I'd like to say welcome to everyone. It's not often we can get everyone at the same place at the same time, but except for Carter, we're all here."

He paused and nodded to the servers, who began passing out drinks.

"I really just wanted to take a minute to say what a blessing all of you are and I'm so thankful that you were all able to make the time to have us come together like this," he went on. "You've all gotten the tour of the house, I know Monica has sent out at least a dozen emails detailing all the local attractions and activities, and I appreciate all the patience because we're going to be putting in some work hours for the next several days."

"As long as you keep it to only several days, we'll keep being patient," Monica teased and everyone laughed.

"If everyone has a glass, I'd like to make a toast," William said loudly. "To family. It does my heart good to see how much we've grown. To look at all these young faces and see this next generation just fills my heart with joy. I look forward to hearing all about what you're doing with your lives and all the exciting things you've been up to!"

"Just don't tell him too much about your personal lives," Jason called out with a mischievous grin and again, everyone laughed. "He may look harmless, but he spent a lot of years playing matchmaker, so unless that's what you're looking for, be careful what you share!"

William didn't let it bother him. He knew it was all said in fun and most of the kids here were too young for him to do any serious matchmaking.

That didn't mean he wasn't thinking about it, though...

"Yes, yes, yes," he said once the laughter died down a bit. "All of your parents owe their happiness to me."

There was a round of light arguments that went on for a

few minutes, but all it did was make him smile. In this room were families that were started because he had been a little crafty. And if they all wanted to poke a little fun at him over it, he'd take it. Their smiles and laughter and the look of contentment on their faces spoke volumes.

"Anyway," William finally interrupted, "I'd like to rase a glass to family. It's everything. Here's to a wonderful retreat and a wonderful holiday. Cheers!"

"Cheers!" everyone called out and then it became a bit of a free for all. The kids ran up to grab snacks and then immediately took their bounty down to the lower level. As much as William wanted to push a little for them to stay up here, it got noticeably quieter, which meant the adults could actually have a conversation.

Then he noticed that Lily was still up here. Kissing Monica on the cheek, he made his way over to his grand-daughter.

"I thought you would have taken off with all your cousins," he said, noticing the glass of champagne in her hands. "Should you be..."

She rolled her eyes while laughing softly. "Grandpa, I'm 22. I'm allowed to drink." Then she leaned in and kissed him on the cheek. "I'm glad I could be here for this. I've missed you."

Was there anything sweeter than hearing those words from your grandchild? He wondered.

"I've missed you too," he told her before leading them over to a sofa in the far corner of the room. "So, tell me all about dancing on a cruise ship. What was that like?"

Her entire face lit up as she tucked her legs under her and got more comfortable. "It felt like I was dancing in a Broadway show every night! The costumes were amazing, the music was awesome, and the audience always seemed to be having a good time." Pausing, she took a sip of her champagne. "During the day we offered dance lessons on the different decks and sometimes we had to step in and help in other areas."

"What areas?"

Now her face scrunched up a bit. "Serving in the lounges or restaurants." She sighed. "I am definitely not a server. I dropped a lot of stuff and messed up orders, but I didn't have a choice. It was one of the reasons it was so hard to get time off. They were always understaffed and guilted us into taking extra trips."

"Well, that's not very professional of them," William chided lightly. "Are you going to go back after Christmas?"

"I don't think so, but...I need to do something."

"Lily, sweetheart," he said with mild amusement. "I hardly think you need to be putting so much pressure on yourself. Your parents would love to have you home for a little while until you figure out your next move. And if you really want to work, we could always find a position for you at Montgomerys."

The laugh was out before she could stop it. "Oh, Grandpa..." she began. "You know I am *not* a finance person or an office one. So, unless you're suddenly hiring entertainment for the office, I am not someone you want behind a desk."

Fortunately, William saw the humor in it as well. "I just thought..."

Reaching out, she rested her hand on his. "I know I can go home with Mom and Dad and it would be great. I could hang out with Sloane and Becca and just relax. But I feel like I need to be proactive. I want to audition for the Rockettes, but that's not until April. There are some other possibilities, but most of them aren't until May. Basically, I've got time on my hands and it's bugging me."

"A typical Montgomery trait, I'm afraid. We don't like to be idle."

"Exactly!" she said with a smile. "So, what about you, Grandpa? What's new with you? I hear there's a big merger and you're all going to be working on it while you're here, but is there anything else exciting going on?"

He glanced around before leaning in slightly. "Well, don't tell your grandmother, but...I'm going to surprise her with a trip to Scotland for our fiftieth wedding anniversary."

Her blue eyes went wide. "Seriously? That's amazing! And totally romantic!"

"You think so, huh?"

"Oh, definitely!" She sighed. "You're one of the good guys. I don't think they make guys like you anymore."

"Why would you say that?"

"I don't know. It just feels like most guys don't want to put any effort into a relationship. It's kind of depressing."

"Maybe you're dating or looking to date the wrong kind of men," he suggested. "Are you currently dating anyone?"

She nodded and smiled. "Ash. He's a bartender on the ship, but he's also one of the mechanics. He's got an amazing motorcycle collection that he's restoring when he has time off."

"Interesting."

Lily sensed a hint of disapproval. "He's a nice guy. Really. He's going to come here for New Year's Eve, so you'll get to meet him."

"I believe the last boyfriend of yours I met was..."

"Gunner," she replied. "He was a drummer in a band."

William forced himself not to cringe. The boy had too many tattoos and a bad attitude. "Yes, I remember. And who did you date after him?"

"Hmm...there was...Troy—he was a skateboarding

champion—and then Jett." She took another sip of her drink. "He was a tattoo artist."

He was beginning to see a pattern here.

"Maybe it's the type of guy you're dating that's the problem, Lily," he said carefully. "Perhaps if you went out with someone who...you know...works in an office or is a little more...I mean...or a little less...?"

Laughing softly, she squeezed his hand. "I get what you're saying, but believe me, the last thing I want is to date a guy who reminds me of my dad. I'm not looking for the suit and tie guy. I want someone who's edgy and fun and artsy and creative! I want someone who would jump up on stage and dance with me. Does that make sense?"

He nodded but refrained from saying anything. She certainly wasn't going to make it easy for him to find someone suitable for her.

"William? Lily? Come have something to eat," Monica called from across the room. "Lily, the stuffed baby porto-bellos are fantastic and I know how much you love stuffed mushrooms. Come taste!"

Before she stood, Lily leaned over and kissed William on the cheek. "Thanks for hanging out with me. I always love when it's just the two of us. Remember when you used to push me on the swing in your backyard?"

Tears stung his eyes because he remembered it vividly. "I do."

"Sometimes, I miss those days," she said quietly, holding out her hand to him as they both got to their feet. "Now let's go grab those mushrooms before they're gone."

And together they walked, hand in hand, to join the rest of the family and William already knew this moment was going to be the highlight of the entire trip.

Two hours later, they were all seated in the massive dining area of the kitchen. It was a wide-open space with two large islands, one that had seating for twelve, and then three long tables that each sat eighteen people. It was loud and boisterous, but it was nice that they could all sit and eat together.

"I didn't think we were getting anything catered," Emma said as she sat down beside her mother-in-law.

"Well, that all sounded good in theory, but the more Janice, Eliza, and I talked about it, we realized that no one was going to want to cook on the day we all arrived."

Emma nodded. "True."

"And even on the second day, we weren't sure we could pull off three solid meals, so the caterer will be back tomorrow night." She took a sip of her wine. "Of course, we all thought Carter would be here and eager to take over the kitchen, so it's really quite fortuitous that we hired a catering company since we don't know when he'll arrive."

"When who will arrive?" Lily asked as she joined them.

"Carter," Monica said with a smile. "Your mother and I were just talking about how lucky we are that we brought in some help with dinner tonight and tomorrow night. Hopefully he'll be here by our third night because even though I know we could all work together to put out a meal, it probably won't be as easy to do for this many people as it would be for Carter."

"True," Lily agreed. "There's always pizza too. I mean, no need to make every dinner a formal affair."

"I'd honestly kill for some pizza right now," Emery said as she came and sat with them. "And not even the ones delivered from some local pizzeria, but just a good, frozen pizza with all the toppings."

Monica froze and so did Emma and Lily, unsure if they should mention what they were talking about.

Clearing her throat, Monica reached for her glass again. "Well, it's not pizza, but it's still Italian. We've got lasagna and meatballs and sausage coming out—plus a garden salad and garlic bread."

"Sounds fabulous," Emery said before taking a sip of her own wine. "I was so stressed traveling alone with the boys that I'm afraid I only indulged in junk food all day. At least...until we had appetizers, so I am more than ready for a real meal."

"Have you talked to Carter?" Emma asked.

Nodding, Emery relaxed a bit in her seat. "I called him after we got here when I had a few minutes to myself in our room." Then she sighed. "I know he's not here for a legitimate reason, but sometimes it's just hard. It's been a while since we had a break so we could all be together for more than a few days at a time. We were really looking forward to it."

"You know how these Montgomery men are," Monica said with more than a hint of sympathy. "Most of them are going to be working for the next few days instead of relaxing with the rest of us."

"Yes, but at least they're here," Emery reminded her. "We already knew Carter would be spending a lot of time in the kitchen helping prepare the meals, but when he wasn't cooking, he would be spending time with the boys. They miss him and they're both at an age where they're starting to resent the fact that he spends more time at his restaurants than he does with us. And honestly, I'm having a hard time defending him anymore."

This time Emma nodded. "I totally understand that. For as much as we can say we've all been there, the fact is, we haven't. Carter's career is much different from the corporate one most of the family shares. There may have been late nights or weekends where they worked, but Carter's job takes him all over the country." She gave Emery a sad smile. "Just know that we're all here if you need to vent."

"Thanks," she replied wearily. "The thing is, I'm tired of hearing myself whine. Over the years, I've worked on the corporate side of Montgomerys and I get being responsible and focused. And I even love the fact that Carter is so hands-on with his restaurants. It's just hard to handle when it interferes with family plans."

"Any word from Carter?" William asked as he took a seat beside his wife. There was a round of groans that left him mildly confused.

"We'll talk about it later," Monica whispered.

The servers began placing plates of food in front of everyone and for a while, all the conversation was focused on that.

At the next table, James and Ryder were listening to their wives' conversation about the reality show while tele-pathically trying to communicate just how much they disagreed with everything they were saying.

Well, telepathically and with nudges and kicks under the table.

"I think we need to get a big SUV wrapped with our logo on it and make sure that's staged in the background as much as possible," Casey said around a forkful of lasagna. "That's just free publicity that we can't get anywhere else."

"You could simply drive around town with the same wrapped SUV," Ryder mumbled.

"I love the idea of the SUV," Selena agreed. "And what about t-shirts? Like...all our staff should wear t-shirts with our logo on it during the setup phase! Again, more free publicity!"

James kicked his brother under the table.

"But they really are looking for drama," Casey reminded her. "I mean...I'm not a fan of the whole crashing into the Ferrari thing, but..."

*Thank God*, Ryder thought.

"I think we can work with it," Selena countered. "As long as it comes out that it was someone else's fault—like the bride's jealous sister or something. Do you think we can suggest that?"

"That's brilliant! Oh my goodness! You know how much viewers love when siblings fight!"

Again, James kicked Ryder under the table.

"Oh, for the love of it, James," Selena snapped. "If you keep kicking Ryder, he's going to walk with a limp!" With a huff of annoyance, she shook her head. "We get it! You don't approve, but you know what? This isn't your call to make!"

All around them, conversation died down and Selena was mortified.

"Sorry," James said, loud enough to be heard. "Just a mild disagreement. Nothing to see here."

It took a solid minute for everyone to start talking again.

"Sorry," he said to his wife. "I just wish you'd let Ryder and I make our case and that the two of you would listen with open minds."

"You're just going to tell us not to do it," Casey said while giving Ryder a hard glare. "We don't tell either of you how to handle your businesses and yet you're asking us to let you tell us how to handle ours. How is that fair?"

The four ate in silence for several minutes, even as conversations carried on around them.

Then, Ryder proposed what he and James were secretly discussing prior to sitting down to eat.

"How about this," he began. "The two of you take some time over the course of the next two weeks to discuss the project with everyone here. James and I will do the same. Then, on say...New Year's Eve, we take a vote and see where everyone lands on this. Okay?"

Selena and Casey exchanged looks, but ultimately agreed.

"Fine, but the two of you need to stop with the childish nudges and kicking when you hear us talking," Selena said sternly. "You guys can talk about it; Casey and I can talk about it. But until New Year's Eve, the four of us will have to find something else to talk about. Agreed?"

Thankfully, it was.

At the third table, all the attention was on baby Cayden and how he became part of the family. Janice was holding him while delicately picking at her dinner.

"Mom, you know you can put him down, right?" Zach asked with amusement. "We have his seat right here. You can still see him while you eat like a normal person."

"Oh, hush. I'm enjoying this. It's been a long time since I've held a baby in my arms," she gently scolded. "And I think I'm still a little in shock."

"Believe me, we are too," Gabriella explained.

"I still can't believe you just went for a casual visit with your family and came home with a baby!" Summer said. "I know we've talked about this, but it still just blows my mind a bit."

"Weren't you talking about how much you were looking forward to retiring?" Alex asked. "Two weeks ago, you and I were planning on taking that trip to Costa Rica for the surfing tournament. Why didn't you mention any of this?"

Beside him, Megan leaned in close and murmured, "Oh, so you don't like it when people make life-altering decisions and then keep it a secret from you? Hmm...go figure."

Yeah, it was heavy on the sarcasm and a direct hit.

Turning his head, he gave her a sweet smile before returning his attention to Zach. "Not that I'm saying you have to share all the intimate details of your life, but..."

"Honestly, it took us both by surprise," Zach said. "We never really talked about having more kids once Skylar turned five. We tried for another baby after she was born because...you know...a boy would have been great...but when it didn't happen, we were okay with it."

"Obviously I had no idea my niece had given birth," Gabriella interjected. "I didn't even know she was pregnant. And judging by the way my family was carrying on, it was clear that no one was on board with the situation at all. I'm still kind of surprised that they hadn't planned for adoption before she gave birth."

"Did they say why they didn't?" Summer asked.

Gabriella shrugged. "Part denial, part defiance, and part indifference," she said sadly. "My family tends to think if they don't discuss things that make them feel uncomfortable, they'll just go away." She shook her head. "I thought my niece would be different, but..."

"We actually talked to her alone," Zach explained. "She's only 17, a little self-absorbed, and had zero interest in Cayden."

"Who was caring for him before you showed up?" Ethan asked. "I know you took him to the pediatrician and made sure he was okay, but I can't imagine what his life was like before you got there, Gabs."

"They had hired a nanny and she seemed perfectly lovely," Gabriella told them.

"And she also seemed perfectly relieved that someone other than Gabriella's niece and her family were going to be raising Cayden." He let out a long breath. "I'm telling you; this has been more of a challenge than any extreme sport I've ever done. It's definitely more of an emotional experience, but..." He wrapped an arm around the back of Gabriella's chair and smiled at her. "We've got this."

"Well, we're all here for you," Summer said. "No matter what you need."

"Thanks. I think it's going to be wild while we're here because it's loud and there are so many people around. When we get back home to Portland, we're thinking it's gonna take a couple of weeks to get him settled into a routine and used to his new surroundings."

"So, we just want to apologize to everyone right now for any lack of sleep you may get while we're all here," Gabriella added with a nervous laugh. "We wouldn't have missed this trip for the world, but we didn't expect to have a newborn with us."

"Don't worry about that," Janice told them. "You've got the first bedroom off the living room, so if you need to get up with Cayden, you can take him out and walk around with him. You're only sharing a wall with one room and the other side is the stairwell and elevator. If you need to swap rooms with someone, we'll make it work."

"And everyone knows we're dealing with a newborn," Summer interjected. "The rooms seem very well insulated too, so I doubt you're going to keep anyone up."

"Well..." Ethan began and instantly closed his mouth when Summer gave him a sharp look.

"Depending on what his schedule's like," Megan said, "and if you're really worried about him waking anyone, I'm sure there will be time overnight when the lower level will be empty." Then she chuckled. "At least, I hope there will. I guess I'm forgetting how teenagers with access to a full game room and movie theater might not be looking to go to bed."

They all laughed, but it was Robert who had the final word on the subject.

"We all made compromises for one another," he said, his voice a little gruff. "Whether it was one of our own children, a grandchild, a niece, or a nephew. Sometimes even for a sibling. So, whatever it is that Cayden needs, that's what's going to happen. Even if it means booting a group of teenagers out of the game room and telling them to go to sleep."

Zach and Gabriella exchanged glances, but figured only time would tell.

And by their watches, they had another six hours before that first late-night feeding to find out.

FOURTEEN

# FIRST FULL DAY

## "ME, YOU, A BOX OF POP TARTS, AND A BOTTLE OF WINE."

AT NINE THE FOLLOWING MORNING, the kitchen had mostly been cleared out of the breakfast crowd, and now William and Robert were ready to begin their first day of meetings. They only had until noon to get their work done, so there was no time to waste.

Looking around, William frowned. They were all seated at one of the long dining tables and since there were only ten of them, there was plenty of room for laptops and tablets and files. He heard laughter coming from the lower level, and part of him felt a little guilty for keeping the group away from their families.

"Dad?" Mac prompted. "Are you okay?"

"What? Oh, of course. Just got a little distracted for a moment. That's all." Pausing, he took a sip of his coffee and then took his place at the head of the table. "I hope everyone got a good night's sleep last night and that your rooms were comfortable!"

Everyone nodded, but William caught Zach's yawn. Poor little Cayden did not have a good night, and he knew Zach and Gabriella had been up most of the night with him.

"Zach, maybe you should go and rest while Cayden's sleeping?" Robert suggested. "I have a feeling today is just going to be us going over the basics and it's nothing you won't be able to catch up on tomorrow."

"I'm good," Zach said before taking a long drink of his coffee. "I'll probably crash later this afternoon, but I'm fine right now. I know Mom and Aunt Monica and Aunt Eliza are going to hold us to being done by noon, so I'd like to get started. Ethan and I have some suggestions on ways we can minimize layoffs while merging staffs in some new locations."

"One of our junior executives in our office did a similar projection," William said. "I'm excited to compare and see what we can realistically implement."

For the next two and a half hours, William, Robert, Mac, Jason, Lucas, Summer, Ethan, Zach, Megan, and Christian shared their research on the best way to handle the merger for not only their own branches, but for the overall company. It seemed like they were primarily on the same page until Noah Wylder called. Normally, William wouldn't have answered a call during a meeting, but when he saw Noah's name, he knew it had to be important.

"Hello, Noah," he said cheerily. "What can I do for you?"

"I hope I'm not interrupting," Noah began, "but Francis Matheson just showed up at the office. He claimed he didn't know you were out of town through the holidays, but I was sitting right there with you last week when you spoke with him and his team and gave them your schedule."

William nodded. "Noah, I'm sitting here with the family and..."

"I really didn't mean to disturb your family time."

"No, it's quite alright. This is very important and when

I say I'm sitting here with the family, I mean the work family," he explained with a small laugh. "So, I'm going to put you on speaker so everyone can hear this. Do you mind?"

"Not at all, Sir. Go ahead."

William adjusted his phone. "Okay, where is Francis Matheson right now?"

"Rose put him in the conference room and brought in coffee and refreshments."

"Did he come alone?" Robert asked.

"No, he's got two associates with him—Logan Joss and Mike Winston," Noah replied. "As you know, we're on a skeleton staff here, so I didn't want to go in there without speaking to you first."

"And we appreciate that," Mac said. "Did they mention why they opted to stop by unannounced?"

"Rose mentioned that they told her they just happened to be in the area visiting with some clients and thought they'd stop in. From everything I've learned in our research, they don't have any clients in this area. The closest that we have on record is in Raleigh."

"That's three hours away," Jason murmured. "That's a long way to drive just to be in the area."

Everyone nodded.

"I figured I'd just go in and tell them you're out of town and remind them of the schedule you'd sent," Noah said. "But..." He paused. "Um...hold on."

"Noah? Is everything alright?"

"Um..." His voice became muffled for a moment. "Rose just came in and mentioned they have some contracts they insist need to be signed. What would you like me to do?"

Everyone looked at one another in confusion before William responded. "Noah, I'd like you to go to the conference room once we're off the phone and set up a Zoom call.

Rather than sitting here speculating, let's just cut to the chase."

"I'm on it, Mr. Montgomery. I'll send you the meeting link momentarily."

"Thank you." As soon as he hung up, William frowned. "I think Matheson is there on a fishing expedition and was hoping to snoop around while we weren't there."

"That seems a little odd, don't you think?" Christian asked. "Did they think they'd get to access computers or something?"

"We won't know until we talk to them, but...let's get ready to find out," Robert said wearily. "I hate working with people you can't trust."

"It's too soon to think about whether this is a trust issue or a simple misunderstanding," William countered. "Either way, we need to keep a level head." He scanned his email, waiting for Noah's link. "Do we want to do this as a group, or should it just be you and I, Rob?"

"Just the two of us. I'll move to sit beside you so it doesn't look like we're ganging up on them with a large group staring them down. Plus, everyone can still be listening."

The email came through and William clicked on it and joined the Zoom meeting with a smile on his face. On the other side of the room in the kitchen, he saw Monica and Janice walk in. Megan got up and presumably explained to them what was going on.

"Good afternoon, Noah," William began as soon as he appeared on the screen. "Thank you so much for getting this set up so quickly!" Then he spotted Francis Matheson and nodded. "Francis, this is definitely a surprise. I didn't plan on speaking with you until after the holidays."

Francis Matheson was in his mid-sixties and although a

brilliant businessman with a good head for finance, he lacked people skills and often came off as cold and condescending.

"As I mentioned to your assistant," Francis began. "We were in the area and thought there was maybe a chance you hadn't left town yet."

It was a lie and everyone knew it.

"So, I hear you have some contracts for us?" Robert asked. "I didn't think we left anything unsigned when we last spoke. Considering we haven't finalized anything, what contracts could you possibly have?"

For a moment Francis didn't answer, but he seemed to shift a bit in his seat. "I'd like something in writing that you're not going to get rid of my executive staff," he finally said. "So I've had our attorney draft up a contract so we know what to expect moving forward."

Doing his best to keep a smile on his face, William nodded. "Obviously I'll have to have our legal team look it over before we sign anything. So why don't you leave everything with Noah and he will personally deliver it to our attorneys and I'll be in touch in a few days. Will that work?"

He didn't look pleased, but he nodded anyway.

"Excellent," Robert said. "Noah, please make sure you handle this personally and call us back as soon as they're done."

"Will do, Mr. Montgomery," Noah said confidently.

"Have a safe trip back to Atlanta, Francis," William said. "And we'll talk in a few days."

As soon as the call ended, he leaned back in his seat and let out a long breath. "That was..."

"It was odd," Jason said. "Why bring up a contract now? Why not call you and request a meeting rather than just showing up?"

"Like I said, I don't trust him," Robert commented.

"Let's put that on hold until after our guys look at the contracts," William said as he caught his wife's eye. "For today, our work is done. Let's go and enjoy some time with the family!"

~

"I don't think this is what anyone meant when they said to rest before dinner," Gina said breathlessly. Mac had her pinned to the mattress while he slowly worked his way down her body, stripping her as he went.

"Doesn't matter," he murmured between kisses along her inner thigh. "This is my interpretation of resting."

"Mac..." But she wasn't sure if she was begging him to stop or begging him to keep going.

"Yesterday was exhausting and by the time we came in here, I barely knew my own name," he told her. "Then I needed to be up early for this meeting and missed being able to just stay in bed with you." Then he hummed with appreciation as he tugged at her panties with his teeth. "And I truly love staying in bed with you."

"Mmm...I love that too." She raked her hands through his hair and it was a little decadent to feel this naughty. The door was locked and there were Montgomerys in practically every nook and cranny of the massive house, and yet right now it felt like they were in their own little world.

And considering the tension between them in the last few weeks, this was a most welcome surprise.

When he rose up over her and kissed her soundly, she simply melted against him. Maybe this little getaway would be good for them. Maybe spending time as a family was what they needed to reconnect a bit. And maybe they could find a little more time for things like this to bring them close like they used to be.

"I love you, Gina," he said against her throat as she arched beneath him.

"Love you too, Mac. I've missed you."

He looked down at her. "I know, and I'm sorry. Things are going to get better. I promise. I want us to find time for it to be just the two of us, and moving forward..."

She pressed a finger against his lips. "No more talking," she whispered. "We don't have a lot of time, and I really like everything we've been doing here so far."

With a boyish grin, he nodded. "Me too." He kissed her again. "It's kind of fun sneaking off like this in the middle of the day like we used to when the kids were small. Maybe we'll make this an everyday occurrence."

"Challenge accepted," she purred, wrapping her limbs around him. And just like that, they were done talking, and it was the closest she'd felt to him in months.

Meanwhile, in another room, things weren't nearly as positive—or as sexy.

"Have you booked your flight?" Emery asked as she slowly paced around her room.

"Not yet, but Uncle William has the Montgomery jet on standby so I won't have to worry about finding a seat. I just need to give a few hours' notice and the plane will be here."

"Why not have the plane there already so all you have to do is call that you're on your way?" she challenged.

"Because the pilot lives in North Carolina and has no reason to be here in New Orleans," he said wearily. "If everything works out the way I'm hoping it will, I should be on a plane tomorrow night. I won't get to the house until after midnight, but..."

She supposed it was something. "Fine. I guess just... keep me posted."

He was quiet for a moment. "How are the boys? Are they having a good time? The house looks amazing."

It was on the tip of her tongue to tell him they'd be having a better time if he were here, but what was the point?

"They are, actually. Tomorrow, I think we're going sledding or tubing or something. James and Selena are coordinating something even as we speak. It's something Isabella researched and now it sounds like everyone's going to go and check it out."

"That sounds awesome! Hopefully everyone will love it enough to want to go back another time or two so I can check it out."

"Mm-hmm..."

"How was the food last night? I heard they hired a caterer for last night and tonight. Were they any good?"

It was such a benign conversation that it bordered on tedious, but she supposed it was better than arguing. "Last night was lasagna with all the usual stuff—meatballs, sausage, garlic bread, and a salad. Emma brought about a thousand pounds of cakes and cookies with her, so we're working our way through that, too. Although I think she's still going to have to bake some more because the kids are really devouring more than their share."

"I'll bet," he said with a laugh. "So, what's on the menu for tonight?"

"Um...I think I heard your mother saying it's Mexican tonight. A big taco bar, enchiladas, a couple of casseroles, and lots of chips, salsa, and guacamole."

He laughed again. "Sounds right up your alley."

"Yeah, well...at least it's not the drive-thru at Taco Bell, right?"

"Em...I can't stand knowing you're still this angry with me," he said solemnly. "What was I supposed to do? Tell me what I should have done differently. If the roles were reversed, you know Max would have had my back."

Sighing, Emery sat down on the bed and then fell back against the pillows. "Logically, I know you're doing what needs to be done, and it's commendable. Emotionally..." She paused as tears stung her eyes and her voice trembled. "Emotionally, I miss my husband and want him here with me and our boys. It's awkward to be here with your entire family without you."

He softly muttered a curse. "Believe me, I would rather be there with you and the boys, Em. You know this. And I swear that things are going to change after this. I'll have a plan in place and hire an extra chef at every restaurant so this never happens again. I just...I need to get through the next day or so and then I promise you, you'll have all my attention."

"Carter..."

"You'll have so much of it that you'll be annoyed that I'm around so much."

She knew he was teasing and couldn't help but smile. "I don't think I'll be annoyed..."

"And I promise to bring an entire case of Pop Tarts and another whole case of potato chips that we'll hide in our room just for you."

Now she laughed. "The chocolate fudge ones, right? Don't try to slip in here with something fruit-filled or I swear you'll be sleeping in the bunk room with all the kids."

"There's my girl." After letting out a long breath, he said, "How about this...when the boys are back in school, we get my folks to come and stay with us, and you and I finally go back to Paris like we've been talking about?"

"Carter, you don't need to do this, and honestly, I don't want you to. Because if things don't work out, it just makes it worse."

"It's going to work out," he said firmly. "You have my word."

Again, it was pointless to remind him of all the other times he'd given his word.

"Let's talk about it when you get here, okay?"

"Okay."

"I can practically hear you pouting," she said with a small laugh. "Tomorrow night, after midnight. Me, you, a box of Pop Tarts, and a bottle of wine. That's all I want."

"Then that's what you'll have."

*We'll see.*

And in yet another room...

"What's going on, Mom? Are you okay?" Megan asked as she walked over and sat on her mother's bed. "You've been acting a little weird all day."

"Have I?" Eliza asked nervously, wringing her hands.

"Um, yeah. Yesterday you mentioned having some sort of announcement or something you wanted to talk about and then you never did."

She hesitated for only a moment before getting to the point. "I had planned on announcing something last night, but then I chickened out. Then I was hoping Carter would show up today, but I don't think that's happening and I'm not sure I can wait for him to arrive."

"O-kay..."

"I met someone. A man. And...and...I invited him to join us for Christmas," she blurted out. "His name is Philip and he's a retired high school teacher. We've been dating now for over six months and I just thought it was time for him to meet everyone." Then she let out a long breath and waited for her daughter's response.

Megan knew her eyes were wide, and it took more than a moment for her to form words. This was all fantastic news and yet it was still a bit...shocking. Her father had been gone for almost fifteen years and it wasn't like her mother hadn't dated at all since he'd died. But this was the first time she was making a big deal out of it, which meant...

It was a big deal.

"Mom! This is awesome!" she said as she came to her feet and hugged her mother. "I'm so happy for you!"

"Really?" Eliza asked nervously. "You're not upset that I invited him to join us?"

Megan pulled back. "Why would I be upset? If he's important to you, then of course he should be here."

"And you don't think your brothers will mind?"

The snort of laughter was out before she could stop it. "Mom, they're going to think this is just as wonderful as I do."

"I'm not sure that's the word I'd use..."

"Okay, well...Christian will probably be a little more reserved about the whole thing, but that's how he is with everything except Sophie and the kids."

Eliza nodded because it was true.

"And Carter? Well...he might be a little shocked, but it will only be for a minute. You know he embraces everything and everyone. He's got a big personality so really, you should be a little more worried about how Philip is going to react to all of us. I mean...we're kind of a lot to handle."

With a sigh, she nodded again. "Which reminds me...I have to apologize for my behavior toward you and Alex yesterday. You both looked so tense and I knew something was wrong and all I could think about was how inconvenient it was for me." Her shoulders sagged. "I was upset that Carter wasn't here with Emery and the boys and then seeing the two of you...well...it was very selfish of me to demand that the two of you go somewhere. I'm truly sorry."

"Mom, you don't have to apologize. We all know our branch of the family seems to have the most baggage." Then she laughed. "Two workaholic brothers and now a daughter who might have to..."

She caught herself before she admitted too much.

"Might have to what, Megan?" Eliza asked gently, before motioning for them both to sit down on the futon.

As much as Megan didn't want to get into this right now, maybe it would help if she talked to someone.

So, she told her mother the entire story about Alex and how he was considering moving them to Colorado. "We actually stopped there so he could do an interview and he wanted me and the kids to see the area and see if we liked it."

"And? Did you?"

"Honestly? I don't know! I couldn't really focus on that because I was so thrown off by his admission that he'd been so miserable. I never saw it! I mean, what does that say about me as a wife if I didn't notice how miserable my husband was?"

"It's not always that easy, sweetheart. And it's not like you've been just sitting around doing nothing. You work full time and have three kids."

"I guess..."

"And I'm really surprised that Alex kept that to himself. That's not like him."

"I know," Megan quietly replied. "The thought of moving isn't scary; after all, I moved across the country once and was okay. I think what's bothering me more is letting everyone else down. This would mean leaving Montgomerys. I've loved working with Zach, Ethan, and Summer. It's the best job I've ever had and the thought of not seeing them every day is…well…"

"You worry too much," Eliza said gently. "Have you been listening or observing what's been going on around here? Zach and Gabriella just adopted a newborn. They're going to have their hands full, and I can guarantee they'll both be excited for you and Alex."

"But by the same token, it's not a great time for me to leave because…"

"You are in IT, Megan. You don't handle the clients or anything on the financial end. Plus, you've got everything running so smoothly that even if they had to train someone, it wouldn't be hard because you'd be leaving them in good shape."

"Maybe. I don't know…it's all just so unexpected!"

Taking her daughter's hand in hers, she squeezed it. "Life is like that sometimes. Things happen that are out of our control and they're not always good. If anyone had told me that trip to San Diego with your father would be our last…that he wouldn't be coming home with me…" She let out a long breath. "It was devastating and awful and so completely unexpected and yet…I survived."

"Now I feel like I'm whining," Megan said. "Moving for a fabulous job opportunity for Alex should be something I'm excited about and celebrating, and instead I'm…"

"Instead, you're grieving a little because your husband was struggling with something and didn't talk to you about it. You're grieving because you'll be starting over with a new job." Then she paused. "Or…you can maybe freelance and cut back on your hours and take some time to get to know this new state and new city and embrace it. I know you're not as adventurous as your husband, but maybe don't say no to this just yet."

"Alex and I agreed to wait until after the holidays to make any decisions."

"That's smart."

They sat in silence for a minute before Megan forced herself to snap out of her funk. "So, tell me more about Philip! When is he getting here?"

# FIFTEEN

# DAY TWO

## "IT CERTAINLY WASN'T A SLAM DUNK."

WHILE WILLIAM and company were up in their makeshift conference room the following morning, Casey, Selena, Gina, Barb, Emma, Lily, Maggie, Sophie, Eliza, Janice and Monica were relaxing in the cozy gathering area on the lower level while half the kids were playing water volleyball in the pool and the other half were in the game room. They were all sipping their coffees and there were at least a half dozen different conversations going on.

And Selena and Casey were about to bring it all down to one.

"Hey, can we sort of get your opinion on something?" Casey asked when she had everyone's attention.

"Of course!"

"Sure!"

"What's up?"

She and Selena shared a smile, and just when Casey was about to speak, Gabriella walked in with Cayden in her arms, followed by Skylar and Willow.

"Sorry, are we...um...interrupting something?" Gabriella asked as she took a seat in the chair Lily vacated for her. Her daughters and Lily sat on the floor in front of her and it was Lily who took Cayden gently from her arms.

"Actually, Selena and I had a question for the group, so really, you're just in time."

"Ooh...color me intrigued. What's the question?"

Again, she and Selena exchanged smiles. "Okay, so...we have the opportunity to be part of a reality show," Casey began. "We were approached to do the wedding of Dana St. Ivy. She does a lot of time travel dramas."

"Oh my God!" Willow said excitedly. "I love her! Have you met her? Can you get me her autograph? Or can we come and work for you so we can actually, like, *be* at the wedding?"

"Willow," Gabriella said quietly, resting her hand on her daughter's shoulder. "Reel it in. I don't think Casey's gotten to the actual question yet."

"Sorry."

But Casey smiled down at her. "Believe me, I was just as excited when we got approached."

"It can be a really big deal for the business," Selena explained, "but it comes with some stuff that Ryder and James aren't on board with."

"Like what?" Janice asked. "I would think two businessmen would see how savvy their wives are being and appreciate it."

"Well...the producers of the show are already scripting the drama they want to see and some of it doesn't exactly portray us in a good way," Casey said. "But Selena and I feel like we can work around that stuff and actually present the producers with better versions, but..."

"But my sons still aren't impressed," Janice stated.

"Exactly. And we made a deal with them that we would

talk to everyone here about it and then get a final vote on New Year's Eve," Selena said. "So...what do you all think?"

Maggie raised her hand. "What sort of drama are they wanting you to be a part of?" Selena told them the scenario with the Ferrari and Maggie's face scrunched up. "That's not cool. And with the way they do things in editing, I don't think you'll get a final say in what they air."

"That's true," Emma chimed in. "Last year, there was a local talk show that came to the bakery to do a segment on women entrepreneurs. I was so excited about it and thought it would be a great boost for business, but when it aired, nothing was like the way we filmed it and some of it really didn't make me or the bakery look great."

"I remember that," Gina said, shaking her head. "They made it sound like Emma had pretty much thrown her daughters to the wolves so she could pursue her own dream."

"Yeah, it wasn't great," Maggie added. "And they portrayed Lucas as a bitter, former athlete. I remember how angry he was about that."

"And the weirdest part was that he was only there for five minutes of the filming and was nothing but friendly to them," Emma said. "But the cameraman caught him frowning over something and they used that in the story. It was..." She shook her head. "I was naïve and had no idea they'd do something like that, so you should make sure you have very specific things put in your contract."

Inwardly, Casey groaned. This wasn't going as great as she had hoped, and it certainly wasn't the slam dunk she anticipated.

"Um..." Lily carefully raised her hand. "We had a reality show film on one of our cruises. It was one of those cheesy couples counseling type ones. Anyway, they asked if

I wanted to be on camera and I thought to myself, yeah! Definitely! But I thought they meant while I was dancing in one of the shows. Turns out, they wanted me to pretend I was actively pursuing one of the guys in the cast."

"What?" Emma cried. "When was this?"

"Last summer."

"Why didn't you tell me? What did they make you do?"

Rolling her eyes, Lily sighed. "Mom, you're freaking out and that's why I didn't tell you." Then she looked at Casey and Selena. "Ultimately, what they wanted was for me to cause a fight between this couple and basically, I could have gotten fired. They swore they'd let my bosses know that it was all pretend, but I didn't trust them. My job wasn't great, but I didn't want to lose it over a lie."

"Okay, whew!" Emma said as she relaxed against the sofa cushions. "That's my girl."

"So...basically you're all against this," Selena said flatly. "I...wasn't expecting that."

"I don't think that's what we're saying," Gabriella commented. "I think we're all just giving you something to think about so you don't go into this blindly and believe that you're going to have the control."

"And as for James and Ryder," Janice said, "this isn't their decision to make. After all, no one's asking them to be on the show."

"Well...actually..."

There was a collective groan.

"We could have totally gotten on board if the guys weren't involved, but if you're thinking of including them, this is never going to happen," Monica said. "And I'm not just referring to them being on the show, but their overall acceptance of it."

"Monica's right," Eliza added. "And I don't understand

why you would want to make yourselves look foolish on TV! I don't watch a lot of reality television, but from everything I've seen, no one comes out looking good. Are you sure this is the kind of publicity you want?"

"Um..."

"We both feel like we're in a bit of a rut," Selena said. "The business is doing fine—we could practically do it all with our eyes closed. We just felt like maybe this would... you know...breathe a little life into things again and make it exciting like it used to be."

"Maybe you just need to come up with a different way to draw attention to the business," Willow suggested. "What kind of social media stuff are you doing? Are you on TikTok? Do you do reels on Instagram?"

"Um..."

Skylar, Willow, and Lily all snickered quietly before Lily said, "We'll take that as a no."

"We have a Facebook page and an Instagram account, but we just post pictures there occasionally," Casey replied.

"What would we have to do to grow our social media? And you think doing that would be better than starring in a reality TV show featuring one of the biggest actresses in the world?" Selena asked.

The three girls conversed quietly for a moment before Skylar spoke. "Okay, over the next few days, whenever there's a meal, you guys need to do something to make it look pretty like you'd do at an event."

"Make a nice presentation, or when we decorate the tree tomorrow, do something with the decorations somewhere else that we can video and post to your accounts," Willow said.

"Treat this house like one of your events," Lily added. "Even something small—if it's even remotely like something you'd do at one of your parties—we'll film it and post it for you. We'll just need access to the accounts."

"Oh, uh...Julie normally handles those things," Casey replied and felt mildly embarrassed.

"Can you just text Julie and ask for the login info?" Gabriella asked with a small smirk.

They both nodded.

William came down the stairs and breezed into the room. "Monica, I was wondering if you would..." He stopped and looked around, his gaze landing on Lily. With a slow smile, he nodded. "I think someone needs to get a picture of this."

"Of what, dear?"

"The oldest grandchild holding the youngest," he said, and there was a slight catch in his voice. "And it's amazing to see."

"Here," Maggie said as she stood up, handing William her phone. "Why don't you get a shot of all of us and then one of just Lily and Cayden and I'll share them with everyone?"

He nodded and then took a few steps back while everyone moved closer and posed. Then, after a few shots, he took a few of just Lily and Cayden before handing Maggie her phone back. "Thank you, Maggie. I can't wait to see them on my phone," he said before walking over to his wife.

"Are you okay?" she asked softly. "You looked a little emotional there for a minute."

"I am," he quietly replied. "This is the sort of thing I was looking forward to the most—the quiet moments where we're all together and seeing this younger generation bond. It...it does my heart good."

She smiled and reached up, kissing him on the cheek.

"And this is just the beginning. Now, what can I do for you?"

"It appears that some of the boys are a little more anxious than the kids to go tubing today. Would it be possible to have an early lunch?"

Chuckling, she nodded. "Of course! But won't that interfere with your morning meeting?"

He laughed with her but waved her off. "We've hit a bit of a snafu, so we'll be done by eleven."

"Then we'll be up there getting everything ready at eleven."

"Thank you." When he turned to walk away, she called his name. "Hmm?"

"Are you planning on going with them?"

"Tubing?" he asked with a bark of laughter. "I wouldn't miss it for the world!"

It was a little like herding cats when they got back to the house a little after four that afternoon, and Christian quietly limped his way through the crowd on his quest to get to the elevator. He just wanted to get to his room and hide in shame. Forty of them had gone to the tubing park and he was the only one who couldn't seem to make it down the hill without bouncing out of the damn tube and hurting himself.

"Landed on my ass every damn time," he mumbled when the elevator doors shut behind him. He'd never been particularly strong athletically, but this was just embarrassing. When the doors opened on the second floor, his wife was standing there waiting for him.

"Hey," she said softly, holding out her hand to him.

"Soph...you didn't need to come up here. I think I can handle walking to our room without hurting myself further."

"Oh, stop. Come on." Hand in hand, they walked the short way down the hall to their room. Once they were inside, Sophie shut the door, leaned against it, and watched as Christian limped over to the bed and gingerly sat down. "Can I get you anything?"

"Maybe a time machine to take me back to around noon when I should have said no to going with everyone."

"Christian, come on," she said as she made her way across the room. "It wasn't that bad, and contrary to what you believe, there were quite a few spills out there today."

"From the kids, Sophie. None of the adults managed to go flying off their tube every time they attempted to go down the hill," he murmured before falling back against the mattress and covering his eyes. "Did you see the way Evan and Brayden looked at me? It was like they were mortified that I was their dad."

"That's not how they feel," she said soothingly, lying down beside him. "What they saw was their father trying something he'd never done before and refusing to give up. Do you remember when I tried surfing?"

Lifting his arm, he stared at her. "That's how we met. Of course I remember it."

Ignoring his surly tone, she said, "I was terrible at it. I fell off the board more than I stayed on it and yet I kept trying. Most people looked at me and wondered why I didn't just quit."

"I know I thought that..."

She shot him a hard glare before going on. "Which is worse—being seen as a quitter or as someone who picks themself up and keeps trying?"

With a loud sigh, he said, "Being a quitter."

"Exactly." Crawling over him, Sophie maneuvered herself until she was straddling him and forced his arms away from his face. "I love how you smiled the entire time and were able to laugh at yourself." Leaning down, she trailed kisses along his jaw. "And when we go back and do it again—because you know that's already in the works—we'll do the two-person tube and go down that hill together. Me and you. What do you say?"

Christian reached up and cupped her cheek. "Always. Me and you, always. Thanks for reminding me of that."

"I love you, wonderful man," she said softly. "Now, tell me where it hurts so we can get some ice on you."

When she went to move off of him, he gently grasped her hips and held her in place. By the sexy grin and the heated look in his eyes, he couldn't be hurting too much, she thought. Rocking slowly against him, she returned his smile.

"Or maybe I can kiss it and make it feel better. The choice is yours," she whispered before lowering her head and kissing him. Sophie still remembered the first time Christian had kissed her and all these years later, she still got tingly whenever he did. It was always a little sweet at first, but then would turn deep and sensual and oh-so-good.

"Lock the door," he murmured against her lips. "And then I'll let you kiss whatever you want before I return the favor."

How could she possibly turn that down?

And while Christian and Sophie indulged in a little sexy private time, downstairs Summer and Ethan were indulging in some frustrating puppy training.

"We should have left her with Olivia and Kira," Ethan said with frustration. "They volunteered and would have had her fully trained by the time we got back."

Summer was busy cleaning up yet another "accident" and was more than a little annoyed by Ethan's condescending tone. "You can at least say her name. Maybe she'd be better behaved if you focused on helping her know who she is."

Groaning, Ethan raked his hands through his hair in frustration. "My failure to use her name—which is a ridiculous name, by the way, and I resent that you and the girls named her without asking me and Jensen for our input!—is not the issue here, Summer. She's a puppy, and this is pure chaos with so many people around. This wasn't the way to get her used to our family."

"I disagree," she said stiffly before picking up the cleaning supplies and putting them in the bathroom. "She's tiny and mostly gets carried around. The kids have all taken turns taking her out for walks. She just gets excited easily and...you know...pees."

"A massive family reunion is not a place for a new puppy. That's all I'm saying."

"Well, it doesn't matter if that's what you're saying because she's here and we need to figure out how to make this work so I'm not cleaning all the floors in the house and you're not walking around saying 'I told you so.' Which, by the way," she mimicked snidely, "is not helpful!"

Now he pinched the bridge of his nose and mentally counted to ten while the puppy yipped and danced around his ankles. Honestly, Lulu was a cute little dog and they—as a family—had taken a couple of years before deciding to get another dog after their precious little Maylene had passed away. If they were home, none of this would be an issue, but it was a lot of work to keep dealing with the messes she was making. "This is like dealing with a newborn."

"And yet Zach and Gabriella are doing just that without

being as grouchy as you are," Summer murmured as she walked past him and sat on the futon. Lulu trotted over and tried to climb up, but she was too small. "Come here, baby. I've got you." Scooping the puppy up, she snuggled her close before glaring at Ethan again. "No one else is complaining about her. Only you."

"I just don't think it's fair to make everyone else have to clean up after her when we're not here. Your mother didn't look particularly thrilled about that when we got back from tubing."

"Oh, please. After breakfast this morning, she was asking if she could take Lulu home with her and Dad after the holidays."

"I hope you told them yes," he mumbled.

"Ethan! How could you even say that? I mean...just look at this smooshy face!" She held Lulu up with their faces pressed together and it was almost comical. The pug was squirming frantically in Summer's arms and soon they were both laughing. "Admit it. She's adorable and you love her."

Slowly, he made his way over to the futon. "She is adorable."

"And you love her."

"I love *you*."

Summer gave him a look that he knew she thought meant she was being fierce, but...it made her look a little silly. "Say it. Say you love her."

"She's a very nice dog."

"Ethan!"

Sitting down, he took the squirming dog from her hands and laughed softly. "Fine. I love her."

Resting her head on his shoulder, Summer sighed happily. "Thank you. That wasn't so hard, was it?"

"No. I just want to be able to go places with you and the

kids while we're here and not have to worry about the dog. That's all."

"I know, I know. I guess I didn't think about it like that. In my head, we were coming to this big house and staying here. The thought of going out for the day didn't really occur to me, so...I'm sorry. We'll figure it out."

"Good." Turning his head, he kissed her as he hugged the puppy close. "How about we put her in her kennel and see what kind of appetizers are out in the kitchen?"

"Ooh...I am definitely hungry. Here, I'll take Lulu and..."

"Shit!" he hissed.

"What? What's the matter?" she asked as she frantically looked him over. But when he carefully placed the puppy back in her hands, she saw it.

The giant wet spot on his shirt and pants.

Summer had to stifle a giggle as Ethan merely glared at her.

"Don't say a word," he warned. "Not one!" Then he stormed off to the bathroom to get cleaned up.

"Lulu," she whispered firmly. "That wasn't very nice. Not when we were just getting him to relax about you being here." The puppy merely yawned as her eyes drifted closed.

With nothing else to do, Summer gently placed her back in her kennel and shut the gate before grabbing Ethan a change of clothes and joining him in the bathroom and said a silent prayer that she'd get him to relax before they joined everyone downstairs.

Jason and Maggie weren't having any problem relaxing.

In fact, they had one of the hot tubs completely to themselves.

Actually, no one was outside with them at all!

There were three hot tubs on the lower-level deck and

while everyone had come back from snow tubing looking to rest, they were the only ones who had thought to think a little outside the box—and house—and hit the hot tub.

"How come we never got one of these?" Maggie asked as she slipped a little lower in the water.

"We had one in our first place, but it didn't seem practical when we moved."

"Our first place was your bachelor pad. I probably associated anything you had there with your playboy ways."

He snorted with laughter. "Sweetheart, I was many things back then, but a playboy wasn't one of them. I was a workaholic who was usually too tired for any kind of playing. Any time I used that hot tub, it was by myself." Then he paused. "Well...almost any time."

Maggie kicked him under the water. "You could have totally left that last part out, you know. It wasn't necessary."

"Sorry."

Her head was thrown back, her eyes were closed, and she felt completely at peace. It had been a great day with the kids, and riding those tubes downhill made her feel like a kid again. But once they'd gotten back to the house, her body reminded her of just how old she really was. That's when the idea of soaking in the hot tub had hit her and it was kind of nice that no one else thought of it.

"I forgot to ask what's on the menu for dinner tonight," Jason said a few minutes later. "Any idea?"

"Last I heard, it was comfort food night."

"Um, yeah, I don't know what that means."

Laughing softly, Maggie turned her head and looked at him. "Meatloaf, mashed potatoes, roasted carrots, biscuits, and gravy. Easy to make and everyone eats it."

"That does sound good. And you know about tomorrow night, right?"

She shook her head.

"Date night. Mom, Dad, Aunt Janice, Uncle Robert, Aunt Eliza, and Barb are on grandparent duty and ordering pizza for them and all the kids so we can go out!"

"Seriously?" she asked with surprise. "How did I not know about this?"

He shrugged. "No idea. But that's the plan and I am looking forward to it. I made a reservation for us at that French restaurant we like so much. The last time we were able to go there by ourselves was around two years ago. Is that okay with you?"

Maggie slid across the seat until she was practically in his lap. "That sounds wonderful! Thank you! Who else is coming with us? Is it everyone?"

"What? No! Of course not. I wouldn't do that. Besides, I think everyone wants a night alone. I guess it's possible that some of us might end up at the same place, but there are enough restaurants in the area that it shouldn't be an issue. Plus, I'm sure everyone has a different idea of what they want to do on a night out. There's so much to see and do in Asheville that it doesn't just have to be dinner."

She laughed as she moved into his arms. "For us it is. We're foodies."

"Exactly. A five-course meal that takes a couple of hours is the perfect night. Well, then coming home and crawling into bed together, then it's a perfect night."

"You know us so well," she teased before leaning in and kissing him. "I already can't wait." Then she frowned.

"What? What's the matter?"

"I'm just thinking about Emery. What if Carter doesn't show up again? How awkward would it be if we all went out doing couple-y things and she had to either go out alone or stay here with all the grandparents?"

"Damn. I didn't think of that."

"I'll quietly mention it to everyone at dinner so we can all be prepared to invite her along if we need to. There's no way we can leave her behind like that."

Jason leaned in and kissed her thoroughly before saying, "You're amazing and I love you. You're always looking out for everyone else." And if his words didn't say it, the look in his eyes did.

"Well, you know the Disney quote about family and how it means no one gets left behind," she said, wrapping her arms around him. "I just really hope that Carter gets here for her sake."

"You and me both." He kissed her again. "Now, let's make the most out this hot tub time before we have to rejoin the masses!" And he sealed that with an even hotter kiss.

# SIXTEEN

# DAY THREE

## "IT'S SERIOUSLY LIKE THREE DATES AND TROUT MOUSSE."

THE CONTRACT NEGOTIATION wasn't going as smoothly as expected, but with any luck, everything would fix itself in the next few days. William had a plan that he was going to share with everyone the next day. For tonight, he wanted to see all of his favorite couples go out and have a good time.

Jason and Maggie were the first ones out the door on their way to their favorite French restaurant, and he had to admit, he was a little jealous. Not that he didn't enjoy a good pizza, but there was nothing like a little escargots à la Bourguignonne followed by some duck l'orange.

But sure. Pizza would be fine.

Gina and Mac were going out with Casey and Ryder, James and Selena made plans with Summer and Ethan, Megan and Alex were heading out with Lucas and Emma, and last he heard, Christian and Sophie were going out just the two of them, as were Zach and Gabriella, and Emery left earlier to pick up Carter at the airport.

"Please don't let him be delayed," he quietly prayed.

Even though Emery left with a smile on her face, William felt like she was putting on a brave front.

Off in the distance, he heard squeals of laughter, several parental warnings, and Janice calling out to the masses about their pizza topping requests. It was going to be a wild night, but he figured between the pizza, the game room, and the movie theater, everyone should be happy.

That's when he heard Cayden crying.

*Well...almost everyone*, he thought.

"Maybe we should stay home," Gabriella was saying as she and Zach were making their way toward the door. William had been standing guard, so to speak, and wishing everyone a good time, but he was also there to reinforce that the grandparents had everything under control.

"He's going to be fine," Zach assured her. "You know he gets fussy while he's waiting for his bottle, and between my mom, Willow, Skylar, Lily, Becca, and Sloane, he's going to be cuddled and rocked and doted on.

Even so, Gabriella halted in her stilettos and looked back toward the kitchen. "We can call the restaurant and tell them we were delayed," she reasoned. "This way, I can feed him and rock him to sleep. And then..."

With his hand resting on her lower back, Zach gave her a gentle nudge to keep her walking toward the door.

"You two should go and enjoy yourselves. We've got everything under control," William said with a smile as he opened the front door. "I heard you have reservations at that farm-to-table place. Monica and I ate there once and I highly recommend it!"

"Thanks, Uncle William," Zach said. "We will."

"But..."

"Gabs, you can FaceTime with the girls from the car if that will make you feel better, okay?"

She nodded and they eventually went out the door.

Five minutes later, Gina, Mac, Casey, and Ryder made their way toward him and they all looked thrilled to be heading out. "You four have fun!" he said as he pulled open the door. "What did you decide on for dinner?"

"Italian," Gina said. "I was telling Casey about the place Mac and I ate the last time we stayed with you and Monica over the summer."

"I looked up their menu online and was sold," Casey said cheerily. "Thank you for being willing to hold down the fort so we can all go out tonight, Uncle William."

"It's my pleasure! Have a great time!" He waved to them as they made their way toward the cars.

James, Selena, Summer, and Ethan left next and were going to a bistro at one of the luxury hotels in the area, and were quickly followed by Lucas, Emma, Megan, and Alex who opted for a casual Korean barbecue place that was all the rage right now. William was about to join everyone in the kitchen when Sophie and Christian came strolling down the stairs, looking very cozy.

"Well, look at you two! You're the picture of a happy couple going out for a romantic evening! Where are you off to?"

"I'm surprising Sophie," Christian said, his arm wrapped possessively around his wife's waist.

"And I'm dying to know where we're going!" she said with a small laugh. "But Christian knows all my favorites and I'm sure wherever we're going, it's going to be amazing."

"Then don't let me stop you," he said as he quickly moved to the door and held it open for them. "Enjoy yourselves and we'll see you later!"

This time when he shut the door, he let himself relax. Now he could go to the kitchen, pour himself a glass of wine, and enjoy the rest of the evening. With any luck, he could convince the kids to watch a movie that he picked and...

*Ding-dong!*

*What the...?*

Could their dinner be here already? It didn't seem possible, but maybe more time had passed than he thought. As he turned around to reach for the doorknob, he could hear bits of conversation regarding pizza toppings still going on, so...who could it be?

Opening the door, he paused with a smile at the man standing there. He was about the same age as William and was also smiling while holding a suitcase.

"Um...can I help you?"

"Hey, I'm Phil. I'm looking for Eliza Montgomery." Then he let out a small, nervous laugh. "I got a little lost on the way up the mountain, so I hope I'm at the right house." Another laugh. "I wasn't expecting to find something quite so big!"

"Um..."

"Oh, Philip! You made it!" Eliza said as she came bustling across the entryway.

And then, to William's surprise, she actually leaned in and kissed this man right on the lips! Passionately!

What on earth was happening right now? Where was Monica? Did she know about this? Who was this guy and why was he kissing his sister-in-law?

"William, what are you doing? Let the man in!" Monica said as she came up beside him.

"Who is he?" he whispered to her.

"Obviously he's someone special to Eliza," she quietly replied. "I mean, have you ever seen her greet anyone else like that?"

"I wish I wasn't seeing it now," he murmured.

Monica elbowed him in the gut as a response.

When Eliza and Philip finally broke apart, Eliza turned and smiled like the happiest woman on the planet. "William, Monica, I'd like to introduce you to Philip Allen, my boyfriend."

*Oh, good Lord...*

Like they didn't have enough to keep them on their toes tonight, Eliza thought *this* was the perfect time to invite her boyfriend to join them? He was about to say something when his wife stepped in.

"It is wonderful to meet you, Philip! And you got here just in time! We're about to order some pizza!" Then she led Philip and Eliza back toward the kitchen, leaving William by himself.

Which was fine.

He was definitely going to need a moment to wrap his head around this new development.

"Good thing we had a reservation. This place is packed," Zach said as he and Gabriella were finally seated.

"Mm-hmm."

They took a moment to get situated and listened to the specials before placing a drink order. Once their waiter was gone, Zach picked up the menu and frowned. "I know I'm normally an adventurous eater, but..."

Gabriella glanced at the menu and her expression matched his. "Maybe this is a sign that we should go. We can pick up something on the way back to the house. There was a Chinese restaurant just a block over. We can grab some takeout and eat it at home. What do you say?"

Chuckling softly, he lowered his menu. "I say that I would rather sit here and try to figure out why anyone would combine seared octopus with trout mousse than cut our evening short." Reaching across the table, he took her hand in his. "Gabs, please try to relax. This is all a good thing—we probably aren't going to have many opportunities for a date night once we're back in Portland. And considering we're now parents of a newborn, we need to make the most of this opportunity to be out by ourselves."

And for some reason, that seemed to work. Her shoulders sagged slightly even as she nodded. "You're right. I talked to Skylar the entire way here..."

"I know. I was listening too."

"And Cayden's fine. He ate, your mom gave him a bath and got him into his little jammies, and he was sitting happily with everyone. I just...I can't help but worry."

"Believe me, I'm worried too, but we need to make sure we're both doing okay too. It's not just about the baby. We need to be able to sit and talk to each other." He squeezed her hand. "I have always loved sitting and talking with you. Our conversations are one of the things I love most about us."

She smiled and she looked incredibly beautiful. "I love them too."

"Then let's enjoy the next couple of hours and eat some weird food and talk about some of the crazy ways our lives are going to change, and then maybe we can take a walk around the town and enjoy the holiday decorations."

"Mmm...that does sound lovely. Thank you."

"For what?"

"For reminding me it's okay to take a little me time. Well...us time."

"I think we're going to have to remind each other of a lot

of things in the coming months," he said with mild amusement. "But we've got this."

Their waiter brought their drinks and a basket of freshly baked bread. "Have you had a chance to look at the menu, or do you need more time?"

"Um...I think we need a little more..."

"Oh my goodness," Gabriella interrupted as she looked just past Zach's shoulder. "Christian and Sophie are here."

Zach turned in his seat and watched as his cousin and his wife spoke to the hostess before he turned back to Gabriella. "Should we invite them to join us?"

"I don't know. They might want some time alone too..."

"Maybe we should..." But he never got to finish because Christian and Sophie were seated at the table right next to theirs. "Hey, funny running into the two of you here!"

"Hey," Christian said, holding Sophie's chair out for her. "I hope you don't mind that we're not only here, but practically sharing your table. We can ask to move if you'd like?"

"Why would we do that? We're family!" Zach said. "And besides, this is a much easier way to have a conversation rather than trying to be heard over forty plus people at any given time."

"That's true, but please don't let us interrupt your date," Christian said easily. "I'm sure the two of you are enjoying having a night out without the kids, just like we are."

Ah...message received. They were looking forward to some alone time too.

"Definitely," Zach said. "We were just going to order, so...we'll chat later."

They all nodded, and Zach put his focus on the menu. "Do you know what you want, Gabs?"

Their server walked over and basically asked that same question.

"I think I'd love to start with the house charcuterie and maybe an order of the oysters," she began. "And then I'll have the wood grilled pork loin with the collard green kimchi."

"Excellent choice," their server said. "And for you, sir?"

"I'm going to have the steak, rare, and...can I possibly get the blue cheese crumbles on the side?"

"Of course." He took their menus and walked away.

"So, where were we?" Zach asked, reaching for Gabriella's hand again.

"Why would anyone combine seared octopus with trout mousse?" Sophie asked, causing Zach and Gabriella to laugh.

"We thought the same thing," Zach told her. "Sorry!"

"It just seems like an odd pairing," Sophie said with a laugh. "Although I'm curious."

"Don't do it," Christian said, shaking his head. "Remember the last time you had octopus?"

"Oh, right. I wasn't expecting it to actually come out looking like an octopus," she explained. "So...maybe I'll stick to the oysters or the hush puppies."

Leaving them to their ordering, Gabriella gently squeezed Zach's hand to get his attention. "Have you noticed how well our girls are getting along since we brought Cayden home?"

"I have. At first, I thought it was just the day we were traveling, but I think this is the longest they've gone in a while where they aren't disagreeing about something."

"Granted, it's not like they seriously fight, but this last year they've been a little snippier with one another than they ever were. This is a nice change."

"Long may it last!" he said before reaching for his glass and taking a sip of wine.

Beside them, they heard Christian and Sophie order almost the identical meal that they did. Once the waiter was gone, Christian looked over and said, "It all sounded so good when you ordered it!" Then he added, "Plus, a lot of the stuff on the menu just looked a little..."

"Weird?" Gabriella finished for him.

"Exactly!" Sophie said before she let out a gasp.

"What's the matter? Are you okay?" Christian asked.

"Carter and Emery just walked in!" she said, waving to them.

*You have got to be kidding me,* Zach thought. *So much for a quiet dinner for two.*

The table on the other side of Christian and Sophie was open, and the hostess sat Carter and Emery there. Carter came around and greeted all of them before he sat, and Zach could tell he was exhausted.

"Great minds, huh?" Carter asked with a laugh. "I hope you don't think we're being antisocial, but I haven't seen my beautiful wife in over a week, so..."

"No worries," Christian said. "We're all just three couples here alone."

"Got it," Carter said. "Thanks."

"That really wasn't very nice," Emery said. "That is your brother and sister-in-law, not to mention your cousin and his wife."

Taking both her hands in his, Carter was practically leaning across the table. "And you were the one who insisted on going to dinner. I wanted to book us a room at that gorgeous little B&B so we could have some privacy. I've missed you and all I've been looking forward to is having you all to myself."

By the mischievous glint in his eyes, Emery knew he was purely thinking about sex.

And honestly, so was she.

So...why had she insisted on dinner?

"The rooms back at the retreat house are actually very private and virtually soundproof. I didn't even hear Zach and Gabriella's baby the last two nights."

"Baby? What baby?" he looked toward his cousin. "How did I miss knowing Gabriella was pregnant?"

"They adopted," she quietly explained. "It's a long story and..."

"Here are your drinks," their server said with a smile. "Have you had a chance to look at the menu, or do you need more time?"

"Um...give us just a minute please," Carter said. Releasing Emery's hands, he picked up the menu. "Wow! This is an incredible variety!" He paused and scanned it some more. "Em, I have to start with the seared octopus with trout mousse. I mean...that is an amazing combination!"

Beside them, everyone groaned.

"What? What did I say?"

"Why do you have such bizarre taste in food?" Christian asked. "We all agreed that the octopus and mousse sounded awful and then you show up like it's a completely normal thing." He shuddered. "And I'm telling you now, if it comes out looking like an octopus, you're going to have to move to another table or risk Sophie either passing out or getting sick all over you. The choice is yours."

"Um..."

"Carter, you can't seriously still be considering it," Emery scolded. "You can't do that to poor Sophie!"

He wanted to argue but considering he'd already ruined

part of his family's trip, he supposed he could compromise. "Fine. No octopus. Why don't we start with...the house charcuterie and the oysters? And then I'll have the steak. What about you, Em?"

"Hmm...you know, the pork loin sounds fantastic. I think I'll have that."

Laughter greeted them next.

"Now what? What did we say that was so funny?"

"We all ordered the exact same thing. From appetizer to main course, all the same," Zach said with another laugh. "It's seriously like three dates and trout mousse!" He shook his head before adding, "You can't deny we're family!"

"And why would we want to?" Carter asked with a hearty laugh. When their drinks came a minute later, he raised a glass and gently tapped it with his spoon to get his family's attention. "I get that we're all here on solo dates, but I just wanted to take a minute to say that I'm happy to finally be here. I love you all, and I am particularly thankful that you took care of Emery and the boys until I could get here." Then he looked at his wife. "And to my beautiful wife...you're everything to me and I'm going to make this our best Christmas ever. I love you."

Everyone raised their glasses and reached out to tap them all together before drinking. Once they all settled back into their own tables, Carter smiled at Emery. "I know we got off to a bumpy start for this trip, but I've still got some surprises up my sleeve."

She laughed softly, crossing her arms, and leaned back in her seat. "I've already seen the boxes of Pop Tarts and potato chips."

That made him chuckle. "I wasn't talking about that—although I did keep to my word on them."

She shrugged and he knew she was unimpressed.

"Tomorrow, a shipment of food is going to arrive at the house. A large shipment along with some kitchen essentials that I knew the rental wouldn't have."

Another shrug. "We already knew you were going to cook, and we all know that you're a control freak in the kitchen. This is hardly news, Carter."

Now he leaned back in his seat and took a sip of wine. He knew food didn't always impress his wife. They'd been together long enough that it normally turned into a playful argument over who had better taste. However, he also knew all her weaknesses—the foods that she loved more than anything else and the foods that came with some of the best memories. He'd spent the last twenty-four hours preparing a menu for the next week that would hopefully do some damage control.

But he was saving his biggest surprise for New Year's Eve. He considered giving it as a Christmas gift, but this was the sort of thing that had to be handled delicately.

Plus, he really couldn't wrap it up and put a bow on it, so...

"Fine. I guess you'll just have to wait and see," he said with just a hint of smugness.

She shrugged one more time. "I guess I will."

"Although...there is one thing that I really can't wait to share."

"Oh?"

Carter leaned across the table and crooked his finger to bring Emery closer. When her face was practically next to his, he whispered in her ear, "I *did* make reservations for us tonight. But not at the B&B, but at that big hotel and spa up the road. We just have tonight and I promised everyone we'd be back at the house for lunch tomorrow, so..." Then he gently nipped the shell of her ear. "And I plan on spending every minute we have there showing you how much I missed you."

He heard her the slight catch in her breath before she moaned softly. "Carter..."

"I'd say we should just skip dinner, but I think we're going to need it to fuel up. But once the entrée is done, we're out of here."

When he slowly pulled away and sat back down, he gave her a very satisfied grin. Watching her squirm for the next hour or so would be satisfying and yet pure torture. The only reason he'd agreed to this dinner was so they could talk things out and truly enjoy their night.

And so far, it seemed to be working.

Their appetizers came out—along with the matching ones for the rest of the family—and they all nodded with approval before digging in.

He made Emery a plate with a little of everything on it before doing the same for himself, and after tasting the oysters, he knew they made the right choice.

Even if he was still wildly curious about the octopus...

"Excellent choice with the restaurant, Em," he said.

"I know you enjoy dining at places that are a little different, and after doing a little research, I thought this one would really speak to you. Did you see anything that you'd want to incorporate at any of your restaurants?"

"Nuh-uh-uh...no more business talk tonight. I already told you that Max is home and doing well and that all the kitchens are covered. Everyone knows not to call me until after January first, so...all I want to talk about over dinner is how you and the boys are and what you've been doing since you got here."

Emery took a sip of wine and nodded. "And after dinner?"

"Hmm?"

"You said that's what you wanted to talk about over dinner. What happens when dinner's over?"

His grin was slow and sexy and downright wolfish.

And she loved it.

"Once we're alone behind closed doors in our suite? The only thing I'm going to want to talk about is how good I'm making you feel."

As much as she sometimes hated his arrogance, this time it excited her. "Mighty confident in your skills, aren't you?"

"I know how to please my wife," he replied.

"Um...TMI, Carter," his brother said from beside him. "TMI. Maybe use your *quieter* inside voice when you want to talk about pleasing...you know..."

Carter laughed loudly before turning and clapping Christian on the shoulder. "When did you turn into such a prude? Or are you just jealous that we get to have a night away from the family circus?"

"A lot you know—Sophie and I made reservations for a night away too."

Carter's jaw practically fell on the floor. "You...I mean... how did you...um..."

Both Christian and Sophie cracked up laughing before Christian put him out of his misery. "Dude, I'm only joking. We're perfectly happy going back to the house and really, the two of you deserve a night with no distractions. It's bad enough you're sitting here with us. We've got another ten days of family togetherness. Take your time tonight and enjoy it."

Carter picked up his glass and grinned. "Believe me, we're going to."

# SEVENTEEN

# DAY FOUR

## "SHE CAN LITERALLY KICK YOU RIGHT BETWEEN THE EYES!"

"I DON'T WANT to do this."

"And what makes you think that I do?"

"Well...you're her mother and you really missed her!" Lucas reasoned. "Besides, she'll take the news much better from you than she would from me."

Emma's gaze narrowed as she paced their room. "I don't understand why this is even a thing! And really, shame on your father! He should be the one talking to Lily right now. If you ask me, he's taking the coward's way out. She'll get mad at me just as much as she'll get mad at you. But her grandfather? She'll never give him a hard time."

As much as Lucas wanted to argue that, Emma had a point. His father was probably the only person in the entire house that Lily wouldn't get snarky with or give a hard time to.

"Is this all really necessary?" Emma asked. "I mean..."

"It's just for one night," Lucas countered. "And it just makes the most sense. Lily's the only one with a room to herself."

"That's not true. Barb's alone too..."

He snorted with amusement. "Emma, come on. Be serious. And where would Barb sleep if she got booted out of her room for a night, huh?"

"The...futon in...Lily's room?" With a brief pause, she let out a long, weary sigh. "Lucas..."

"Noah Wylder is taking time out of his life to come up here with the contracts. He's essentially been holding down everything at the Charlotte office, and it's only fair that we invited him to spend the night. This way, we can meet with him this afternoon and again tomorrow morning, and then it should be the end of us having to work. It's a small sacrifice to pay for our daughter to give up her room for one night. Besides, it's not like we're forcing her to sleep on the floor or something. She's literally staying across the hall with her sisters and sleeping on the futon."

"I know, but..."

A knock on their door interrupted them, and Becca stepped inside. "Hey. Do you guys have a minute?"

"Of course, sweetheart," Emma said. "What's up?"

She nervously walked across the room and let out a huff of annoyance. "So there's some sort of rumor going around that some random guy is coming to stay and that he's taking Lily's room," she blurted out. "Now Lily's freaking out and saying she doesn't want to stay with Sloane and me and she's pacing and waving her arms around and just...*ugh*...it's a lie, right?"

"Um..."

"Oh my God!" she whined. "Do you guys realize how...I don't know...*feisty* Lily gets when she's pissed? Like...you don't want to get too close. She can literally kick you right between the eyes! It's insane!"

"Okay, okay, okay," Lucas said, raking a hand through his hair. "No one's getting kicked between the eyes. I guess…I'll go talk to her." He looked at Emma one last time and hoped she'd tell him she'd go instead but that proved pointless.

He was on his own.

*Crap.*

Since their room was only a few doors down from Lily's, he checked for her there first.

Except…he hesitated at the closed door and wondered what he should say.

"I hear my granddaughter is a little miffed," William said as he came strolling down the hall.

"That's what I just heard," Lucas murmured. "This house is so damn large; are we sure there isn't another spot we can make for Noah?"

"Lucas, I believe your mother heard you tell Lily that she was going to have to be flexible when you all arrived. It's only for a night."

"I know that and you know that, but I find it funny that you didn't want to be the one to break the news to her. You told me to handle it."

"And yet here I am. I heard part of the conversation between your girls. Lily took off running up the stairs and then Becca huffed that she was going to talk to you and Emma. So…I was ready to go in and talk to her myself."

"Great. I'll see you later…"

"Lucas!" his father said with just a hint of shock. "You'd leave me here by myself?"

Before he could answer, the door swung open and there stood his definitely ticked off daughter.

All five feet and four inches of her.

Tapping her foot in a sign of annoyance, Lily started, "For the most part, these rooms are exceptionally quiet, but when people are arguing right outside your door, you hear it." Crossing her arms, she stared at them both. "So? Is it true? I have to move out of my room for the night so some weird guy can sleep in my bed?"

"Lil, no one said weird," Lucas gently corrected. "Noah Wylder works for us and he's a very nice guy and..."

"And he can't stay at a hotel?" she interrupted. "I mean...this is supposed to be a *family* trip and suddenly we've got Aunt Eliza's boyfriend here and now this Nolan guy..."

"Noah," William murmured. "His name is Noah, Lily, and he's a very nice young man. He's doing me a favor and I'd greatly appreciate it if you would do this for me." Stepping in close, he took one of her hands in his. "You know I hated to bring work with us for this trip, but some things came up that couldn't be avoided. Noah's been working closely with us on this merger and he's volunteered to give up part of his vacation time to come up here for a few days."

"*A few days?*" she cried, staring incredulously at him and then at her father. "I thought it was for one night! Now suddenly it's a few days?"

"Okay, poor choice of words," Lucas chimed in. "What your grandfather meant was that Noah's arriving today, spending the night, working with us in the morning, and then leaving tomorrow afternoon. So...technically...two days. Really, it's just one if you add it all up. And one night. Surely you can handle sharing a room with your sisters for a single night."

Her foot started tapping again as her gaze went back and forth between them.

"I'm not packing up my room," she said defiantly. "He'll just have to deal with having my stuff everywhere."

"I'm sure it will be fine," William told her. "And maybe you can put some fresh sheets on the bed?"

Her gaze narrowed.

"Or I believe the housekeeper can do that. It's her day to be here anyway. I'll just ask your grandmother to let her know."

"Lily, you're behaving like a brat," Lucas said to her. "As it is, you're the only one with a room all to yourself. Some of your cousins are three to a room."

"Barb has her own room. Why doesn't Nathan switch with her?"

*Like mother, like daughter.*

"It's Noah, and you realize you're just proving my point. That was a totally bratty comment to make. You'd rather throw an 80-year-old woman out of her room than be the one to make the sacrifice. That's incredibly childish and rude," Lucas said sternly and almost sagged with relief when he saw the remorse on her face.

"Sorry. You're right. It's just...I haven't had any real privacy in over a year. This has been a great way to decompress and I guess I didn't expect some stranger to be the one to boot me out of my room."

"One. Night," he reminded her. "For the love of it..."

"If you don't want to share the room with your sisters, I'm sure you could sleep on the futon in Barb's room," William suggested. "She goes to bed early, is a little hard of hearing, and wouldn't be much of a bother. I could ask her if you'd like."

"Grandpa, be serious. I'm not going to intrude on Barb."

"I'm just trying to come up with a solution that is the least offensive for you."

"There's always the couch," Lucas said sarcastically. "There are about a dozen to choose from."

"Dad..."

"We're done discussing this, Lily. Clean up the room,

clear up a little space for Noah, and we'll ask the house-keeper to come up and change the sheets. But you need to be out of the room in two hours. Understand?"

For a moment, he thought she was going to argue, but she simply nodded and turned and shut the door on them.

Loudly.

With a weary sigh, Lucas leaned against the wall. "It's been a long time since I've had to negotiate with her. Becca and Sloane aren't nearly as argumentative with me. They give Emma hell, but with me..."

"Lily's always been more independent and unafraid to speak her mind. I'll make this up to her. Once Noah leaves, I'll take her out for an afternoon. Just the two of us."

The snort was out before Lucas could stop it. "And you think that's going to work?"

"Oh, I know it will. Lily and I were just talking about that exact thing a few days ago—how she missed the times when we'd do stuff, just the two of us. So...I'll find something extra special for us and no one else will be invited."

They turned and walked toward the stairs to rejoin the family on the main level. "I guess that will be nice."

"I just hope she'll forgive me by then."

"And I just hope that she doesn't give Noah an attitude when he gets here or say anything offensive. Like you said, she's unafraid to speak her mind."

William smiled to himself as an idea began to form.

Granted, Noah Wylder wasn't the type of man his granddaughter would be drawn to, but there was something to be said about opposites attracting and all that. With any luck, the next two days would be highly informative—and entertaining.

His smile grew as they reached the bottom of the stairs.

"What are you so happy about?" Lucas asked with a small laugh.

"Just thinking about some of the things Lily and I are going to do. I remembered how I used to take her to lunch at that big hotel high up on the mountain. She used to enjoy going there for lunch and afternoon tea. I thought maybe that could be something special."

Fortunately, Lucas nodded. "I'm sure she'd love that."

And with a little luck, maybe she'd be making a memory with someone new.

Someone who could be her forever person.

It was after four when everyone started to scramble. Noah looked around in mild confusion as everyone began collecting their tablets, laptops, and folders as if some silent alarm had gone off.

"Um..."

"Sorry, Noah," William said with a soft laugh. "My nephew told us we'd all need to be out of here by four-fifteen so he could start preparing tonight's dinner and..."

"I need everything put in the kitchen right through there," someone called out. "And be careful with the refrigerator! It's going out on the deck right outside the sliding kitchen doors!"

Suddenly there were a dozen extra people in the house carrying boxes and appliances and, in fact, a massive refrigerator.

"Carter! Good Lord, what are you doing?" William asked.

"I spoke to my mother a few days ago and she mentioned how full the refrigerator always was and I knew if I was going to cook the way I wanted to, I was going to need more space. And there was no way I was going to shop for groceries every day. So, I arranged to have some supplies shipped from my Orlando restaurant and then rented some things as well. Now we'll all be able to relax and spend only minimal amounts of time ordering food and whatnot."

"I have to say, I'm impressed," William told him. "And we'll get out of your way like we promised."

"Thanks, Uncle William. I appreciate it." Then he paused and nodded at Noah. "Hey, I'm Carter Montgomery."

"Noah Wylder," he replied, shaking Carter's hand. "Nice to meet you."

"Same!" And then he turned away and began directing people all over the place.

"So, umm..."

"Why don't I show you to your room, Noah? This way you can relax for a bit and then join everyone back here in an hour," William explained as they walked to the stairs. Noah had left his overnight bag there when he arrived, so he picked it up and followed. "We meet for drinks and appetizers every night around five, but with Carter getting a late start, I'm guessing it will be closer to 5:30. But don't let that stop you from exploring a bit. The house can be a bit intimidating. Most of the bedrooms are on the upper level, but there are also several on the main floor. Then, down on the lower level, we have a game room, another gathering area, a movie theater, a gym, and a pool. You didn't happen to bring a pair of trunks with you by chance?"

He shook his head. "No, I didn't. I figured I'd be working the whole time and I feel a bit awkward interfering with your family time. I can totally go out and explore the town on my own. It seems like you're a bit crowded here."

"Nonsense! You already met a large part of the group already!"

They were halfway up the stairs and Noah could hear laughter coming from just about every direction. A couple of kids ran past them on their way down the stairs, quickly followed by a few more.

"There's also an elevator," William was saying. "I'm not saying you have to use it, but just know that it's there if you do."

"O-kay..."

At the top of the stairs, they walked past a large bunkroom and then to the end of the hall. "This one's yours." William motioned to the open door and Noah stepped inside. "Housekeeping was in and put on clean sheets, but my granddaughter Lily has been staying in here, so I'm afraid you'll be dealing with a lot of her things being in here."

"Well, there was no point in making her completely move out. I'm only here for the night," he said as he looked around the large room. It had a king-size bed, a futon, a full bathroom, plus the equivalent of a small kitchenette. It was bigger than the apartment he lived in while he was in college!

"That's what we told her, but I'm hoping you'll find the room comfortable, even with all her stuff scattered around."

"I'll be fine, Mr. Montgomery. Thanks," he said with a smile. "It's only for tonight."

"Excellent," William said with a nod. "Then I'll leave you to it. When you're ready to come downstairs, you can..."

"I know—elevator or stairs to the kitchen." Putting his bag down, he slid his hands into his trouser pockets. "Got it."

"Perfect. I'll see you soon. And if you need anything..."

"Oh, hey, Grandpa. I just needed to..."

A beautiful brunette stood in the doorway. She was younger than him—but not by much, if he had to guess. Her hair was long and slightly wavy and she was a little on the petite side. Noah smiled and took a step toward her to introduce himself, but her expression went from somewhat neutral to mildly hostile.

Weird.

"Lily, this is Noah Wylder," William said, and Noah heard just a touch of hesitation there, which was even weirder. Mr. Montgomery was the most confident person he'd ever met. "Noah, I'd like you to meet my granddaughter, Lily. This is her room you're staying in."

"Hey," he said softly as he approached her and held out his hand. "It's nice to meet you."

"Mm-hmm," she replied stiffly and made zero attempt to shake his hand.

"Uh, yeah, so...thank you for lending me your room for the night. I would have been fine going to a hotel, but your grandfather assured me this was the best setup."

She nodded with a curt, "Yup."

William quietly cleared his throat. "Well, if you two will excuse me, I'm going to grab a little nap before dinner."

Noah started to wave to him and then realized how lame that looked.

Then he realized he and Lily were standing in the doorway as if having a battle of wills.

"So," he began in an attempt to break the ice, "I really appreciate the room. Was there something you needed?"

For a moment, he didn't think she was going to answer him, but she seemed to reconsider and relax a bit. "Um... yes. I'm just staying across the hall with my sisters, but I wanted to grab my tablet and a few other things before you got settled in."

He stepped aside and watched as she walked around and grabbed a pair of shoes, a few garments of some kind from a drawer, and then she walked into the bathroom and came out with a small zipped-up bag. When she made to walk past him and out the door, he stopped her.

"Look, I get that you're being a little inconvenienced, but you have to know that I really did plan on staying somewhere else for the night."

"Then why didn't you?" Okay, there was definitely a bitchiness to her tone that he just didn't get.

"Your grandfather is very persuasive," he replied. They stood there awkwardly for another moment or two before he tried a different approach. "So how many Montgomerys are actually here?"

Lily's gaze narrowed briefly, but then she seemed to resign herself to having a conversation with him. "There's 54 of us, plus a newborn. He was a last-minute addition and a total surprise."

"Wow, that's...intriguing."

She nodded. "Zach and Gabriella adopted him. It's a long story, but it all happened in the last week or so and none of us were aware of it. Not that it matters because Cayden is absolutely adorable and a great baby."

Noah had no idea how to respond to that, so he decided to find out about the rest of the family. "Mr. Montgomery said the house was intimidating. I've only really seen the kitchen—I guess it's your cousin Carter who's currently moving an 18-wheeler full of food and kitchen equipment in—and whatever rooms we passed on our way up here. Is there really a movie theater downstairs?"

Another nod. "Oh, yeah. And we can all sit in there and

watch a movie. It's crazy. This is a little like having a hotel to ourselves, minus the room service." Then she smiled, and she had a really great smile.

"But apparently there's housekeeping?"

"I guess you could call it that?" she said with a laugh. "But there's a team of three people who came in today and changed some sheets and did some basic cleaning. The rest of the time, we're fine cleaning up after ourselves. There's so many of us that it's not a big deal."

"I guess you're home from college then?"

Now she laughed harder. "Seriously? Um, no. I graduated two years ago from UNCSA—University of North Carolina School of the Arts. I could have gone for a four-year degree, but I was tired of being in school and wanted to actually go out and perform."

"So you're an...artist? Actress?"

"Dancer," she told him. "I've been taking dance classes basically since I was three years old."

"I would have thought you'd follow in the family footsteps and go into business and finance. It seems like most of your family has done that."

She made a face. "Ugh...no thank you. I have zero interest in any of that. The thought of sitting at a desk all day would make me want to scream." Then she chuckled. "My dad only went into it because an injury took him out of the NFL, so I guess I take after him a bit in that we're both athletic."

"I guess that makes sense, but can you really make a career out of dancing?" He tried to discreetly check her out and she didn't seem like a ballerina, so what did that make her? "What kind of dancing do you do?"

"I can do all of it," she said confidently. "I've done ballet, tap, jazz, hip-hop, contemporary, ballroom..." She shrugged. "For the last year, I've been working on a cruise ship performing in shows six days a week. It was grueling and the money wasn't great, so I decided to come home and see what I can find here."

"And if you don't, I'm sure you could always go back to school and get a degree in business or something," he suggested. "Although, with your family connections, you could probably pick whichever branch you wanted to work at and find something there."

With a frown, she studied him. "First of all, I already said I'd never go into the family business and I wasn't joking. It's a hard no for me and the last thing I want is to be around uptight people wearing suits all day. No, thank you. I prefer to be around creative people and hearing laughter and watching art and music and colors evolve around me. Having an uplifting environment is everything to me. Why would I want to stifle myself in a cubicle? That is a total ick factor to me." Then she shuddered dramatically. "I don't even like to date guys who work in that world—much to my father and grandfather's dismay, but...I find it totally unattractive."

If her words didn't convey that message thoroughly, the look of utter disdain on her face certainly did, and Noah took offense to it.

"Okay, wow," he murmured. "Some people actually *enjoy* the business world and corporate life. People—like me —happen to excel at it and find it feeds *our* creative side. And considering that corporate and business world essentially pays for everything you have and gives you the opportunity to twirl around on a cruise for a year before coming home and probably flitting around from one whim to another before finding something to hold your interest, you'd think you'd show it a little more respect."

"Hey!" she snapped. "What the hell? Who are you to judge me?"

"I could ask you the same question!" he countered, but before he could say anything else, Lily turned and stormed off across the hall, slamming the door behind her.

*Great. Insult the boss's granddaughter. Brilliant move, genius.*

He considered walking across the hall and apologizing, but he had a feeling it wouldn't do him much good. Turning, he walked back into his own room—or...Lily's room—and shut the door and began to have a mild panic attack.

Awesome.

He *needed* this job with Montgomerys.

He'd been working his ass off since he was fifteen to make something of himself. He'd put himself through college and ate more ramen than any human being should have to, just to stay alive. And now, when he was finally on track to make an impression on the executives, he had to go and get into a verbal war with the boss's granddaughter.

Muttering a curse, Noah forced himself to sit down on the futon. What he really wanted was to collapse onto the bed, but it suddenly felt weird to do that. It was Lily's bed, and she clearly had a massive gripe against him—and not just because he was borrowing her room for the night, but simply because of who he was and what he did for a living.

"She's rebelling," he mumbled, leaning back and closing his eyes. "Typical trust fund brat rebelling against her family."

That made the most sense, and it almost made him feel better.

Almost.

Still, he had to prepare himself to potentially be invited to leave when he went downstairs for dinner.

"So...hold off on unpacking anything."

With nothing left to do—except hide in the room to go undetected for a little longer—he pulled out his phone and researched some things to do in the area. Christmas was only a few days away, but...he wasn't going home this year. His mother and brothers were all doing their own things and while he didn't begrudge them their plans, it left him completely on his own for a holiday for the first time in his life.

And he wasn't quite sure how he felt about it.

When William Montgomery had asked him to bring some contracts here to Asheville personally, Noah took that as a sign that he should do something other than sit home for the holidays by himself. He hadn't made any hotel reservations because he wanted to explore and see what drew his attention, and he wasn't afraid to wait until the last minute to find a place to stay.

Looking around the room he sighed.

*Must be nice to have a place like this to spend time with your extended family...*

Then he snorted and shook his head.

*Must be nice to actually* have *an extended family.*

Pushing the negative thoughts aside, he focused on the local sites and finding something to do tomorrow after his work here with the Montgomerys was done.

# EIGHTEEN

# DAY FIVE

## "STILL... THE COMPARISONS ARE THERE."

LAST NIGHT'S dinner consisted of seafood Alfredo with spinach salad on the side. It was some of the best food Noah had ever eaten. Then, luckily, Christian, Ethan, Ryder, and James had invited him to join them out on the heated deck for an after-dinner drink. He was beyond relieved to have someplace to go where he couldn't see Lily. She shot daggers at him all through dinner and he had feared she went back and told her father and grandfather how he'd insulted her.

But so far, no one had threatened to throw him out.

Now, this morning, Carter had prepared Belgian waffles and fresh fruit for everyone, but by nine o'clock, everyone had left the dining area except for their small group who had work to do. Noah's plan was to leave after lunch, so he was eager to get things going. Last night's research showed some interesting things for him to do. He was considering going skiing and possibly on a tour of the Blue Ridge Mountains. On top of that, there were a lot of great restaurants and galleries for him to check out. Sure, it would be nice not to do it all alone, but...sadly...he was used to that.

"Okay, let's get things started," Robert Montgomery said as he came back to the table. "William and I have been on the phone with our legal team and we think we've come to an agreement on almost everything."

It still seemed weird that Noah had to be here. With technology being what it was, there was honestly no reason the lawyers couldn't have simply emailed the contracts to them. But William had mentioned that there weren't printers here and both he and Robert were a little old-school and preferred to hold the papers in their hands. The upside to the whole thing was that it gave him a little more face time with the owners. Someday he hoped to be one of their executives—a top-tier executive who maybe had his own office and maybe even ran his own branch of Montgomerys.

Dream big. That's something his mother always said to Noah and his brothers. So far, it worked for two of them. Simon was a runner-up in *America's Next Singing Sensation* and was currently on a solo tour after signing with agent and manager Mick Tyler. It was crazy that his little brother was possibly going to tour the world.

Then there was Jax. He inherited his athletic ability from their deadbeat father, but whereas their father failed to play anything professionally, Jax got a football scholarship for college, and after two years, was drafted into the NFL. He was currently playing for the Wichita Warriors. It was a topic he considered sharing with Lucas Montgomery; after all, Lucas had played in the NFL back in the day, but Noah feared it would make him sound like he was kissing up to the bosses.

So, yeah. He kept that to himself.

And about Simon too.

They were both such major successes, and he was just... not. Well, okay, he was working his way up through the ranks, but he didn't have the skills and talents his siblings had. Sometimes it bothered him, but Noah was a numbers man. He was the math nerd growing up, and someday he hoped it would pay off. There was a part of him that knew and accepted that he would never be as rich or as successful as his brothers, but that was okay. As long as he loved what he did, he would be a success.

*The thought of sitting at a desk all day would make me want to scream.*

Lily's words from last night came back to him and he frowned.

*Why would I want to stifle myself in a cubicle?*

That certainly wasn't a great part of his job, but it was only temporary. He could handle being a little stifled if it meant he was moving forward.

*I don't even like to date guys who work in that world—much to my father and grandfather's dismay, but...I find it totally unattractive.*

And why that particular statement stuck with him, he had no idea, nor was he willing to examine it too closely.

"I'm going to go over all the changes to the contracts with our team after we all agree on it," Robert was saying. "After that, we are officially off the clock and can enjoy the rest of our holiday vacation."

Everyone politely cheered.

"And I'd like to once again thank Noah for making the trek up here to help us with this," William chimed in. "I hope we didn't interfere with your family's plans."

"Not at all," he assured him. "I'm on my own this year, so...this trip gave me something to do." With a small smile, he added, "I'm planning on checking out everything that Asheville has to offer over the next several days before heading back to Charlotte."

William frowned. "Does that mean you'll be spending the holiday with some friends?"

Noah shook his head. "Sadly, no. Everyone had plans, so..."

"I see," William murmured before looking at everyone at the table. "I guess we should go over these contracts so we can finish up, have some lunch, and formally start our vacations."

For two solid hours, Robert Montgomery read out loud every line of the contract and discussed all the changes. At one point, they started a video chat with the legal department and Noah—again—had to wonder why he needed to stay for all of this. But when it was all finally done, Carter announced he was serving chili and cornbread for lunch, which made him happy he'd stayed.

After running up to his room and grabbing his bag, he came back downstairs and put it by the front door. When he walked into the kitchen, he found the only available seat was next to Lily.

Who was sitting beside her grandfather.

*Awesome.*

She was glaring at him and William must have noticed because Noah heard him say, "Stop scowling, Lily," he gently scolded. "Is that how we treat guests?"

Noah nervously took his seat and waited for her to rat him out, but she didn't.

Not exactly.

"I was scowling because Noah and I had a disagreement over careers yesterday," she said matter-of-factly. "I told him I was opposed to corporate jobs and he thought dancing was frivolous."

Everyone grew silent around them and he seriously wished a hole would open up in the floor and swallow him.

"I never said frivolous," he quietly corrected.

"You implied it," she countered.

"After you insulted pretty much everything I do for a living."

William leaned back in his seat and grinned.

Broadly.

Then he laughed. "Well, I always said you were outspoken, Lily." Then he looked over at Lucas. "Weren't we just saying that yesterday?"

Fortunately, Lucas nodded and chuckled. "Yes, we did."

"Don't let her words offend you, Noah," William told him, even as he smiled fondly at his granddaughter. "Lily is a bright, talented, and outspoken young woman and we respect her for it and we're proud of all of her accomplishments. Even if she doesn't particularly share our interests, we still love her." He winked at her.

"I share some of your interests," she murmured.

"I know you do, sweetheart. Maybe don't attack anyone who chooses a career different from your own. We all can't be dancers," William teased, and Lily looked over at him and laughed. "Although I did try."

And for some reason, that seemed to make her relax a bit. She turned to Noah and, for the first time, didn't look quite so hostile. "When I was five, I had a recital. Mom just had Sloane and was still in the hospital and I was staying with my grandparents. Well, they brought me to the auditorium, and they were in the audience with Becca. I was backstage, and I just didn't want to go on. So my dance teacher went out to talk to them in hopes of my grandmother coming and talking to me."

William picked up the story from there. "Well, Becca started crying when Monica tried to get up, so I went back to talk to Lily. I asked her why she didn't want to dance and she told me she wanted her daddy because he had been practicing with her."

"To be clear," Lucas interjected. "I did it because Emma was on bedrest."

"Don't worry, Dad, I think everyone knows you weren't into ballet," Lily said with amusement. Then she looked at Noah again. "So it was almost time for me to go on and we were standing behind the curtain and Grandpa asks me to show him my routine. I did and then he tried to learn it. It wasn't overly complicated, but..."

"I think I did pretty darn good!" William declared. Then he chuckled and explained, "I motioned to the teacher to raise the curtain and Lily and I danced for the audience for a solid minute before she realized what was going on. Then I took my bow and twirled off stage."

Beside him, Lily nodded before reaching for William's hand. "That is one of my best memories of us. I still can't believe you did that."

Leaning in close he said, "I would have put on a tutu and performed Swan Lake if that's what it took to make you smile."

Noah swallowed hard. He'd never known unconditional love like that, and it was hard to wrap his head around. Did these people realize how lucky they were? How blessed? There wasn't anything he could say at the moment, so he focused on enjoying his meal while counting down the minutes until he could leave. Everyone had been really great to him—well, almost everyone—but this was all just a giant reminder of his own dysfunctional family.

He had a mouthful of chili when William asked, "Tell us about your family, Noah! Where is everyone at this year and how come you ended up on your own?"

*Crap.*

It took a minute to finish chewing and then, with dozens of Montgomerys listening, he gave the briefest explanation he could think of.

"My brother Simon is a singer and is currently on tour. My other brother, Jax, is an athlete and he's spending the holiday preparing for the playoffs."

"He plays football?" Lucas asked, the surprise written all over his face. "You never mentioned that before."

"Honestly, it never came up," he replied. "Anyway, Jax plays for Wichita and they've been doing well this season and he just felt like he needed to stay disciplined and not take any time off."

Lucas nodded.

"My parents are divorced, and my mother is a nurse who also works as a personal support worker. Right now, she has a patient who needed to travel up to Boston to be with their family and asked my mom to go with her."

"A personal support worker?" Lily asked. "Is that the same as a home health companion?"

"Um...I believe a home health companion doesn't deal with the actual medical stuff. A personal support worker looks after the physical, mental, and emotional well-being of a patient who really can't do that for themselves. Most of the time, her patients are elderly. Mom makes sure her patients have healthy and nutritious meals, helps them with daily tasks, and works with an interdisciplinary team to ensure the best quality of care." Reaching for his glass, he took a long drink of his soda before shrugging. "She's got her nursing degree as well, but she spent a lot of years as a support worker and I think she truly enjoys the one-on-one aspect of it."

"That's very impressive," William said before looking around. "We're an eclectic group here, but only a couple of the spouses are in the medical field. Christian's wife, Sophie, is a nurse, and Megan's husband, Alex, is a brilliant physical therapist. I'm a little in awe of both of them."

"We're all in awe of my mom, too," Noah admitted. "She had been going to nursing school when she got pregnant with me and had to drop out. That's when she went into the support end. A couple of years ago, my brothers and I encouraged her to go back to school to get her degree and were blown away by how she aced all her classes."

"Good for her!" Emma said. "And that's incredibly sweet that her sons all encouraged her. I'm sure that meant a lot."

All he could do was nod and hope the conversation moved on to something else.

Which it did.

For the rest of the meal, he was able to just sit back and listen to everyone else talk about their plans to go snow tubing and maybe snowmobiling, and how they were going to decorate the massive twenty-foot tree tonight.

That last one seemed odd to him because there were already decorations on the tree.

Beside him, Lily nudged his arm. "Aunt Monica mentioned the whole tree decorating thing to us and we all wondered what she was talking about since there's already stuff on it," she said quietly, as if sharing a secret with him. "I'm guessing it's just some token stuff so we all feel some sort of connection to it. I know my family makes a big deal out of decorating our tree at home. My mom still has all the ornaments from when we were babies."

Noah laughed softly. "Yeah. Mine too." Then he paused. "I didn't even put up a tree this year. There didn't seem to be a point."

She looked at him. "Well that's just sad. I mean, just

because you're not with your family doesn't mean you shouldn't celebrate—even if you just put some silly stuff under the tree for yourself."

"It's a little late for that. By the time I get back to Charlotte, Christmas will be over."

Lily continued to study him for a moment longer before returning her attention to her lunch with a shrug. "I guess."

Everyone finished their meals and began cleaning up. Lily took Noah's plate and, after thanking her, he walked over to William and Robert to thank them for their hospitality.

"Noah, we cannot thank you enough for coming to the rescue," William said. "If you wouldn't mind—since you're heading into town—can you stop at the post office and get the contracts in the mail?"

"Next time we need to make sure any house we rent comes with a home office," Robert murmured. "This all just seems like a lot of extra work."

Noah smiled. "No problem. I'm just going to go and say goodbye to everyone and I'll meet you by the door."

William shook his hand, and so did Robert, before they walked away. Fifteen minutes later, Noah had his bag and the contracts in his hands and was heading out the door. Snow was starting to fall, and he hoped it was just going to be a couple of flurries.

He was halfway to his car when Jason Montgomery came walking out and slowly jogged over to him.

"Hey," Jason said when he caught up. "Listen, I was just checking the weather and it looks like the snow is going to get a bit heavy. If you can't find a place to stay or it gets too intense for you to drive home, please know that you can come back here."

"Thanks, but I'm sure it's going to be fine."

Sliding his hands into his pockets, Jason nodded and walked with him to his car. "Still, just know that the offer is out there. My mom is upset that you're going to be alone for Christmas and so are my aunts," he explained. "And my dad didn't want you to feel pressured, but...you and I work together every day and I want you to know the invitation is sincere. There's room here for you if you decide to come back."

Although he smiled, there wasn't a doubt in Noah's mind that Lily had moved all of her belongings back into her room the moment she was done cleaning up the lunch dishes.

"I promise to keep that in mind, Jason. And really, thanks." They shook hands and Noah tossed his bag into the back seat of his SUV. "Have a merry Christmas."

"You too, Noah," Jason said as he took a step back and waited as Noah pulled out.

With a final wave, he pulled away, staring at the massive house in the rearview mirror. It might have been nice to spend the holiday with the Montgomerys, but this was for the best. He'd been alone before and one more quiet holiday wasn't going to kill him.

The snow was coming down hard and fast.

It was getting darker out and even though everyone had a lot of fun playing in the snow this afternoon, now that it was approaching dinnertime, William found that he couldn't relax.

"Dad?" Mac asked as he joined him beside one of the tall windows. "Everything okay?"

"I hope Noah found someplace to stay or simply drove home."

"Have you called him?"

"Not yet," he said with a sigh. "I know he's a grown man and what he does in his free time shouldn't concern me, but..."

"But you're concerned," Mac finished for him. "Nothing wrong with that. Lucas and I were just thinking the same thing." He looked over his shoulder and saw his brother hold up his phone before talking into it. "Actually, I think he's calling Noah himself."

That made William smile inwardly. He'd raised good men—compassionate men. It was a good feeling.

"What about you, Mac? You doing okay?"

He shrugged. "Gina and I are..." He paused. "We're in a weird place right now."

"What do you mean?"

"She wants Barb to move in with us and..."

"You don't."

Mac chuckled. "Hell no!" Then he laughed softly. "I just...we're almost empty nesters. I've worked hard and I know I've worked a lot of long hours that didn't make her happy, but...I'm ready to cut back a little."

This was news to him. "Really? I had no idea!"

He nodded. "Yeah, well...I was going to talk to you after the merger. But really, what's the point in me cutting back if Gina and I aren't going to have any time together? She's the one I want to spend time with once the kids are all in college, not her and...you know...her mother."

"So Barb's pushing pretty hard for this, huh?"

"That's just it; I don't know. I haven't heard her say anything and you know she's a fairly vocal woman. I'm not sure if she's just whispering this all in Gina's ear, but..."

William placed a hand on his son's shoulder. "Let me see what I can find out. Barb's been very chummy with your mother and your aunts. If she's planning on moving in with you and Gina, I'm sure she would have mentioned it to them. The bunch of them have been curled up around the fireplace every afternoon chatting away since we got here."

"Look, we both know I'm not going to tell her she can't live with us. If she needs to and it's what Gina wants, I'm going to agree to it," Mac said before letting out a long breath. "I just...I had hoped to spend some time making things up to my wife and doing some of the things she's been wanting to do for years that we just didn't have time for because of me."

"That's very commendable, but if Barb moves in, the three of you are going to have to talk about expectations. You and Gina shouldn't have to stop your lives or cancel your travel plans just because she moves in. Your mother and I live close by, so it's not exactly like Barb would be completely alone."

"I appreciate that, Dad. I really do. I just wish I hadn't been so neglectful."

"Mac, you and I both know that wasn't the case. You changed after you and Gina got together. You cut back on your hours a lot! There was a time when I couldn't get you to leave the office!" William assured him. "Sure, every once in a while you worked late or you had to travel, but you were always there when you needed to be."

"That's not what Gina says..."

"Then you need to prove to her that you're committed to making her happy from this point forward, but not to the point that you make yourself miserable. The two of you will need to find a balance."

"I know," Mac quietly agreed. He was about to say more

when Lucas and Emma joined them. "Did you get Noah on the phone?"

"I did," Lucas said. "He was sitting waiting for a tow truck because someone hit his car and he went down a small embankment."

"Sounds wildly familiar," she murmured. "Luckily he wasn't hurt, but..."

"I told him to have the driver bring him back here. All the forecasts say this snow is going to continue for the next couple of days so it just makes sense for him to stay with us. He said he couldn't find a hotel with any availability."

Beside them, Emma chuckled. "Sorry, it just really sounds so much like the trip where I got stranded with Lucas." She hooked her arm through Lucas' and smiled up at William. "Of course, we later found out that it was all part of your very first attempt at matchmaking and that's definitely not the case for poor Noah. Still...the comparisons are there."

"Well...I'm just glad he has someplace to go," William said solemnly. "After he talked about being alone on Christmas, I really wanted to do more to convince him to stay." Then he looked up at the three of them. "And you certainly can't accuse me of orchestrating a snowstorm and an accident."

Emma reached for him with her free hand. "Of course not. You're just concerned about an employee. There's nothing wrong with that. Besides, it's not like there's anyone here you can play matchmaker with."

That's when she felt her husband tense up.

"Lucas?"

But he was staring at his father. "You're not trying to match Noah up with anyone, are you?"

William laughed nervously. "Of course not! No one here is even old enough, and Lily has a boyfriend."

"She does?" Emma asked in confusion. "She didn't mention that to me."

"Dad..." Lucas warned.

"What?" William challenged. "I'm telling you; that's not what's happening here. We genuinely needed Noah's help with the contracts. You saw for yourself that there wasn't any office equipment here in the house. It all was going to work out with everyone working and then him going on his way. None of us were watching the weather, so..."

"Lucas, you need to calm down," Emma said softly. "You're letting your imagination get the better of you."

"I just want to make sure he's not trying to play match-maker with our daughter," Lucas argued. "Don't get me wrong, Noah's a great guy, but Lily's too young for him and I don't like the idea of her getting manipulated."

"You're sounding a bit paranoid," Mac chimed in. "It's just a weird set of coincidences. That's all."

"Didn't we all think that at one time?" Lucas challenged. "Didn't we all tell each other that?"

"We were grown men," Mac went on. "And you know Dad wouldn't do anything to hurt Lily."

For a minute, Lucas didn't appear to be convinced, but he did start to relax. "He better not." Then he looked at his father. "Do not let me catch you trying to orchestrate anything between Lily and Noah, Dad. I'm serious."

William held up his hands in surrender. "You have my word, Lucas. I'm not orchestrating anything. All I'm trying to do is put business behind us for the next ten days and enjoy the holiday."

Lucas narrowed his eyes, but ultimately had to take his

father at his word. "Okay, then. If I had to guess, I'd say we should expect Noah within the hour, depending on the roads."

"Do you think we should go get him?" Mac asked.

"None of us have vehicles that are better than the tow truck. I told Noah to tell the driver that he was coming to the Montgomerys and to mention me and Dad specifically. Hopefully that will go a long way in getting him here sooner rather than later."

Just then, Monica walked over and smiled at their group. "I hope I'm not interrupting, but Carter said dinner will be in ten minutes."

"It's a little early, isn't it?" William asked.

"It is, but because of our tree decorating tonight, I asked for him to prepare something easy so we could eat earlier."

Mac shook his head. "Did he enjoy being told what to do? We all know Carter had everything planned out with his menus and doesn't like it when things don't go his way."

"Oh, hush," Monica said, even though she laughed softly. "I mentioned it to him last night so he had time to get mentally prepared."

"So, what is on the menu tonight?" Emma asked.

"Lemon chicken with scalloped potatoes and asparagus."

"And that's what he considered easy?" Lucas asked with a laugh. "Good grief, that sounds complicated to me!"

"It does not," Emma playfully reprimanded. "You used to do a lot of cooking—and quality stuff, not just frozen dinners—when you were single."

"That was a long time ago, and believe me, I'm sure what Carter's doing is going to taste better than anything I ever made."

"Dinner in five!" Carter called out at the same time that the doorbell rang.

"I've got it," William said as he made his way to the front door and found Noah on the doorstep. "Welcome back!"

"I'm really sorry to impose, Mr. Montgomery..."

"Noah, you're going to be here with family for several days, so please call me William," he said jovially, shaking Noah's hand. "Now come on in and get warmed up. Tell me, are you hurt?"

"What? No. Not really. They hit me from behind and I went down a small embankment. I slammed the steering wheel, but other than being a little sore, I'm fine."

"Be sure to tell us if that changes. Like I told you earlier, Sophie's a nurse and she'll be more than happy to talk to you if you need anything."

Nodding, he said, "I will. Thanks."

"You lucked out and got here just in time for dinner. Go run your bag back up to your room and I'll save you a seat."

"Oh, um..."

"Go on. Carter just gave us all the five-minute warning!"

With another nod, Noah simply smiled and walked over to the stairs and jogged up, even as some of the Montgomery kids were on their way down. They all said hello as they ran down and he had to admire their manners. At the top of the stairs, he paused and let out a long breath. His shoulder hurt more than he was letting on and what he wanted more than anything was to just be alone and relax, but that clearly wasn't going to happen.

Walking to the end of the hall, he found the bedroom door open and stepped inside, stripping off his coat the instant his bag hit the bed. He let out a groan as he moved his shoulder and heard a gasp that didn't come from him.

Lily stepped out of the bathroom and stared at him in wide-eyed shock. "*You!* What are you doing here?"

"Um..."

"Did you forget something?"

"Uh...I had an accident," he told her, grimacing as he tried to roll his shoulder. "It looks like I'm going to be spending Christmas with your family."

And with a muttered curse, she stormed out the door.

# NINETEEN

# DAY FIVE—PART TWO
## "PUNNING? IS THAT EVEN A WORD?"

THE MAIN LIVING area was almost comically crowded. It didn't matter how many chairs and sofas there were, people were spilling out all over them. As Monica looked out and around the room, her heart had never felt fuller. The tree wasn't lit, but there was a fire roaring in the fireplace, Christmas music softly playing on the sound system, and the snow was still coming down heavily outside.

"If I could have everyone's attention please," she called out, and it took almost a full minute before the room was quiet. "This night is almost fifty years in the making. From the moment William and I were engaged, I dreamed of big family holidays like this. It seemed like every year there was someone missing or someone couldn't make it, so to stand here and see the faces of everyone I love just makes this moment feel like everything."

William came to stand beside her, wrapping his arm around her waist. "When Monica told me what she wanted to do this year, all I could think was, 'Good luck!' but I was just as determined as she was to make it happen. So thank you to each and every one of you for making this dream a reality for us."

There was a flurry of comments and it took another ten minutes before Monica spoke again. "We all have our holiday traditions and the things that mean the most to us during the holidays and we wanted to be sensitive to that. I'm sure it feels a bit weird to all of you because you don't have your own tree or your own ornaments, and while this tree behind me is rather impressive, it's also fairly generic." She paused and smiled. "Until now."

One of the servers they'd hired to come in and help with dinner every night walked into the room with an armful of boxes before walking away to grab another. They were all on the end table closest to Monica.

"I have to admit, this was all William's doing. He got the idea and ran with it and I'm a little disappointed I didn't think of it myself!" she joked. "I hope you'll all indulge us, since I'm sure we're going to get a little sappy up here." Then she motioned to William to pick up the first box.

"My wife and I talked a lot about the things we were most looking forward to with this trip," he began. "And we both agreed it was just the joy of getting to see all of you together. But...being who I am, I took a few moments to pat myself on the back for making most of your relationships possible."

There was a collective groan throughout the room, followed by laughter and a bit of heckling, before Monica chimed in.

"Yes, yes, my sweet husband is still basking in the glow of playing matchmaker," she said. "But let's not forget that I contributed to a couple of happily-ever-afters myself." With a wink, she took the first box from William's hand. "This is for Lucas, Emma, and the girls." She took the lid off and pulled out an ornament—a beautifully intricate crystal snowflake. "This is to remind you how it was the snow..."

"And a bit of poor planning on my part," William added.

"That finally got the two of you together," Monica continued. "We had your wedding date engraved on it for you. And there are matching snowflake ornaments in the box with charms on them representing each of your girls." Stepping through some of the crowd, she handed the box to Emma. "We love you all so much."

"Thank you," Emma whispered with tears in her eyes.

"Jason and Maggie," William said in a bit of a booming voice. "The two of you were awfully fun to watch, and I love how one little lie of omission wasn't enough to stop a great love story." He picked up the second box and gently removed the lid before picking up an ornament—a miniature airplane. "I chose this to remind you of the whirlwind business trip the two of you took that turned into so much more. And like the snowflake, we had your wedding date painted on it." He smiled at them. "The matching ornaments are actually shaped like airplane tickets to represent each of your children."

"I love that!" Maggie said as she stepped forward to accept the box. After kissing William on the cheek, she went and hugged her mother-in-law.

Once she was seated, Monica took her turn again. "Mac and Gina...the two of you were probably the most personal match for us because of how much we loved Arthur." She paused because even after so many years, she and William missed their dear friend and Gina's father. "I know the timing was wrong on so many levels, but it was lovely to see the way that you leaned on Mac for support and the way he took care of you."

"Mac, you accused me of orchestrating getting you and Gina together," William said gruffly. "And I never told you this, but...the day Arthur told me of his diagnosis, that's exactly what we were talking about—setting you and Gina up together." He paused for a moment to compose himself. "In a million years, I never imagined our conversation taking such a sad turn, but I know Arthur has been looking down all these years and smiling at the beautiful family the two of you created."

Monica opened their box and held up their ornament. "Gina, you actually get two ornaments. The first is a miniature of one of the paintings you originally did when you stayed with us all those years ago. It was going to be one of your gifts before William came to me with this idea about personalized ornaments for everyone." She met Gina halfway across the room and handed it to her before hugging her. "You've always been family."

"Thank you," Gina whispered tearily before looking at the ornament. "This was so incredibly sweet of you."

Cupping her face, Monica smiled. "I love you."

"Love you too."

As she made her way back to her husband's side, William was explaining what ornament they had made for Mac and Gina. "The story goes that one of the things that ultimately got these two back together was an 80s movie that Gina loved so much, *Say Anything*. And I have to admit, I've watched it several times and thoroughly enjoy it." He winked at Gina. "So, your family ornament is this ceramic boombox with your wedding date on it." He paused and chuckled. "And each of the ornaments representing your children are matching cassette tapes."

Mac was laughing and shaking his head as he walked up and hugged his father. "Brilliant, Dad. Very clever."

After that, it went on with each couple and family getting ornaments that were extremely personalized to them. And once they were all handed out, Monica invited each family to come up and put their ornaments on the tree. As soon as they were all done, William asked everyone to stand back while he stepped behind the tree and plugged it in. All twenty feet of it lit up and, with the addition of over fifty ornaments, seemed to give it a new life.

Everyone was talking at once, saying how great it looked and what a wonderful addition all the ornaments were. Then there was a flurry of activity as they all began bringing Christmas presents out of their rooms and placing them around the tree in a somewhat organized fashion.

"It's beautiful," Monica sighed as William came back to her side. "I know in the grand scheme of things we didn't add a lot, but…"

"It was the perfect amount," he told her, kissing the top of her head.

"Everyone!" Carter called out. "We've got hot apple cider, a hot cocoa bar, and about a thousand Christmas cookies waiting in the kitchen, so go and help yourselves!"

But William and Monica stayed where they were while everyone made their way toward the kitchen. "This was a good night," Monica said as she hugged her husband close.

"It definitely was. And it's all thanks to you."

She looked up at him and smiled. "It was a joint effort." He held her a little tighter. "I love you so much. You've made me so happy, William. Almost fifty years of it being the two of us. It's hard to believe sometimes."

He kissed her again. "The best is yet to come, my dear. The best is yet to come."

～

It was after midnight when Mac and Gina stepped back into their room. It had been such a great night and as much as he was relaxed and happy, there was something on his mind that he needed to discuss.

Gina was standing by the window looking out at the snow, and he came up behind her and rested his hands on her shoulders. "A white Christmas," he said softly. "I don't think I can remember the last time we had one of those."

She nodded before resting her head against his chest. "I think it was when Tanner was five." Mac began to gently knead her shoulders, and she let out a throaty hum. "Mmm...that feels so good."

Smiling, he kissed the top of her head. "I was thinking about our ornaments and that day I came to you on the tarmac playing music on the boombox."

"You didn't have a boombox, you had two small speakers attached to your phone," she teased. "And it was the most romantic thing anyone had ever done for me before."

"I'd like to think I didn't peak with that. I hope that wasn't the only romantic thing I ever did to show you how much I love you."

Slowly, Gina turned in his arms, looping her arms around his broad shoulders. "You've done so many things, Mac. Big and small...a million little things. Your love for me was never in doubt."

"Are you sure? Because lately it feels like..."

"I know," she quickly interrupted. "And I want you to know that a lot of that's on me. I'm the one struggling with stuff and I'm taking it out on you."

"Gina..."

"Not that you're totally blameless, but...I keep thinking of these scenarios for our lives—things that haven't even happened yet—and I'm projecting a mood or a situation when there's no reason for it."

"Um...I'm confused." Taking her by the hand, he led her over to the bed. "What's going on?"

With a loud sigh, she shifted on the bed and got comfortable. "For years, I was fine with my mom being in San Francisco and us being in Charlotte. I would travel to see her, she'd come and stay with us, and it's been fine. But the last few times she stayed with us, I felt guilty sending her home. She's a little frailer and she talks about being lonely and...I don't know...it makes me feel like a bad daughter."

"Gina," he said, caressing her cheek. "You have never been a bad daughter. Ever. Even when you were mad at Barb, you were still being a good daughter."

"It doesn't feel that way," she murmured. "She goes to these senior groups and then tells me about the things all the other kids are doing for their parents, and then..."

"You feel guilty." He paused. "Okay, but that's a game she's been playing for years. You and I both know that. She's famous for tossing guilt around as far back as when she was married to your father. You shouldn't let that get to you."

"And normally I don't, but now that she's so much older..." Another sigh. "I'm torn, Mac. What if something happened to her and she was all alone back in California? It would take almost an entire day before I could get to her."

It was something he hadn't thought about in a long time. Years ago, Barb needed hip replacement surgery and Gina went to stay with her, but after that, she'd been fairly healthy. But hearing his wife put it so plainly, he could understand why she'd been a little more emotional lately.

"So, when does she want to move in?"

Gina looked at him like he were crazy. "What? She...I

mean...she hasn't asked. This is something that *I'm* struggling with because I feel like I need to ask her this."

It would be wrong to sag to the floor with relief, but...

Carefully, he maneuvered them until they were lying on the bed and he had Gina pressed up against him. "How about this—you stop being so hard on yourself and you relax? You are the best wife, the best mother, and the best daughter anyone could ask for. And when the holidays are over, we'll sit down with an architect and see about adding to the house so Barb can have her own space on the main floor."

Those beautiful eyes went wide as he gently combed her curly hair away from her face. "You mean that? You'd... you'd really be okay with this?"

"Gina," he said gruffly, "there isn't anything I wouldn't do for you. I know I don't always show it and sometimes I still put my job ahead of things that are more important, but those days are gone. This new year is a new beginning for me. For us. And if moving your mother in with us is going to give you peace and make you happy, then that's what we're going to do."

She laughed softly and pressed closer to him, her hand smoothing over his chest. "Well...I didn't say it would give me peace. You know how much she can make me crazy."

He opted not to jump on that bandwagon...

"Whatever you want, beautiful girl," he said as he slowly rolled her beneath him. "Whatever you want."

Staring up at him, she reached up and caressed his stubbled jaw. "Does that only apply to our living situation, or could it be something right now?"

Resting his forehead against hers, he whispered, "What do you want right now?"

Releasing a shaky breath, Gina's gaze met his. "I want

you, Mac. I've always wanted you, and I'm always going to want you."

"You have me, Gina. Always." And then he was kissing her, but she quickly took control, rolling over until she was straddling him and kissing him senseless. His hand fisted in her glorious mane of hair as they each fought for breath.

This was what had been missing in their marriage for a while—passion. And now that they were finding it again, there was no way he was ever going to take it for granted and let it go.

She lifted her head and gave him a sexy smile. "Make love to me, Mac."

"With pleasure," he growled.

And what followed made an already great night spectacular.

But Mac and Gina weren't the only couple getting their groove back...

Down the hall, Carter carefully slipped into his and Emery's room while balancing a small tray and then quietly locked the door. Things had been better between them the last few days, but because of all the cooking he was doing, they hadn't had any real quality time to themselves except when they came to bed.

And even though they'd had a fantastic night at the resort a few nights ago, he was still doing everything he could to make things up to her.

Tonight's effort: Emery's favorite Christmas cookies with a snifter of brandy.

Even though Emma had baked almost a thousand cookies, he knew for a fact that she hadn't made the Italian Christmas cookie that Emery absolutely adored.

Actually, he'd called her a few weeks ago and asked her

specifically *not* to make them because they were one of his specialties.

He'd made this batch while making dinner—which was no easy feat—and now he was ready to feed them to her in bed.

"Em?" he casually called out as he pushed away from the door. Glancing around the room, he wished there was a fireplace or something to make it a little more romantic in here. Placing the tray on the bedside table, Carter turned and was about to call her name again when she stepped out of the bathroom wearing red flannel pajama pants with snowmen on them and a white t-shirt.

Definitely not seduction attire, but he still found her sexy as hell.

"There's my girl," he murmured as he walked over and kissed her like he hadn't seen her in days rather than minutes.

"Wow," Emery said breathlessly when they broke apart. "That was quite the greeting." Smiling, she stepped around him and took a few steps toward the bed when she froze. "Are those...?" Pausing, she looked at him over her shoulder. "Where did you get the Italian Christmas cookies? Emma said she didn't bake any."

Grinning, he sauntered toward her and wrapped his arms around her waist. "They're freshly baked," he said, kissing along the slender column of her throat. "I know they're your favorite, and I didn't want you to have to share them with anyone."

Her laugh was low and throaty and sounded sexier than it should have. "Is that a little extra frosting I see on that tray?"

He hummed between kisses. "It is."

"Mmm...and brandy?"

"Naturally."

"Not milk?"

"I thought I'd class up our snack a bit. But if it's milk you want, I'll go to the kitchen and…"

Emery spun in his arms and cupped his face. "Don't you dare leave this room." Then she led him across the room before playfully pushing him onto the bed. "This was all incredibly sweet of you." She crawled on top of him. "But you didn't need to do this. You've been cooking all day and…"

"Shh…" Placing a finger over her lips, he shook his head. "You're worth it, Em. I wanted something that was just for you."

"There were a lot of cookies out there earlier. I definitely don't need any more sweets…"

Reaching over to the tray, he grabbed one of the cookies and held it up to her lips. "Take a bite."

When she did, Emery moaned with pleasure. "Why are these so good?"

"You were expecting them to be bad?" he teased.

"No, just…I shouldn't want to eat any more cookies, and yet…" She finished the rest of the cookie he was still holding up for her. "Damn you, Carter. I'm going to have to wear yoga pants to Christmas dinner."

Shifting beneath her, Carter scooted them both up toward the pillows where he awkwardly sat up, but kept Emery firmly seated in his lap. "No, you won't. Because we're going to snack, and then we're going to make love and burn those calories off. Then we'll snack again and make love again. See where I'm going with all of this?" He waggled his eyebrows playfully until she laughed.

"You're ridiculous," she said, licking his fingers when he brought another cookie to her lips. "But I love you."

His free hand anchored into her hair, his expression fierce. "I love you too, Em. And I want you to see how much I'm trying to make things up to you. I want..."

This time it was her fingers over his lips. "We're not talking about his again," she whispered, resting her forehead against his. "You're here, and that's all that matters, okay? Just relax and stop trying so damn hard."

Then she took a bite of the cookie and moaned again.

"But maybe keep a batch of these in here just for us."

"Anything for you." Then he grabbed a cookie for himself and took a bite. "Damn, I am good!"

"Ugh...that ego..."

"Yeah, but it's part of my irresistible charm," he said confidently.

"Carter..."

"Here." Handing her a glass, he took one for himself and looked up at her. "To us and to a very satisfying night."

"Mighty confident, aren't you?"

"Are you doubting my ability to satisfy you? Because I am up for the challenge. Again." Gripping her hips, Carter held her firmly against him.

"I'd make a comment about the pun, but it's too obvious." Tapping her glass to his, she added, "But I'm challenging you anyway, just to see how hard you're willing to work."

"Now who's punning?"

"Punning? Is that even a word?" But Emery was smiling and gently rocking against him. They could continue with this playful banter or they could do what they do best.

Each other.

Taking a sip of her brandy, Emery crawled off the bed and stripped off her pajama pants. Carter came up beside her and kicked off his shoes, then pulled his shirt up over his head. In less than a minute, they were naked and kissing and rolling on the bed.

"Wait a minute, wait a minute, wait a minute," Emery chanted with a huff. Then she took another sip of brandy and smiled at Carter. "Okay, now I'm ready."

"Life is never boring with you, Emery."

"Would you want it to be?"

He shook his head. "Never. We're perfect just like this."

"Carter?"

"Hmm?"

"Less talking, more kissing."

Chuckling, he rolled her beneath him. "You're on."

Upstairs, there was a battle brewing.

"I don't understand how you could possibly come all the way to Asheville at Christmas and not book a room in advance," Lily said as she stomped around the room that was supposed to be hers, but now wasn't, scooping up all the things she was going to need. "What kind of person doesn't plan ahead?"

Noah sighed wearily. "I hadn't *planned* on coming up here at all. Everything was last minute and considering I'd never been up here before, how was I to know that all the hotels would be booked?"

"Um, maybe because it's the holidays and most hotels usually are?" And she wasn't even trying to hide her sarcasm. It was late, she was tired, and she had really been looking forward to being back in her own room tonight, but thanks to Noah and his failure to plan, she was stuck on the futon in her sisters' room.

"What is it you want me to say here?" he snapped. "I've

apologized, and in case you haven't noticed or weren't paying attention, I was in a car accident. Believe me, this wasn't part of my plan either, you know."

She crammed a bunch of things into her suitcase before glaring up at him. "Yes, but at least you have a great room all to yourself for the next few nights, whereas I have to share a room with my sisters."

It was on the tip of his tongue to match her sarcasm, but he wasn't that guy. Hell, he still couldn't believe he'd argued with her yesterday and he refused to take the bait again. "Believe me, if there was a sofa bed or someplace in this house that was remotely private, I'd sleep there. But there isn't."

"There are, like...a dozen couches down in the living room," she stated. "I'm sure we can find you some extra pillows and blankets."

Crossing his arms, he stared at her for a moment. "I said private. I'm not going to get any sleep in the middle of the main room in the house. Even I know that most of your cousins run down to the kitchen every few minutes for snacks and drinks."

The sound she made was almost like a growl as she stomped her foot. "You are seriously ruining my entire vacation." Zipping the suitcase shut, she spun around and faced him again. "Just...you need to be gone before New Year's Eve."

"And why is that?"

"Because my boyfriend is coming and I highly doubt he's going to want to share a room with you."

Noah took a moment to fight every urge to argue with this woman, but...

"Can I ask you something?" he finally said.

Lily looked at him hesitantly. "Um...I guess..."

"How old are you?"

"Why?"

"Just...how old are you?"

"Twenty-two. Why? How old are you?"

"Twenty-nine," he said.

She continued to look at him expectantly. "And...?"

He wanted to point out how childish she was acting but decided against it. She was young and spoiled and he had no doubt that this was how she acted all the time. It was better to just let her get the rest of her things and leave than prolong this conversation.

"Just curious," he finally said. "Do you have everything? I'm exhausted and I need to ice my shoulder."

"What's wrong with your shoulder?" she asked as she grabbed the handle of her suitcase, but she didn't sound the least bit interested.

"I banged it hard on the steering wheel when my car went down the embankment." He rolled it just to test the pain level and instantly winced.

"Are you sure it isn't broken? I'm sure Sophie could come up and look at it?"

"Um..."

"Just wait here. I'll go get her. She's just down the hall."

"It's okay, you don't..." But it was too late, she was already gone. With nothing left to do, Noah kicked off his shoes and then walked into the bathroom, where he carefully pulled his sweater up and over his head. The angry bruise he saw wasn't a surprise. He just hoped it was just a bruise and nothing more.

"Knock, knock!" Sophie called out. "Noah?"

"Yeah, hang on," he called out and wondered if he should put his sweater back on, but ultimately decided against it. Stepping out of the bathroom, he gave her a nervous smile and was instantly uncomfortable when Lily came back into the room. Her eyes went wide when she spotted him, but she didn't look away.

"That is a nasty looking bruise," Sophie said as she stepped closer. "Do you mind if we go into the bathroom where the lighting is a little better?"

All he did was nod and follow her.

For the next several minutes, she poked at him and made him carefully lift his arm in different directions while asking a ton of questions. By the time she was done, she concluded he needed to see a doctor, but it seemed like nothing was broken, and he was more than likely just badly bruised.

"Do you have an ice pack up here or do you need me to make you one?" Sophie asked as they stepped out of the bathroom. There was no sign of Lily, so Noah felt himself relax a bit.

"I made one earlier and used it while you were all doing your Christmas ornament thing, but it was kind of melted by the time I was done. I can go down and make another one."

"Do you have an ibuprofen with you?"

He shook his head.

"Okay, you go make the ice pack and I'll go grab you some ibuprofen. Be sure to bring a couple of bottles of water up here for yourself too."

Nodding, he grabbed his bag from the floor and pulled a t-shirt out. There was no way he was going to walk around the house shirtless.

"I'll be back in a few minutes," she said with a smile before walking out the door.

Noah made quick work of putting his shirt on and

heading downstairs. It was weird to find the kitchen deserted, but it was nice not to have to make small talk.

He filled a Ziploc bag with ice, grabbed a couple of bottles of water, and then—just because—he also took a handful of sugar cookies, before heading back to his room. He met Sophie at the top of the stairs, and she followed him to the room.

"I want you to take some ibuprofen," she began, "and then ice the shoulder for twenty minutes every hour until you go to sleep. Don't leave it on for longer than that, okay?"

He nodded.

"You're going to be sore tomorrow, so hopefully this will help a bit." Looking around the room, she let out a soft sigh. "Is there anything else you need?"

"I think I'm good. Thanks, Sophie."

"You're very welcome. I'm sorry you got hurt. What are you going to do about your car?"

"I have to call the mechanic tomorrow and see what the damage actually is, and then I'll see about renting a car to go home as soon as the snow stops and the roads are clear."

She looked at him oddly. "You're not going to stay for Christmas?"

"Probably not. It feels a little...I don't know...weird. Besides, Lily's boyfriend is coming to join her for New Year's Eve, but I don't know exactly what day he's coming, so...you know...not enough rooms and all."

That made her laugh. "It's crazy when you think about how many bedrooms there are and how many beds, but I get what you're saying." She yawned. "Oh my goodness, sorry!"

"No worries, it's late. Thanks for your help and I guess I'll see you at breakfast."

She nodded before yawning again. "Sounds good. Goodnight, Noah."

"Night, Sophie."

Closing the door behind her, Noah kicked off his shoes, shirt, and stripped out of his jeans. In nothing but his boxer briefs, he took the ibuprofen and washed them down with a half a bottle of water. With the ice pack in his hand, he was ready to slide into the bed when there was a knock at the door.

"You have got to be kidding me..." he muttered before walking over to it. "Who is it?"

"It's Lily. I forgot my robe. It's on the back of the bathroom door."

"Hang on. I'll get it for you." Without offering to let her in, he quickly slid his jeans back on without zipping or buttoning them and grabbed her robe from the bathroom. At the door, he only partially opened it and held the garment out to her. "Here you go."

Her eyes were wide again as she openly stared at his chest. Noah knew he was in decent shape, and yet he couldn't remember a woman ever checking him out so brazenly.

Then, as if someone flipped a switch, she licked her lips and met his gaze. "Um...thanks. Goodnight." Then she basically ran back across the hall to her room and slammed the door.

Smiling to himself, he shut his own door and locked it. When he was back down to his boxers, he grabbed the ice and crawled into bed. Turning on the TV, he got comfortable, but he wasn't paying attention to what he was watching. He was thinking about the beautiful spoiled girl across the hall.

# TWENTY

# CHRISTMAS EVE

### "JACK FROST CAN SUCK IT."

"CHESTNUTS ROASTING ON AN OPEN FIRE? CHECK," Ryder said cheerily as he sat down with a glass of wine.

"And freaking Jack Frost can suck it," James muttered as he sat down beside him. "How much snow is too much? I mean...it's been coming down for days."

Ryder shrugged. "It really hasn't dampened anyone's mood. Except yours. What's going on?"

"This is the third day in a row that we've been stuck in the house. It's just...it's a lot, that's all. I prefer things to be a little more..."

In the distance, Cayden let out a loud wail, and both James and Ryder groaned.

"Peaceful," James said. "I prefer things to be a little more peaceful."

"Dude, he's a baby. Your kids cried too."

"Yeah, I know, but I thought we were all past this stage. I have no idea how Zach and Gabriella are handling it."

"The same way we all handled it," Ryder casually

replied. "Plus, they have two teenage daughters who are willing to help out, so..."

"What are we talking about?" Ethan asked as he joined them.

"Babies," James said. "And how loud they are."

Ethan chuckled. "Yeah, Zach's looking a little frazzled, but Sophie talked with them earlier and it's just colic. They're working on ways to help the poor little guy since we can't seem to get out of here and to a store."

James' head slowly lolled back against the cushions as he groaned.

"Yeah, James isn't a fan of all the noise," Ryder said, smirking.

"I get that. Personally, I'm not a fan of all the puppy training. I wish Summer would have left the dog at home with the trainer so we could have simply gone home to a dog that knew not to poop in the house." Sighing, he shook his head. "With the snow and all the people, the poor thing isn't going to know which end is up by the time we get her back home with us."

"Hopefully she'll be a little more agreeable to house training by then," James said. "You know Summer's good with animals. Always has been."

"She's practically like a damn Disney princess with them," Ethan grumbled. "You have no idea how many pets I've had to talk her out of. I'm pretty sure if she had her way, we'd be living on a farm with a menagerie of animals."

"You must be talking about Summer," Alex said as he took a seat on the sofa opposite theirs. "She's got a serious gift."

"Sure, if you don't mind finding a baby goat in your bathtub," Ethan told him.

"Okay, that would just be weird," Alex said before

pausing and looking around the main floor. With the space being so open, you could see all the different groupings of people and he found it mildly fascinating.

Off in the distance, Zach came out of the bedroom hallway and stretched. Alex laughed to himself because he could tell just how beat his friend was. He was about to wave him over to join them, but watched as Zach made his way to the kitchen, undoubtedly to grab himself something to drink.

"Hey, so what's going on with Selena and Casey?" he asked instead. "They've had their heads together for days and every time I see them, they look fierce and always talking to one small group or another. Right now, they're sitting with Maggie and Emma and looking pretty intense."

"Reality TV," Ryder said with a shrug before explaining the situation. "Basically, the two of them want to do it and they're trying to convince the entire family to side with them."

"And...the two of you are against it?"

"Hell yeah," James said. "We're supposed to take a vote on the whole thing on New Year's Eve and see which side wins."

Alex stared at the two of them for a moment. "Have you guys campaigned at all?"

"Some," Ryder said before taking a sip of wine. "We're just being less obvious about it."

"Ah. Got it." Looking around the room some more, he spotted Lucas talking with Noah. The two of them had been spending a lot of time together since Noah came back and he had to admit he was mildly curious but didn't know either of them well enough to simply plunk himself down next to them and find out.

"What about you guys, Alex?" Ryder asked. "How's

Megan handling this whole thing with Eliza and her... uh...boyfriend?"

Raking a hand through his hair, he let out a long breath. "Well...it's not particularly shocking. Eliza's dated a bit ever since Joseph died, but this is the first time she's brought anyone to a family thing, so I think that's where the real issue is."

"Issue in a bad way?" Ethan asked.

"Issue in an...awkward way. I think Megan's trying to figure out the shift in dynamics and if this is something truly serious."

James snickered and then caught himself. "Let's be honest here, Aunt Eliza is in her seventies. I think we can all agree that it's great that she found someone and I'm sure the companionship aspect is a good thing. I would think Megan, Christian, and Carter would be happy for her."

"And they are," Alex countered. "I'm guessing it's just got to be a little weird to think about their mother married to someone other than their father. Even after all this time."

"I would imagine, especially after all this time," Ryder said solemnly. "I know Uncle Joseph wasn't the nicest guy or a particularly good father, but...that's all they've known."

At that, they all simply grew quiet and nodded.

That's when Zach walked over and plopped down on the sofa beside Alex. "Please tell me we're talking about sports or something exciting," he said with his head thrown back and his eyes closed. "If I have to talk about baby gas or poopy diapers, I may lose my mind."

"We're discussing Aunt Eliza and her new boyfriend," Ethan said with a hint of amusement.

"Bloody hell," Zach murmured as he sat up and opened his eyes. "Where the hell can I go for some manly conversation?"

Christian came up behind him and said, "That would be Lucas and Noah. They're talking football."

Zach got to his feet. "Then that's where I'm going," he said before walking away, leaving Ryder, James, Ethan, Alex, and Christian staring at one another in confusion.

"Well, that was a little rude," Christian said as he took Zach's spot on the sofa.

"He's cranky," James said. "I think the baby's keeping him up."

"Thank God for excellent soundproofing in this place," Alex commented. "We haven't heard Cayden at night. During the day, however..."

"Yeah, we've all heard him," Christian said with a small laugh. "And we've all been there, so..."

"Exactly," Alex agreed. He took another look around and couldn't help but smile. Christmas music was playing, at least a dozen people were in the kitchen helping with dinner preparations, and other than poor little Cayden being cranky, everyone looked genuinely happy.

In the kitchen, however, there was one other cranky person.

Carter.

He had everything under control for their dinner tonight, but apparently his mother and aunts didn't get the memo. There was more than enough room for everyone, but they were starting to encroach on his space and it was ticking him off.

"Oh, stop frowning, Carter," his mother scolded. "Just because you have your menu covered doesn't mean we didn't have things we wanted to make."

Pinching the bridge of his nose, he mentally counted to ten. "I realize that, but you should have talked to me so we could have staggered the prep time so it wasn't so crowded in here."

Both Janice and Monica laughed, but it was Monica who spoke up. "Carter, both of these islands are almost twenty feet long. There is more than enough space."

"We thought we were helping, dear," Janice said.

Barb and Eliza were at the second kitchen island prepping the salad—three large bowls per table—while his mother and Monica had been working on charcuterie boards, which they were going to serve momentarily.

"Honestly, Carter, you'd think you'd be a little thankful for the help," his mother went on. "Besides the help we hired."

"They couldn't make it here because of the snow, Mom," he reminded her.

"Still...it's the thought that counts."

This conversation was getting him nowhere, so he turned toward the ovens and went to baste his turkeys.

And speaking of turkeys...

"So, we were thinking we'd pitch the idea of menu options," Casey was saying to Maggie, Emma, Summer, Megan, and Gina. "And we'll suggest having turkey at the carving station, and Dana will insist that we only use fresh turkeys!"

"Ones we'll have to go to a farm for and then we can chase the turkey around!" Selena said, cracking herself up. "And then Dana will see the little guy running around and decide she can't let us kill him and maybe want him as a pet. Won't that be sweet?"

"Um..." Emma began hesitantly. "That just sounds..."

"You can't let them mistreat the turkey!" Summer exclaimed. "That's just cruel!"

"Oh, we wouldn't mistreat him," Casey assured her.

"We'd make sure he was taken to a zoo or a farm where he wouldn't be killed! I mean...that would just be crazy!"

Megan leaned forward a bit. "You guys do realize we're having turkey for dinner tonight, right?"

"Oh, hush," Summer said. "We know, but we didn't go out and pick them out for the sole purpose of killing them. Sheesh!"

"Okay, I hate to be the one to say this," Maggie began hesitantly, "but...this just doesn't seem like either of you. Actually, it sounds the opposite of the two of you. You're intelligent, levelheaded businesswomen. Why are you going out of your way to look so scatterbrained?"

"And Lily was serious the other day about wanting to help with your social media stuff," Emma added. "Maybe after tomorrow, you can spend some time with her and see what else she can do."

Casey and Selena exchanged glances. "Her stuff is already getting way more interaction than anything we've been doing," Selena said. "It just..."

"We really loved the idea of being famous for a little while," Casey finished. "We spend so much time being behind the scenes that the thought of being the ones in front of the camera sort of dazzled us."

With a weary sigh, Selena nodded. "I really was dazzled. It all just sounded so exciting, but..." She looked at Casey. "I don't think it's right for us."

"I have to agree." She paused and looked across the room to where her husband was sitting with James and several of the guys. "You know James and Ryder are going to gloat about this, right?"

Summer stood. "Don't say anything to them yet. Let them sweat it out a little longer and then I'll deal with them." She gave them an impish grin. "It's been a long time since I've had the opportunity to put some fear into my big brothers." Picking up her glass of wine, she took the last sip. "Now, if you'll excuse me, I need to let Lulu out before we sit down for dinner."

As Summer made her way across the room, she saw Lucas, Zach, and Jason talking with Noah, and as she walked by, she quickly leaned in and said to Jason, "Your wife is kind of a genius. Never take her for granted." And then she went on her merry way.

"What the heck was that about?" Jason asked, looking across the room at his wife, who looked like she was enjoying a light conversation with everyone.

"She probably gave someone advice," Lucas said before taking a pull of his beer. "You know Maggie's brilliant when it comes to that sort of thing."

He knew his brother was right, but now he was mildly curious about what the advice possibly could have been.

*Note to self: find out when we go to bed.*

"So you never had any interest in playing football?" Lucas was asking, and Noah shook his head.

"Nope. I'm not particularly coordinated and I'm much better with books and numbers than I am at catching a ball." He let out a mirthless laugh. "I got teased for that plenty, believe me, but..."

"I feel your pain," Jason said. "Mac and I are both okay athletes, but nothing compared to Lucas. I think Mac was more like you and he just embraced academics. I played baseball in high school, but I was never going to get drafted into the big leagues, that's for sure."

It was on the tip of his tongue to mention how the Montgomerys didn't have to worry about their futures the way he and his brothers did. Noah had worked his ass off to get every scholarship he could and then he worked two jobs while going to college just so his mother wouldn't have to struggle while his brothers were still at home. And while he appreciated Jason trying to say he understood, the fact was, he didn't.

"Jax got the bulk of the athletic skills," Noah went on. "And I love watching him play. He makes it look effortless."

"That's what it was like watching Lucas," Jason said as he looked at his brother with pride. "No one else in the family—even the extended family—ever came close." He paused. "Well, maybe Zach."

In response, Zach snorted and shook his head. "I was an adrenaline junkie for years, but I never took an interest in any one particular sport. I wanted to experience everything."

"Nothing wrong with that," Noah told him. "I know my limits and it's safer for myself and everyone if I stick to finance." He laughed and took a sip of his own beer.

"It's good to know your limitations," Zach assured him. "No need to get unnecessarily hurt or cause someone else to get injured."

"He's speaking from experience," Lucas said solemnly. "Zach survived falling off a mountain. Half the team he was climbing with went down."

"Holy shit! Seriously?"

Zach nodded. "The recovery was hell and there was a time I didn't think I'd ever walk again. I owe my life to the team of rescuers and Alex." He motioned to where Alex was sitting across the room.

"So...wait...Megan introduced you to him?"

"Actually, Zach was the reason Alex and Megan met," Jason explained. "Alex was his physical therapist."

"He's the only reason I'm walking today," Zach said

quietly. "Then, when Gabriella and I got married, he met Megan at our wedding."

Laughing softly, Noah shook his head. "I don't think I'll ever remember all the names and relationships. There are too many of you here."

"I'll drink to that," Lucas said, tapping his bottle of beer against Noah's.

"Everyone!" Monica called out. "Appetizers are on the table! We have assigned seating tonight with each table designated for each branch of the family, and some of the kids will be seated at the island!"

As everyone began making their way toward the dining area, Noah had to wonder who he was going to sit with. When he got closer to Monica, she called him over.

"You're sitting with us," she told him. "I hope you don't mind."

He smiled at her and held out his arm. "I am honored. May I escort you?"

She blushed and even giggled. "Such a charming boy. Thank you." Together, they walked to their table, where he held out her chair for her.

"Thanks for taking care of my girl!" William told him. "I hope you don't think we're monopolizing your time. We just figured you work with us and maybe were more comfortable sitting with people you knew."

"Absolutely," he told him and was about to sit when Lily came up beside him. They were going to be sitting side by side again. Was anyone aware that it kept happening or was it just a coincidence? But, since he was raised to be a gentleman, he took a step back and held out her chair for her.

"Thanks," she murmured with a tight smile.

"No problem."

As soon as everyone was seated, William stood and tapped his wineglass. "If I could have everyone's attention for a minute," he said loudly. "I just wanted to say how wonderful this week has been. It has been an absolute joy to get caught up with all of you and talking to all the kids and hearing about what's been going on in their lives. I see a lot of unique personalities and some familiar ones, and I'm fascinated to see where life takes them." He paused and looked around and felt so much love that it threatened to overwhelm him. "So, thank you for indulging us in coming together to celebrate the holidays. You all mean the world to me and even though we'll probably be saying this at least a hundred times between now and tomorrow night, I wanted to wish you all a very merry Christmas. Cheers!"

Everyone held up their drinks, and it was a full chorus of *cheers* and *Merry Christmas*.

After that, everyone enjoyed the charcuterie boards on their tables, along with some of the best wine Noah had ever tasted.

"Noah, you mentioned one of your brothers was a singer who was on tour, right?" Maggie asked.

Ugh...he knew what was coming and forced himself to smile.

"That's right," he replied.

"Would we know him?" she asked.

"Um...did you ever watch *America's Next Singing Sensation*?"

Maggie's smile grew as she nodded and suddenly it felt like everyone at the table was watching him and anxiously waiting for his next response.

"My brother's Simon Bennett. He was a runner-up on season..."

"Oh my God! You're Simon Bennett's brother?" Sloane asked excitedly. "We love him! He's so freaking amazing!"

"Can you call him?" Becca asked, equally excited. "Like...could you FaceTime with him right now so we can meet him?" She stood up and called out to...her cousins...for the life of him, Noah couldn't remember their names. "You guys! Noah's related to Simon Bennett!"

There was a round of screams and a bunch of questions he did his best to answer.

Yes, he could call him.

Yes, he could FaceTime with him so they could all see him and say hello.

Maybe he could get him to sing.

No, he himself could not sing.

Yes, he could probably get them tickets.

William must have sensed his unease and finally put an end to the insanity. "Okay, everyone, let's give Noah a break. We've got an enormous meal coming and no one's making any calls until later, so enjoy your food and let's save any more questions until after dessert."

And just like that, the questions stopped.

"Thank you, sir," he whispered. "I never know if anyone's going to recognize Simon's name, so I'm always hesitant to bring it up."

"No worries. I'm just sorry it turned into a bit of a mob mentality there for a few minutes," William replied. "Now you can relax for at least another couple of hours."

"Thanks." He finished the assortment of meats and cheeses on his plate and felt himself relaxing again.

"So, one brother's a football star, the other's a pop star," Lily said as she swirled her wine in her glass. "With talent like that in the family, how did you end up working at Montgomerys?"

It was nice that she didn't come right out and mock him for not having any talent, but he knew she was thinking it, so he decided to beat her to the punch. "Can't catch a ball and can't carry a note," he said with a shrug. "But I can manage both of their financial portfolios and make sure they don't lose any of their hard-earned money."

"Good answer," Emma said from across the table. "You're a good brother to be looking out for them."

Luckily the conversation moved away from him and on to previous holidays and some of their favorite memories. It was interesting to listen to, and it made him miss his family more than he already did. Not all the memories from his childhood were bad. Hell, some of them were actually pretty good. He knew there was some family tradition in the Montgomery family of opening one gift on Christmas Eve and he planned on heading up to his room so he didn't have to sit and feel left out.

But now he had to wonder if anyone was really going to leave him alone until he at least called his brother.

*Guess I'll have to wait and find out...*

The charcuterie boards were cleared away and then Carter announced that he'd prepared turkey with apple dressing as their main course, along with roasted vegetables with a pecan topping, and a few other sides. Noah had heard all about Carter being a world-famous chef, and it felt pretty cool to get to experience his food like this.

It was—as expected—spectacular, and by the time they were all done eating, there wasn't much left. Everyone worked together to clear the tables and clean the kitchen. There was still dessert to be had, but that would happen after the traditional opening of the gifts. Noah excused himself and was thankful no one stopped him as he made his way up to his room. He had just settled in when there was a knock on the door.

Standing, he went and opened it and was surprised to see Lily standing there. "Hey."

"Hey," she said, and she looked a little nervous. "So um...I wanted to say that you don't have to hide away up here. I know we're opening gifts and all, but it's just pajamas. It's a silly tradition we've had since forever, so it's not like you're interrupting anything overly personal." She paused. "It just seemed wrong for you to have to come up here just to avoid watching us open presents."

"It's fine. Really. I'm not used to this sort of thing. I don't come from a big family, so this has all been a bit overwhelming." He laughed softly. "Coming up here and having a few minutes of quiet was kind of nice."

Fortunately, she laughed with him. "I totally get that. I've been working on the cruise ship for the last year and had a roommate so I was looking forward to just being able to go to sleep without having to deal with anyone else."

Noah let out a long breath. "I've apologized for taking your room like a dozen times! I didn't..."

"No, no, no! Let me finish," she said firmly. "I was definitely annoyed that you took my room, but it forced me to spend more time with my sisters and that's actually been very special. I didn't realize how much I missed them until we had to bunk together, so...thank you."

He dramatically held his hand to his chest. "Wait...I think I'm in shock..."

Rolling her eyes, she said, "Knock it off. I'm trying to apologize here. I...I was kind of being bratty, but it all worked out so...sorry."

He relaxed. "Apology accepted."

"So? Are you going to come back downstairs?"

He made a face. "I'll be back down for dessert. I just need a little time to myself."

"You're going to call your brother and warn him, aren't you?" It wasn't a question.

That made him laugh. "I wasn't, but that's not a bad idea."

"Noah! You can't give him a heads up! We need to surprise him!"

"We? Are you telling me you're a Simon Bennett fan too? Because you didn't let on downstairs."

"Well...okay, I saw the way everyone was carrying on and I kind of felt bad about it. I didn't want to pile on or anything, but...yeah. I'm totally a fan." She paused and studied him. "And now that I know the relationship, I can sort of see a resemblance."

Great.

"I'm guessing he took a stage name?"

Noah nodded.

"But...with a last name like Wylder, I would think that would be perfect for a performer."

"Everyone said it sounded too much like a rock star— like a hard rock star—and his image was supposed to be softer. They wanted him to be like Ed Sheeran, so he had to change his last name."

"Ah. But his real first name is Simon?"

"Yup."

"Okay, that's the last question I'm going to ask because I'm sounding like my sisters and cousins." She took a step back. "And you promise you'll come down for dessert?"

"Absolutely. Those pies all looked amazing."

She smiled. "Thanks! I made the apple pies and the s'mores ones. They're my specialties." Then she shrugged.

"That's what happens when your mother owns a bakery and you spend a lot of time there growing up."

"Good to know." Then he paused. "Will there be ice cream to make the pies à la mode?"

She nodded. "You know it!"

"Then I'll see you for dessert."

"Okay. Um...yeah. Give it like...an hour."

Now it was his turn to nod. "Sounds good." And then he watched as she walked away and smiled when she turned around and waved before heading down the stairs.

Stepping back into his room, he found he was still smiling.

This was turning out to be a pretty good Christmas.

# TWENTY-ONE

# DAY EIGHT: CHRISTMAS DAY
## "UGH...FINE! I'LL LET HIM BUILD THE SUPERIOR SNOWMAN!"

IT WAS CHAOS, pure and simple, but the best kind.

The room was covered in wrapping paper and filled with laughter.

Basically, it was the perfect Christmas morning.

The snow had finally stopped; the sun was shining, everyone was on their second cups of coffee, and as soon as everything was cleaned up, there was brunch to be served. Everyone had contributed to the menu—with Carter's approval, of course—and the rules were you could make yourself a plate and eat anywhere in the house that you wanted.

Personally, Zach wanted to take his plate back to bed and eat it after he got maybe another four hours of sleep. Naturally, that wasn't going to happen, but he could dream, right?

He was yawning broadly when Gabriella came back to sit beside him with Cayden in her arms. "He's clean and dry now," she said, kissing the baby's cheek. "I think he'll go down for a nap just as we sit down for brunch. At least... that's the plan."

Nodding, Zach took a sip of his coffee before smiling down at his son. He was definitely getting more alert and interested in his surroundings. He reached out and touched Cayden's hand and felt his heart swell with love when the baby wrapped his entire hand around his finger. Their gazes met and at that moment, Zach felt a connection that hadn't been there before.

"You okay?" Gabriella asked.

He swallowed hard and nodded again. "Yeah. I'm...I'm great." Carefully, he put his coffee down and then took Cayden from her arms. "Let's go look at the tree, buddy." Standing, he maneuvered their way between piles of wrapping paper, stacks of boxes, and general debris from this morning's gift opening extravaganza. When he reached the tree, he found where his family's ornaments were and frowned. "Next year, you'll have an ornament on the tree, I promise. Every tree we have from now on, little man, you're going to be on it."

He felt Gabriella standing beside him. "We'll have to ask your uncle where he got the ornaments made so we can add Cayden's to it."

"Exactly. That's what I was telling him. Next year, he'll have one of his own on the tree."

"You don't think we're going to do this again next year, do you?" she asked. "I mean, this has been wonderful and a lot of fun, but...I kind of miss our traditions." Resting her hand on his arm, she smiled up at him. "I like the life we created and the things we've done with the girls."

"Me too," he replied softly. "And I don't know if this is going to become an annual thing, but I'm sure we're not the only ones who are missing their usual Christmas morning traditions. Maybe we should suggest doing this at different times of the year. Maybe one year we do it for Thanksgiving, another year we do it during the summer…"

"I think those ideas sound lovely." Resting her head on his shoulder, Gabriella let out a quiet sigh. "I know this hasn't exactly been a relaxing vacation and you're not really getting a lot of sleep…"

"Hey," he whispered, turning so he could look at her. "Yeah, it's been a little harder than I remembered, but it's not going to be like this forever, right? We thought the same thing about the girls and eventually, they slept through the night. Now they sleep so much we often wonder if they'll ever get out of bed!"

That made her laugh. "I know, but…"

"Gabs, we're gonna get there. And if a bunch of sleepless nights is what it takes to make sure this little guy knows he's wanted and loved, then it's worth it."

Tears shone in her eyes and all she could do was nod.

"Are you crying?" Summer asked as she walked over. "There's no crying on Christmas morning!" Then she glared at Zach. "What did you do to make her cry? Are you whining because you're tired? Because listen up, buddy, that poor little baby is relying on you to keep him safe and to love him! He has no idea that he's keeping you awake or what his days and nights are yet! So you just better knock it off and…"

"Summer, Summer…" Gabriella interrupted as she wiped her tears. "It's fine. Zach wasn't complaining at all. We were just standing here talking about how overwhelming this all is, but how it's all worth it."

Summer's shoulders dropped and she had the decency to look a bit chagrined. "Oh. Okay. Sorry." Then she looked up at her brother. "But you totally get why I made that assumption, right? You're just always so moody and growly and complaining...ugh...honestly, you're exhausting and I don't know how Gabs puts up with you."

And before he could come up with a response, she just sort of flounced away.

"If anyone in this family is exhausting, it's her," he grumbled.

"Poor baby," Gabriella cooed. "Now, why don't you and I try to get this little guy down for a nap so we can eat?"

"I'm not done holding him yet."

This time when she sighed, she felt lighter. And as she wrapped her arms around both of them, she finally started to believe that they were going to be okay.

Willow and Skylar came up to them and also wrapped their arms around them—forming a family hug. "So, um... we were thinking," Willow began. "How about tonight you let Cayden sleep with us?"

Both Zach and Gabriella looked at her like she were crazy.

"What? I'm serious!" she argued. "Skye and I can totally take turns feeding and changing him, and this way, you both can get a solid night's sleep. Plus, we are literally in the room right above you. If there's anything we need, we can run down to you."

"Girls, that is incredibly sweet of you," Zach said, "but..."

"Dad, come on," Skylar said firmly. "You know we stay up late all the time, so it's not even like we're going to miss out on a lot of sleep. Then, tomorrow morning when the two of you get up, you can come and get him and then we'll grab a few extra hours of sleep if we need to." She looked up at him pleadingly. "Please? Please let us do this!"

Zach looked at his wife. "Well? What do you think?"

"I don't know..."

"Just...think about it, okay?" Willow prodded as she somehow maneuvered Cayden out of Zach's arms. "Now, why don't the two of you go and finish your coffees and we'll get our brother down to sleep? We'll see you when brunch is served."

And before either of them could react, the girls and Cayden were halfway to the bedroom.

"I guess it's not the worst idea," Gabriella said reflectively.

"No, but...does that make us selfish?"

Sophie was picking up some of the wrapping paper that was strewn all over the living room and when she got closer, she smiled up at them.

And then frowned.

"Wow. Are you guys okay? You look like you're deep in thought."

Gabriella shared what the girls wanted to do for them.

"Oh my goodness, yes! How wonderful! And what a great bonding experience for them to have with Cayden!" she said excitedly.

"I know it would be good for them, but...we kind of feel guilty," she explained.

"Nonsense! This is such a unique situation and it's incredibly sweet that they actually want to help the two of you." Her hand went over her heart and tears stung her eyes. "What a beautiful, selfless act. You don't see that a lot in teenagers. You are raising some seriously amazing girls."

Of course, with so many people milling about, more people joined the conversation.

"That is just incredibly sweet," Gina said.

"You two are so lucky!" Maggie added.

"That's the beauty of having older kids when you also have little ones," Sophie said.

"It's no different from if you were home," Selena said. "If the girls were up and the two of you were sleeping, they'd take care of him. You need to take care of yourselves, too."

"Dude, why are you even worrying about this? There's fifty-plus people in this house and half of them are parents," Ethan reasoned. "Do yourselves a favor and get some sleep tonight. It's all under control."

The conversation transitioned to some funny stories when siblings babysat for one another, but fortunately, none of them were horror stories. By the time brunch was being served, they both felt better about taking their daughters up on their suggestion.

Until...

"Remember the time you had to babysit me and I ran out of the house naked and the neighbors found me in their hot tub?" Summer asked with a grin as she walked past them on the way to the kitchen. "Of course, Cayden's way too young to give your girls any real trouble yet, but...someday..."

"Oh my God," Zach groaned even as his sister laughed her way to the buffet line.

****

Much later, the house was fairly quiet. Dinner and dessert had been eaten, the kids were all off enjoying their gifts, and the adults were gathered in the living room enjoying the peace and the fire roaring in the fireplace.

Except Zach and Gabriella, who promptly went to bed after dessert.

"Well, now we can have a few days to really relax

before we gear up for New Year's Eve," Janice said as she got comfortable next to her husband. "I think tomorrow we should be able to finally get out and maybe go into town, don't you think?"

"The plows have been out all day," William commented. "I'm sure that by lunchtime tomorrow it would be safe to go out driving." Then he looked over at Noah. "I'm sure you're eager to hear about your car. If you need a lift into town tomorrow, just let us know."

Nodding, Noah smiled. "Thank you. I'm guessing since the mechanic was closed for the holidays that he'll be a little behind. My plan is to see about a rental and head home. I can come back when the car's fixed." He paused. "I mean...if it's something that requires a few days in the shop."

"Well, if it's only going to be a day or two, you're more than welcome to stay," Monica said. "I know you were probably planning on working the rest of the week, but I'm sure the boss will be flexible, all things considered." She winked at him. "And if he's not, just let me know and I'll talk to him."

"Thanks, Mrs. Montgomery," he said with a laugh. "I'll keep that in mind."

"I think we should definitely make tomorrow an outdoor day," Alex said from his spot on the floor closest to the fire. "I think it could be fun to maybe go tubing again and then at some point we'll see about going skiing later in the week."

"It's not like they haven't had a way to burn off their energy," Ethan commented. "The pool has been a great distraction and the snowman building contest the other day was epic."

"If by epic you mean the adults got way too competitive

and the kids all opted to come back inside and swim," Christian said with a laugh, "then yes, it was epic."

"You're just upset because your snowman's head fell off and you lost," Ethan said with a grin.

"Care for a rematch?"

Ethan looked toward the windows and then back at Christian. "You and me. Right now. No one else. What do you say?"

"I say you're both insane," Sophie interrupted. "It's like twenty degrees out and we're all relaxing." She squeezed Christian's knee. "Don't go out and do this. It's ridiculous."

That's when Ethan made a clucking sound like a chicken.

"Okay, that's it," Christian said as he jumped to his feet. "I have gotten thrown off of snow tubes, four of the kids beat me at chess, Brayden swam more laps than me, I tripped going up the stairs this morning, bit my tongue at dinner, *and* lost my snowman's head, so dammit, I *need* to do this!"

"Christian..."

"No! I'm serious, Soph! I am going to go out there and build the best damn snowman this family has ever seen!" Then he glared at Ethan. "I'll see you outside in five minutes!" Then he stormed off to change into warmer clothes.

It wasn't until he was up the stairs and they all heard the bedroom door slam shut that everyone stared at Ethan.

"Ugh...fine! I'll let him build the superior snowman!" he said with a huff. "Jeez. I wasn't going to hold him to the competition. I just figured we'd go outside and mess around for a bit."

"Babe, let him build the snowman, but don't make it look like you're *letting* him do it," Summer instructed. "I mean, he's smart and he'll see right through a sympathy snowman."

"Anyone else want to come outside and join us? Maybe cheer him on so that will boost his confidence too?" Ethan asked as he slowly made his way toward the stairs.

"I would, but it's so cold out there and so warm in here," Summer told him.

"I probably should go," Sophie murmured, even as she pulled her pashmina tighter around herself. "But maybe I'll let him get started so I don't make him nervous."

Pretty much everyone had a reason why they didn't want to go outside and most of them involved the temperature, but ultimately Lucas, Jason, Carter, and Alex went outside in a show of support. Once they were all out the door, there seemed to be a collective sigh of relief.

"Are we bad people for not being more supportive?" Eliza asked. "I mean, Christian's my son. I probably should go out there."

"Eliza," Phillip began, "it's freezing outside. No one expects you to go and stand in the snow."

But as much as everyone tried to assure her, she still felt bad. "What if we turned on the heat lamps out on the deck and watched from there?" she suggested. "We can make more coffee or warm up the cider and sit outside and just cheer Christian on a bit."

"If that's what you want to do, then I'll go with you," Phillip told her, and the two of them went to the kitchen to refill their drinks.

"I like him," Janice said when they were out of earshot. "I know Eliza has dated some, but I think this one is serious." Then she looked at her husband. "How do you feel about this?"

Robert shrugged. "Joseph was my brother and, of

course, it feels a little strange to see Eliza with someone else, but…he's been gone a long time. She deserves to be happy."

William agreed. "It's been nice to see her looking so at ease and smiling more. I always felt like she was putting on a brave face whenever we got together."

"I think she was," Monica said quietly. "After all, it has to be hard to be with other couples when your spouse is gone."

"For years, Mom said she had no interest in dating," Megan said, her own voice low and reflective. "At first, I figured that was just something most people said after losing their husband. Then I wondered if maybe she just felt like she was too old to start dating again."

"Old insecurities held her back," Emery said boldly. "Carter and I got to spend a lot of time with her those first few years after Joseph died, and she was always apologizing for everything and second-guessing everything she did. I used to feel so bad for her. It's been nice seeing her come out of her shell and look so happy."

"Did you know about Phillip?" Janice asked.

Emery shook her head. "Not specifically. We knew she was dating someone, but she was a little secretive about it." Pausing, she took a sip of her tea. "But that just had me feeling like this one was different. So I wasn't totally surprised by her news, but I was surprised that she invited him to join us here."

"How does Carter feel about it?" Monica asked.

She shrugged. "I think he's just happy that she's happy. We both obviously worry about her and hate that she's alone—well, *was* alone—so he sees this as a good thing."

"Megan," Janice began, "how do you feel?"

"I think it's great," she replied. "We've been trying to get to know him these last few days, but it's hard because there's so much going on." She sighed. "But from everything we've learned, he seems like a genuinely nice guy."

"Do you think we should maybe...find out for sure if he's a nice guy?" William asked carefully.

"William!" Monica hissed softly, nervously glancing toward the kitchen. "What in the world are you even suggesting?"

"Already on it," Robert said as he stared into his brandy. When he looked up at all the shocked expressions, he asked, "What? I'm looking out for Eliza. That's what Joseph would want us to do."

"I cannot even believe you did that," Janice huffed. "Honestly, did you consider maybe just having a conversation with him before you went the PI route?"

"Actually...Christian suggested the same thing," Sophie quietly added. "I told him not to, but..."

"See? Even her son wanted me to do it," Robert quipped.

"It just feels...I don't know...wrong," Monica said. "Very, very wrong. And invasive." She was ready to say more, but Eliza and Phillip walked back into the room wearing their coats and carrying steaming mugs of coffee.

"Anyone want to join us?" Eliza asked as she slid open one of the back doors. "Those heat lamps are really quite wonderful."

"You two enjoy yourselves!" William said, waving to them. Once the door was closed, however, he faced the rest of the family again. "He seems nice enough, but...you just never know."

"So, um...Grandpa," Lily began as she popped up from the couch she'd been reclining on. "Who else have you investigated here? Any of the spouses before they were married? Any former boyfriends or girlfriends?" Then she paused. "Any of the guys I've dated?"

"Well, I...um..."

"Grandpa!" she cried, sitting up straighter. "Did you?"

"You never dated anyone long enough for them to be a concern," he replied diplomatically. "But this young man you've invited for New Year's...well...if things are serious, we might have to."

"You wouldn't!" Then she looked over at her mother. "Mom! Tell him not to do that!"

Emma laughed as she shook her head. "Oh, no. I'm not getting involved in this."

"There is nothing wrong with Ash," she said defensively. "He's a great guy and if you did any kind of investigation, you'd be seriously disappointed because you wouldn't find anything bad about him."

"Wouldn't that make them happy?" Becca asked from another couch. "That would mean you were dating a good guy."

With a huff of annoyance, Lily got to her feet and walked over to William. "Just...don't do it, okay? Please?"

He nodded solemnly. "If it makes you this upset, then I won't. I promise."

She relaxed slightly. "Thank you." With a yawn and a stretch, she looked at her sister. "Want to go watch a movie?"

"Down in the theater? I think Logan said they were doing some sort of Marvel marathon down there," Becca said as she got to her feet. "Want to watch something up in our room?"

"Definitely. Good night, everyone!" Lily called out as she walked out of the room. "I'm going to grab some snacks and drinks, Becs. Want anything?"

The two of them giggled as they went to raid the kitchen.

Emma waited a minute before looking at William. "You're totally going to look into this character, aren't you?"

William glanced over at her. "Would you like me to?"

"Let's just say I'm not impressed with this Ash person or the fact that Lily invited him to join us. Lucas was going to talk to her, but..." She shrugged. "I didn't want to cause a fight."

"He's either brave or stupid to want to show up when her entire family is here," Maggie said with a laugh. "The last boy Mila brought home to meet us, she made me swear that no one other than Jason and I were going to be there. She didn't even want her brothers home!"

"Well, being the only girl and having three brothers would certainly intimidate most guys," Emma said.

"I know it did with almost every guy I dated," Summer chimed in. "And Ethan saw that happen all my life. It's one of the main reasons he never hit on me when we were growing up."

"Because we would've had no choice but to kick his ass," James said before yawning. "So if this guy Lily's dating is willingly showing up here, um...yeah...brave or stupid, and only time will tell."

"When is he supposed to show up?" Megan asked.

"Thursday," Emma murmured. "The day before New Year's Eve." Groaning, her head lolled back against the cushions. "Someone's going to have to help me distract Lucas."

"Where is this boy supposed to sleep?" Janice asked.

"I'm guessing on one of the couches or possibly one of futons that isn't being used?" Emma suggested before looking over at Noah. "Any chance you want a roommate for a few nights?"

His eyes went almost comically wide. "Oh, uh...I don't plan on being here for New Year's Eve. Once I know what's going on with my car..."

"You really don't have to leave, Noah," William said. "The office will be just fine without you. That is...unless you have plans for New Year's Eve."

He shook his head and immediately cursed himself for responding without thinking. He was sure they were going to pity him and ask him to stay so he wouldn't be alone for yet another holiday.

"Then it's settled!" William said happily. "You'll stay and celebrate with us!"

"I don't think..."

"Oh, don't even try to argue with him, dear," Monica said sweetly. "One thing you should probably know about your boss is that he doesn't take no for an answer where family is concerned."

"Yeah, but...I'm not family."

"Nonsense! You fit right in!" William told him. "Trust me. We have a lot of great stuff in the works for this week and you'll have a great time. Besides, you work too hard. This way, I know you'll be well rested by the time we all go back to work. It's not every day that I get the opportunity to get to know one of my employees so well. This has been a wonderful experience, don't you think?"

"Oh, um...absolutely! I really appreciate you opening your home and letting me be a part of your holiday," Noah said and then felt like he was sounding a bit like a suck up. "I mean...I...I..."

"Relax, Noah," Mac said from across the room. "We appreciate all that you did to help us with the contract stuff.

We're all just glad we were able to help you out after the accident."

It would be wrong to point out that there wouldn't have been an accident if he hadn't had to come up here to the mountains...

"I'm just glad you didn't mind having another person staying here," he said with a small laugh.

"What's one more when there's so many here already?" Janice said. "And besides that, you've been a real sport with all the games and activities the kids have dragged you into."

Yeah, he'd played video games, had snowball fights, done relay races in the pool, played poker, and sat through a marathon of *Star Wars* movies.

Basically, he'd been having a blast.

"You never called your brother though, did you?" Gina asked.

He shook his head. "I did text him to see what his schedule was like, but we haven't been able to work out a time yet. But don't worry, I won't leave without making it happen. Simon was actually flattered that so many of you wanted to meet him."

"The girls have been talking about it almost nonstop," Maggie told him. "All the girls. I hope they don't start screaming when you put him on speaker."

That made him laugh. "I'm sure he's used to it."

"Sloane played a couple of songs for us earlier," Megan said. "I have to admit, I didn't know who exactly he was, but then I realized I recognized some of his music. He's got an amazing voice."

"It's crazy because no one else in the family can sing," he told them. "But Simon's been singing since he was little. We just never thought he'd make it to this level. We're all just so proud of him."

The conversation moved off of him—thankfully—and changed to speculation on the snowman building outside.

"I think I should step out onto the deck and see how it's going," Sophie said as she stood and stretched. "With the heat lamps, I should be able to do it without getting bundled up, right?"

Emery stood too. "I'll go with you, but I need to freshen up my tea. Give me two minutes."

A few more people stood and murmured about grabbing a coat or a sweater and being curious about how it was all going, and before long, they were all out on the deck. The heat lamps were definitely effective, but they were still fairly huddled together while sipping hot beverages.

"At least Ethan's attempting to look like he's trying," Robert whispered.

"But Christian's doing a great job," William countered. "I don't know what he was so worried about."

"He hates being rushed," Sophie told them. "So if Ethan's taking his time, I can guarantee you that Christian isn't feeling the pressure." Then she leaned over the deck railing. "Looking good, baby! I'm so proud of you!"

Everyone cheered with her, but also said some encouraging words to Ethan too.

"Yeah, yeah, yeah," Ethan mumbled as he smoothed his snowman's middle for the tenth time. He was freezing his ass off, but...this was for a good cause.

"And...done!" Christian called out a few minutes later. Looking up at the crowd on the deck and then his brother and cousins down on the ground with him, he said, "So? How did we do?"

Lucas, Carter, Jason, and Alex all stepped out and examined both snowmen before unanimously declaring Christian the winner.

"*Yes!* Yes, I knew it! I knew I could do it!" Christian said excitedly. Looking up at Sophie, he said, "Brace yourself, beautiful! We are celebrating tonight!"

"Yay!" she clapped. "Come inside and I'll warm you up anyway you want!"

"TMI, you guys," Ryder murmured as he began to walk back into the house. "T-M-I."

# TWENTY-TWO

# DAY TEN

## "THIS IS THE EQUIVALENT OF A PAPERCUT TO HIM. TRUST ME, HE'S FINE."

THE HOUSE WAS UNUSUALLY QUIET.

Almost too quiet.

But as Eliza, Janice, Monica, and Barb sat down in their favorite little nook on the lower level with their cups of tea, it felt perfectly peaceful.

"It's hard to believe that everyone went out," Monica said, cupping her mug in both hands. "I thought for sure there'd be a few stragglers."

"Well, I think with the temperature being above forty, they all thought it was a good time to find some outdoor activities to do," Janice replied. "I think Gabriella will bring Cayden back first."

"I wouldn't be so sure," Eliza added. "I heard Zach saying they were actually doing a drive to see the Blue Ridge Mountains. I was surprised that Willow and Skylar opted to go with them instead of skiing."

"It's so wonderful to see that the girls genuinely still want to spend time with their parents and help with Cayden," Janice went on. "I was afraid there was going to be some resentment, but it seems like they're all really settling in and accepting this new family dynamic."

"It makes you wonder what it must feel like to suddenly have a new person in the house when it's just been the four of them for so many years," Monica said. "A baby changes everything. You can't just get up and go like you used to." She paused. "I think it's an amazing thing they're doing."

"I agree," Eliza said. "But I think any time the dynamics change, it's a big adjustment." Pausing, she took a sip of her tea. "Look at what's going on with Phillip and me. My kids are sort of tiptoeing around us trying to figure out how they're supposed to act." She shrugged. "Heck, I'm trying to figure it out too!"

"I thought it was very nice that William and Robert invited him to tour the Biltmore Estate with them," Barb said.

So far on this trip, she'd kept to herself. After all, she was the outsider. Without Gina's marriage to Mac, she would have lost touch with William and Monica many years ago. So she tended to sit back and observe, but this time it was such a small and intimate conversation and she felt like she had something to contribute.

"Oh, don't let them fool you," Eliza said with a small laugh. "They're probably interrogating my poor Phillip, but he's prepared for it. He knows they're just looking out for me and doing what they think Joseph would want them to do." She glanced over at Monica and Janice. "Did they already run a background check on him?"

Monica sputtered and Janice nearly spit out her tea. "Wh...why would you even ask such a thing?" Janice cried. "I mean...that would be...it would seem..."

But Eliza waved her off. "Please. I've been part of this family almost as long as I've been alive. I know how protective William and Robert are of everyone." She took a sip of her tea. "And believe me, I'm not offended at all. I think it's kind of sweet."

"You're a better person than I am," Janice murmured. "I don't think it's anyone's business but your own where Phillip is concerned."

"Not every man is an honorable one," Barb commented and you could have heard a pin drop in the room. With a slight sigh, she went on. "Several years ago, I dated a man who many of my friends had been begging me to go out with. I reluctantly agreed, but he was charming and friendly, and...well...he literally swept me off my feet."

Leaning forward, Monica studied her. "You never mentioned dating anyone."

With a shrug, Barb replied, "I know I'm not anyone's favorite. If there had been a choice of me or Arthur to leave this world all those years ago, I know I would have been unanimously voted to go."

"Barb..."

But she held up her hand. "It's okay, Monica. I've learned to accept who I am, and who I was, and I was a complete and total bitch."

This time Janice did spit out her tea before muttering multiple apologies before running to grab more napkins.

"Arthur was always the good guy, and I was always difficult," she went on. "I didn't really see it until he was dying and Gina came back here to be with him. She told me off a time or two and it forced me to realize some hard truths. And while my daughter has forgiven me, it was very hard for me to come around and spend time with you and William again because I knew I was a reminder of the friend you both loved and lost."

"I'll admit in the beginning it was hard," Monica admitted. "But you're Gina's mother and that makes you family. I've enjoyed getting to know you again, Barb, and I wish you were comfortable enough to confide in me if something important was going on in your life."

She couldn't help but smile. "I appreciate that, but it was so embarrassing and I didn't want to admit it to anyone."

"What did he do?" Eliza asked. "If you don't mind my asking."

"He wanted someone to take care of him. It was suddenly like being married again, but to a stranger. He was always there and expecting me to wait on him hand and foot." She shuddered. "One day he got hold of my ATM card and tried to withdraw a very large sum of money from my account. Fortunately, everyone at the bank knows me and they blocked the transaction and called me." Shaking her head, she sighed. "I had to call the police and have someone at the house with me for when he came back."

"Did you press charges?" Monica asked.

She shook her head again. "No. I was just so humiliated. The police officers stayed while I made him pack up his things to make sure he didn't steal anything else. Once he was gone, I changed my passwords on everything and even requested new cards. It was awful."

"Oh, Barb, I am so sorry!" Janice said as she sat back down.

"The thing is...after that I started coming and visiting with Mac and Gina more and more, but I never explained why. And now I feel like I'm ready to make a change and I don't know how to present it to them without it turning into...you know...a big thing."

"What are you looking to do?" Monica asked.

For a moment, Barb simply stared into her mug just to

fortify herself. When she looked up, she said, "I want to move back here to North Carolina, and I'd really like to..."

Three phones rang simultaneously, causing them all to jump.

"That can't be good," Janice said as she reached for her phone. Monica and Eliza did the same as they all stood and walked in different directions. "Hello?"

"Okay, don't get upset..." It was Ryder.

"Oh my God. What happened?"

"There was an accident at the ski resort," he began cautiously. "There was a problem with the lift and...I still don't know how it happened, but...it broke down and then a couple of the chairs just sort of...snapped."

She gasped. "Who...? Who got hurt?"

"Christian, Lucas, Lily, and Autumn," he said solemnly. "They just took them all away in ambulances, and we're following them to the hospital now. Well...James stayed behind to make sure we didn't miss anyone."

"Okay, okay, okay...we're on our way," Janice said, and heard Eliza and Monica saying the same. "We'll see you there soon."

"What's going on?" Barb asked.

"An accident at the ski resort. Lily, Lucas, Christian, and Autumn are hurt and on their way to the hospital," Janice said. "I need to put on shoes and grab my purse!"

"Same!" Monica cried as she walked hurriedly toward the stairs.

"Should I stay here in case anyone comes back?" Barb asked, following them all. "Should I call William?"

"Jason took care of that," Monica told her, pausing to take Barb's hand. "Thank you, but I think we are going to need you to drive. None of us are in any condition to get to the hospital safely right now."

With a curt nod, Barb pulled her in for a hug. "Then I'm your girl!"

~

It was after eight when everyone was finally back at the house. Carter and Emery had taken the lead in making sure there was food waiting for them all since the majority hadn't eaten all day. There were platters of sandwiches, several frittatas, and a massive pot of soup.

Fortunately, no one had to stay overnight in the hospital and their injuries weren't nearly as bad as they all feared. Lucas and Autumn each had a broken arm, Christian broke his ankle, and Lily suffered a mild concussion and a broken collarbone. It was a relief to see them all come through the door and Carter ushered everyone into the kitchen and began making plates of food for them.

"I hate that the day turned out like this," he murmured to Emery. "If we thought my brother was a mess the other night with the snowman, he will never go anywhere with snow ever again after this."

"He seems to be okay," she whispered. "He may surprise us."

"I think they gave him the strongest pain killers because he complained the loudest. Trust me. Christian will never do a winter sport again."

"Well that's just sad."

"Believe me, I know. I'm just relieved it wasn't worse for any of them."

"It's going to be worse for that ski resort," she said firmly. "Your uncles have already been in touch with their lawyers."

"Good. Faulty equipment is a crime. It's a miracle more people weren't hurt."

Emery had to agree.

Across the room, Emma was fussing with Lily's dinner plate. "What can I do to help you?"

"Mom, it's fine. You don't have to hover. It's my left shoulder, so I'm perfectly capable of using my right hand."

"I know, but...I just know you're uncomfortable," Emma reasoned.

"So is Dad. I bet he could use a hand." But when she looked down the table, her father was eating a sandwich with gusto and laughing at something someone was saying. It was like he wasn't even hurt.

"Your father played professional football and got hurt a lot during his career," Emma said with a grin. "This is the equivalent of a paper cut to him. Trust me, he's fine."

As if sensing their conversation, Lucas looked over at the two of them and gave them a thumbs up with his good arm. "How are you feeling, princess?"

"Pretty crappy," she replied with a laugh. "I guess it's a good thing I don't have a dancing job to go back to, huh?"

She meant it to be light and funny, but it suddenly hit her how this injury had the potential to derail her plans for the spring. The doctor assured her it would take six to twelve weeks to heal, but it was also too soon to know how it was going to affect her dance career. Suddenly, tears stung her eyes and she lost her appetite.

Swallowing hard, she carefully pushed away from the table. "Um...you know what? I'm not very hungry. I think I really just want to lie down."

"Okay, but remember what the doctor said—you'll need to be woken up every couple of hours because of the concussion," Emma reminded her.

"Um..."

Her sisters were immediately at her side, helping her up. "We'll keep an eye on her, Mom. Don't worry," Skylar said.

"You take the bed tonight," Becca said. "Me and Skye will sleep on the futon. You need to be comfortable."

*I'd be more comfortable if I had my own room...*

And yeah, that was fueling her emotions right now. What she wanted most was to be alone, but that wasn't going to happen—especially since Noah was still here. Why didn't he just leave already? His car was being worked on and he could have easily rented a car and gone home.

*Jerk.*

They took the elevator up the stairs and her sisters flanked her and walked slowly with her as if she were made of glass.

And she loved them so much and was so happy they were there with her. If she couldn't be alone, they were a pretty great consolation prize.

In their room, Skylar fixed the bed and stacked some pillows while Becca moved some things around to make Lily more comfortable. Once she was settled on the bed, she realized just how uncomfortable a broken collarbone could be.

"Do you want to sleep? Watch some TV? Want me to grab us some ice cream?"

What she wanted was tissues so she could cry, but...she didn't want them to know how upset she was. "I think ice cream and some TV sounds good."

"I'll be right back!" Becca said as she ran from the room.

Skye turned and faced her. "I can easily distract her for a few minutes if you need some time alone."

All she did was nod, even as the first tear fell.

Skye gave her a gentle hug. "We'll be back, but not too soon, okay?"

Another nod.

But as soon as she heard the door click shut, the tears fell in earnest. And they didn't stop for a long time.

Downstairs, Summer was hovering around her daughter who, like Lucas, was unbothered by her injury. "Mom, we all fell to the left and I'm right-handed. This is kind of annoying, but I can still eat and do just about everything. Plus, I broke this wrist when I was doing gymnastics in the fifth grade, remember? I'm fine. Please sit and relax."

But Summer simply sat beside her and was extremely aware of Autumn's every movement and sound. "You can sleep on the futon in our room tonight if you want," she suggested.

Autumn fought the urge to roll her eyes. "Um...thanks, but Ariel and Nora already agreed to let me have the bed to myself so I don't bang my arm, so...I'm good."

"Oh."

At the table behind them, Sophie was happily making sure her kids had their dinner and only giving Christian a small amount of her attention.

He shifted uncomfortably in his chair with a huff. Luckily, he was at the end of the table so he could keep his leg out of everyone's way, but...

"Can you pass me the salt?" he asked Sophie.

Turning her head, she looked at him like he were crazy. "Are you kidding me right now?"

"What? What did I say?"

"The salt is literally inches from your plate," she hissed quietly. "I get that you're hurt, but you're not an invalid. Besides, it's important to keep moving everything else so you don't get too stiff."

"I fell off a damn ski lift today, Soph," he snapped. "Can you cut me a break here?"

"And I'm a nurse and have been for almost twenty years, and I'm telling you to stop being such a baby. You can certainly reach for your own salt!"

The room grew quiet and they both looked around awkwardly.

It didn't take long for everyone to take the hint and start up their own conversations again.

"All I'm saying is that you've been a bit whiny this trip and while I get that now you're genuinely hurt, you've just been...well...a lot this past week."

His eyes went wide. "Seriously?"

She nodded. "Christian, I love you, but...oh my goodness...the whining!" She tugged at her hair in frustration. "You carried on over everything and it's a little like the boy who cried wolf, you know?"

"But...I was in an actual accident today!" he argued. "This isn't me whining! I fell and got hurt!"

"And so did several members of your family," she countered. "Everyone's feeding themselves and refusing to be fussed over—and they all have arm and shoulder injuries. Yours is your ankle and last I checked, you don't need your ankle to help you eat or reach for the salt shaker."

Groaning, he shook his head. "Some bedside manner you have, *nurse*," he huffed, grabbing the salt. "Last time I ask you for anything."

Reaching over, Sophie patted his hand. "I believe in tough love. You're fine, Christian. I know you're uncomfortable, but you're fine. And when we go to bed later, I promise not to be so tough, okay?"

He eyed her warily. "Yeah, I'm not sure I believe you."

She gave him a sassy grin. "I guess you'll just have to wait and see."

With no other choice, he turned his attention to his dinner.

"She's right, you know," his mother said from beside him. "You're going to be incredibly sore if you don't keep moving."

"Mom, I think I'm going to be sore no matter what." He put his utensils down. "And you know what would have been great for that?"

"No, what?"

"The hot tub. If I had broken my arm, I still could have soaked in the hot tub and helped the rest of my body, but no. I had to go and break my ankle."

Eliza was quiet for a moment before looking up at him. "Sophie's right. You're whining."

Great, now even his mother was against him.

*Ugh...I loathe myself...*

Since dinner was a bit informal, everyone got up at different times, cleaning up their own things. When Christian was finished, that's when Sophie helped him. "I know you can't carry all of this while on crutches," she said with a serene smile that did nothing to help his mood.

Slowly, he got to his feet and reached for his crutches—because he'd look like a jerk if he asked anyone to hand them to him—and carefully made his way out of the kitchen. There were people in the living room, people downstairs, and there was another movie marathon just starting up down in the theater. He wasn't feeling social, so he made his way to one of the chairs tucked away in the corner and figured he'd do some reading on his phone.

Or...that was the plan until Phillip came to sit in the only other chair in that particular place in the room. He placed a glass of amber liquid on the table between them. "Thought you could use this," he said."

Christian eyed the glass before looking up. "Um...I can't drink any alcohol. I've taken some painkillers already, but... thanks." Then he went back to scrolling on his phone.

"It's not alcohol; it's ginger ale," Phillip said. "A lot of those painkillers can upset your stomach, so I thought you might need a little something." Then he relaxed in his own chair and pulled out his phone and began scrolling.

For a minute, Christian wasn't sure if he was supposed to say anything else or just sit quietly, but it didn't take long for the silence to feel awkward.

"So, um..." Pausing, he cleared his throat. "How was the Biltmore tour? Did you get to finish it?"

Placing his phone down, Phillip nodded. "It was very interesting. We were about three-quarters of the way through when we got the call. I know your mother's been there before, but I was thinking it was something we can go back and see maybe before we head home. Have you been there before?"

He shook his head. "We've never been here for vacation before." Then he let out a mirthless laugh. "I guess I should have gone with you and my uncles today, huh?"

But Phillip didn't laugh. He did, however, offer a sympathetic smile. "That's one way of looking at it, I suppose. Although I'm sure you would have been bored walking at such a slow pace."

"I doubt it. Probably safer for me too..."

"Christian, may I ask you something?"

"Um...sure?"

"What's troubling you?"

That...wasn't quite the question he was expecting.

"Right now, my ankle."

This time, Phillip did laugh. "I don't mean physically, I mean...dig a little deeper. It seems like you've been having some issues since you got here." He casually relaxed, crossing one leg over the other. "I'd say that maybe you have an issue with me, but from what I heard the other night with the whole snowman thing, you were struggling before I got here."

Crap. That would have been the easy excuse to give, but it also would have been a lie, and Christian prided himself on being honest.

Shifting slightly in his seat, he winced as his foot hit the floor, but didn't talk about the pain. "I'm at an age where I'd like to think about retiring," he began slowly. "I don't need to work as much as I do."

Phillip nodded. "Your mother mentioned your struggles with your work-life balance."

"Exactly. Well...now I really would like to cut back. Our kids are all in high school now and there are a lot of opportunities for us to travel and really be involved more in what they're doing in their lives."

"Okay. That all sounds good."

"I thought so too until we got here. We flew in, drove from the airport, and...I don't know...I got here and just..." He was at a loss for words.

"You don't know how to relax."

"No. Yes. I don't know. Maybe..."

Phillip chuckled. "Want to try that again?"

And for some reason, his gentle tone really seemed to touch something in him. "I know I can relax. We've traveled dozens of times before. But I think because of the crossroads I've put myself at, I thought I'd be...more capable of keeping up with my kids." Shaking his head, he explained further. "That damn tubing hill really did me in.

I'm one of the youngest Montgomerys of my generation and that was the first time I couldn't keep up with my peers."

"It's a tough spot for a man to find himself in. And when something like that happens, we tend to overcompensate and end up doing more harm than good." He laughed softly again. "Trust me. I know."

"Did you fall off a tube in front of your kids too?" Christian asked with a hint of amusement.

"No, but..." Now it was Phillip's turn to shift in his seat. "Before my wife died, I remember her telling me we needed to hire someone to build some new shelves she wanted. I had always been handy and took offense to her suggesting that I couldn't do it." He shrugged. "So I went and bought all the lumber, got a new saw, and I thought I was all that." Then he shook his head. "It took me over a month to build six shelves and I nearly cut off one of my fingers, and then fell off the ladder when I was installing them. It was a bit emasculating."

"Okay, but...how old were you? Because I'm going to be..."

"You're going to be fifty next year," Phillip finished for him. "I was fifty-two when it happened."

"Wow."

"Exactly."

"Did you get the shelves hung?"

"I did. And they're still up and probably the most level thing in that house."

"Oh, so you still live in the same house?"

He shook his head. "No, but my son and daughter-in-law do, and every time I visit them, I marvel at my handiwork while remembering my stupidity. They might have just been shelves, but...I should have hired someone." Then he held out his hand to Christian. "You can see the scar on this finger here. I severed a nerve and can't really feel it."

And sure enough, there was a scar and it was a bit gnarly. "Holy crap, Phillip."

"Believe me, I know. It's my own daily reminder to know my limitations. I may not be able to build anything, but there are so many other things I can do." He sat back and got comfortable again. "So you can't ride a snow tube. Who cares? Not all dads are athletic. Do you love your kids? Do you talk to them and encourage them?"

"Every damn day," he said gruffly.

"That's more than most men do. Anyone can throw a ball or swim in a pool. It takes a real man—a real father—to be someone their kids can come to just to talk or for advice. It's a gift to be able to guide them on how to simply exist in this crazy world."

Christian was speechless.

"I've had the pleasure of spending some time getting to know your kids," Phillip went on. "And I have to tell you, they're really great kids. I'm not just saying that because you're their dad and I'm talking to you; I genuinely mean it. They are great kids. They're polite and respectful and they all have a great sense of humor."

"They get that from Sophie. Trust me," he said with a laugh.

"Christian, be the dad that you've always been. Be the dad that you're comfortable with. You've been doing that all along and look at the results! They're not asking you to become someone different just because you're working less." Then he leaned forward and gave him a friendly pat on the knee. "You're doing a wonderful job. Know that." Then he got to his feet. "Not everyone can be a great father, but...you seem to have that locked down. Keep it up."

When he turned to walk away, Christian called his name.

"Hmm?"

"You're an awesome father too," Christian said.

Even in the slightly dim light in the corner, it looked like he was blushing. "Well...I don't know about that."

"Trust me. You are. Thank you." He reached out his hand to shake and smiled when Phillip obliged.

"Get some rest while you can. Sleeping with a cast will be a challenge."

"I will. And again, thanks." Phillip walked toward the kitchen and Christian sat where he was for several minutes and realized just how much that one conversation did for him. When his father was alive, he had never been that compassionate or encouraging, and he never knew how much he needed that sometimes.

Like right now.

"Hey, there's my patient," Sophie said as she came over and crouched down beside him. "How about we go upstairs so you can elevate this foot? I found some extra pillows and I made you a nice cup of tea, and I thought we could snuggle in bed and watch some TV. What do you think?"

A little while ago, he probably would have had a snarky comeback for her, but thanks to Phillip, he was in a much better headspace. "I think that sounds fantastic. Let me just grab my crutches and..."

"No, I got them," she said quickly as she got to her feet, but Christian stopped her.

"It's okay, Soph. I got them, but thanks for wanting to help." When he was on his feet and balanced on the crutches, he leaned in and kissed her. "I love you."

"Aww...my sweet man. I love you too." Her smile was

everything. "Now come on. Let's go and maybe get semi-naked and I'll see what I can do to make you feel better."

That made him laugh as they made their way to the elevator. "There are no strings attached to us going up to bed. I'll be happy just having you pressed up beside me."

"If you say so..."

But a little while later, he was more than happy with his wife's brand of making him feel good.

# TWENTY-THREE

# DAY TWELVE

"IS THERE a reason we're all hiding out here in our room?" Jason asked. He was staring at his brothers and their wives, plus Maggie. "What's going on?"

"We needed a place to talk without an audience," Mac began. "And since the accident the other day, it feels like no one's going out as much."

"I saw Dad and Noah leave earlier," Lucas said. "Were they picking up his rental car?"

"That was the plan, but he seems hesitant to let the poor guy leave," Mac said with a laugh. "I think he's enjoying having someone like Noah close at hand so he might prepare him to be part of the next generation of executives at Montgomerys."

Jason nodded with a chuckle too. "You know how Dad is about having the best team possible for the company."

"And the family," Mac added. "He certainly has a thing about handpicking people and I guess it's not just in match-making, right?"

"Oh, no," both Lucas and Emma mumbled.

"What? What's the matter?" Maggie asked.

Lucas jumped to his feet. "I really think he's trying to set Lily and Noah up, and I'm not gonna stand for it!"

Emma tugged on his hand—hard. "Just sit down," she ordered. "I'll admit that I'm starting to feel the same way, but I think we're getting a little ahead of ourselves. Lily has shown zero interest in Noah, and her boyfriend is arriving tomorrow."

"Don't remind me," Lucas murmured.

"Let your father spend his time getting to know Noah and we'll just hope he's looking at him as someone he's potentially promoting at work," Emma said.

"Um...I hate to sound like a jerk," Mac interrupted. "But we kind of had our own stuff we needed to talk to you guys about."

"Oh, right! Sorry!" Emma said. "Go ahead."

"We think my mother is going to ask to move in with us," Gina said. She and Mac were sitting on the futon and everyone was just sort of staring at them. "According to your mother, she was about to tell everyone that the other day, but then the call came in about the accident."

"Okay, but...maybe that wasn't what she was going to say," Maggie reasoned. "I mean...maybe she just wants to stay for a longer visit after the holidays."

But Gina was shaking her head. "She specifically said she wants to move back to North Carolina. And honestly, I don't know what to do!"

"Wait...I thought you wanted her to move in with you?" Jason asked. "At least, that's what Mac was telling us."

Groaning, Gina held her face in her hands as Mac took over.

"She thought that's what she was supposed to be doing. Barb's never mentioned moving in with us, but...she's getting older and once Gina and I sat down and talked about it, we realized that it just made sense. She's been living in San Francisco for so damn long, and up until recently, she's been fairly independent."

"So what's changed?" Emma asked.

"It's little things that I notice," Gina replied. "But before the little things become big things..."

"You want to make sure she's close by," Maggie finished for her. "So...okay, what's the problem then?"

"We just..." Gina paused, looking at Mac. "We just don't know if we can handle this. We're watching Zach and Gabriella with the new baby and everyone's talking about how much the dynamics change when you bring someone else into the home, and..."

"And while we realize Barb isn't a newborn baby, sometimes she requires just as much attention," Mac said flatly. "So what we need is a little...I don't know...input. Are we doing the right thing? Is this what's best for our family and for Barb? This is all brand-new territory and we're kind of floundering here."

"Plus, Mac was really looking to cut back on his hours so that we could travel a bit and have some quality time with the kids before they're all out of the house. If we move my mother in..."

"Then it's less quality time and more having to cater to her," Maggie said. "Got it." She let out a long breath. "My suggestion would be to sit down with her and have an honest conversation about your fears and concerns. If she knows going in how you feel, it might help."

Gina wasn't so sure. She knew how demanding her mother could be and there was a part of her that really had reservations about opening that door.

"Maybe..."

"I suggested we put an addition on the house so Barb

has her own space—a suite of rooms that are all hers instead of moving her into the guest room. A place that's separate from ours, but still part of the house," Mac said.

"Maybe ask Mom and Dad if she can move into the guest house," Lucas put out there. "No one really uses it. Hell, I think the last time anyone really used it was almost twenty years ago when Gina stayed there."

"Oh, I couldn't do that to your parents," Gina said. "She's my mother and…"

"And our responsibility," Mac finished for her. Then he looked up at them. "If it were any of you, what would you do?"

"It's not really a fair question because all our parents live close to us," Jason replied. "And—no offense, Gina—none of us have a…contentious relationship like you've had with Barb."

Nodding, she agreed. "I know. That's the part that's bugging me. I just wish…"

A knock on the door had them all freezing.

Jason walked over and pulled it open partially, "Oh, hey, Mom. What's up?"

Monica tried to look beyond him into the room. "I was trying to figure out where you and your brothers went. I knocked on Mac and Gina's door and then came up here. I was going to Lucas and Emma's next. Is everything okay?"

"Um…"

"Let her in," Mac said as he got to his feet.

"My goodness. This looks like quite the intense little gathering. What's going on?"

"We were talking about my mother," Gina said. "Mac and I said we'd deal with it after we got home, but…I feel like it's just hanging over my head and I wanted some input from everyone."

"You poor thing," Monica said, sitting on the futon beside her. "I think it's something you and your mother need to sit and talk about sooner rather than later. We're all prepping for our big New Year's Eve party, and I'd love if you were able to fully enjoy it."

"I know, but..."

"I'm not saying you have to talk to her right now, but... before Friday, okay?" Then she kissed Gina's cheek and looked up at her sons. "We're barbecuing tonight and Carter's in all-hands-on-deck mode. There are five grills and since he's handling all the sides and everything in the kitchen, and Christian's hurt..."

"Um...so am I," Lucas reminded her.

"Yes, dear. I know. I was going to suggest that Jason and Mac handle one of the grills. Zach and Ethan have one, James and Ryder have one, Alex and Noah have one, and Phillip and Robert have one. It only seemed fair that the two of you..."

"We're on it," Jason said and was about to walk out of the room when he looked at Mac and Gina. "Are we good here?"

They nodded, and then Mac followed him out the door.

"Two men per grill?" Lucas asked with amusement. "Seems like overkill."

"Well...it was easier to team everyone up so they could limit the amount of people milling around and asking when things were going to be ready. Plus, you're all competitive with your grilling skills so...I guess we'll find out who's truly the grill master," she explained with a wink. "Now if you'll excuse me..."

"What's Dad doing?" Lucas asked. "If Uncle Robert and Phillip are sharing a grill, where does that leave Dad?"

"He and Christian are playing a game of chess." Getting

up, she walked over to the door. "You should go and sit with them and relax until dinner's ready."

"What's Carter making for sides?" Emma asked.

"Ooh...baked beans, potato salad, coleslaw, homemade onion rings, and a Mexican street corn salad with couscous." Shaking her head, she added, "I swear I don't know how he does it."

"He's not cooking for New Year's Eve, is he?" Maggie asked. "I hate that he's not having time to relax."

"We made an agreement with him on how many meals he could prepare, because if we had everything catered, he would have picked it all apart. But New Year's Eve is being catered with a full serving staff. New Year's Day, Carter insisted on making this rather eclectic meal that is supposed to bring good luck, but I can't remember everything that was on it."

"I'm guessing we'll eat leftovers earlier that day since we're all leaving on the second, right?" Gina asked.

"Almost everyone," Monica replied. "And that sounds like the most practical idea with the food. But William and I aren't heading home until the fourth, and the same with Janice, Robert, Eliza, and Phillip. We all decided to stay a few extra days to unwind."

"That sounds wonderful. I think we could all use a few days to unwind before returning to our regular schedules," Emma said. "I'm just worried about Lily."

"She has been a little quiet since the accident," Monica said with a sigh. "You know she's got to be worried about her recovery and what it will mean in terms of her career. Maybe when you all get home and she sees the orthopedic doctor for a follow up, she'll feel better."

"I hope so," Lucas said solemnly. "But I remember how I felt every time I had an injury while playing football. You think it's a career-ending thing every time. Maybe I should talk to her?"

"I'm sure she'd appreciate that," Emma said. "But maybe see how she is at dinner. Just...observe before you jump in with a 'you know how she feels' speech."

"On that note, I need to see where I'm needed downstairs. Dinner should be in about thirty minutes. Don't be late!" And with a wave, Monica was out the door.

"What's the movie marathon tonight?" James asked.

"Harry Potter," Selena replied as she made herself a cup of tea. "Last I saw, there was a massive amount of pillows and blankets going down to the theater, and Casey just popped an almost obscene amount of popcorn for the kids. I'm guessing they're pulling an all-nighter."

"It's cool that they're all getting along so well and finding stuff that's of interest to everyone," James said as he made his own cup of tea. "Plus, with them all down in the theater, it makes everything peaceful up here."

"That is the truth." Picking up her cup, Selena turned and motioned to Casey, who was sitting across the room. "Do you know where Ryder is?"

"Um...last I saw, he was out on the back deck. How come?"

At that moment, Casey walked over to them. "I just texted Ryder and asked him to come in and join us."

James frowned. "What's going on?"

The girls exchanged glances before Selena spoke. "We wanted to talk to the two of you about the whole reality show thing."

He chuckled. "I know you've been campaigning since

we got here, but I thought we weren't going to talk about this until New Year's Eve."

"What about New Year's Eve?" Ryder asked as he walked into the room. He immediately walked over to the refrigerator and pulled out a bottle of milk. "Are there any cookies left or did the kids eat them all?"

"There's a box over there in the corner on the counter," Casey told him. "We had it hidden until after they all went down to the theater."

That made him laugh. "Smart!" Pouring himself a glass of milk and preparing a plate of cookies, he asked, "So... what's going on?"

"Why don't we sit down?" Selena suggested and as soon as the four of them were seated, she nodded at Casey.

"It has come to our attention that...there are more negatives than positives to us doing this show," she murmured, hating that the guys were essentially getting their way. "The more we talked about it with everyone, the more we realized that...you were right. You were both right."

"Over the last week, Lily, Becca, Willow, Skye, and Autumn have been helping us with our social media content and we've gotten more engagement than we've ever had," Selena explained. "And while it's not on par with being Dana St. Ivy's wedding planners, we think it's better for our brand."

Then she sat back, held her breath, and waited for the "I told you so" speeches.

And waited.

And waited.

James and Ryder exchanged glances, and Ryder spoke first.

"You both need to know that it doesn't give us any joy to hear this. If anything, we were hoping someone here was going to come up with a way for you to have your cake and eat it too. We know it would be a huge coup for you to be associated with a celebrity wedding."

"And you still can be this Dana person's wedding planners," James went on. "But you need to tell the producers that you're unwilling to be on camera. Let them hire someone else to play the part of whatever drama they need. The other people—the DJ, the caterer, the florist—let them play into that nonsense. Go in there and be the ones who fix all the other buffoons' mistakes."

The girls both frowned. "I...we didn't think of that," Selena murmured. "I mean...what if we were the ones who only came on to fix everything?"

"I don't even know if the producers will go for that," Casey argued. "They seemed pretty intent on how they wanted the drama to unfold."

"Yeah, but...they also told us to think about things. If we sit down with them next week and lay out our plans, who knows? They might agree?" Then she shrugged. "And if they don't, we know we're going to be okay. It's not like we're running short on events."

"That's true," Casey agreed. "It just...I'm afraid they'll say yes, but then put us in awkward positions anyway that we can't get out of."

"Then we walk away right now," Selena said firmly. "I'm tired of stressing out about this. I'd rather hire one of the girls to keep helping us or find someone locally who can do this sort of thing and move on. I feel like we missed out on some of the fun on this trip because we were wrapped up in Dana's wedding drama. We're only here for a few more days, and I want to enjoy it."

It took a moment, but Casey finally nodded. "Okay

then. We're done. We're going to find a social media millennial and keep doing what we're doing."

"I feel like we need to toast this with something more than tea and cookies," James said with a laugh. "Let me get us some wine to make it official."

"I'm not going to argue with that!" Selena said as she sat back in her chair and grinned. "I feel like a giant weight has been lifted, don't you?"

"I hate to say it, but...yes," Casey replied. Then she looked over at Ryder. "And you're not allowed to gloat at any point about this. Ever. Agreed?"

He held up his hands in surrender. "Agreed. I'm proud of both of you for really thinking this through from every angle." Then he took Casey's hand in his. "And I would never gloat about this. I know it was a big deal for you."

James came back with a bottle of Prosecco and four glasses. "I didn't tell anyone what we were doing because I kind of feel like this is just for us."

"I'm good with that," Selena said.

He popped the cork quietly and poured them each a glass. With his drink in his hand, he held it up to toast. "To two of the most amazing women in the world. We are in awe of you both every day and we know even bigger things are coming your way. Cheers!"

"Wine and cookies?" Zach asked as he strolled into the kitchen. "How come no one told me?"

"Oh, it was...I mean, we just..." Casey stammered.

"No worries," he told her as he walked over and grabbed a cookie off the plate. "I was just coming in to grab some dessert for me and Gabs. We're just chilling in the room with Cayden."

"Hey, how did that go the other night when the girls had him? Did it all go okay?" Selena asked.

He grinned before popping a cookie into his mouth. "Better than okay. I think the girls didn't get much sleep though because they didn't want Cayden to cry. So someone was always awake and waiting to get him whatever he needed. But Gabriella and I got almost twelve hours of sleep that night. I felt like a new man!"

They all laughed. "And now?" Ryder asked. "How've the nights been since?"

"We developed a family system for the rest of our time here. Obviously, when we go home, the girls will go back to school and need their sleep more than we do. So basically, until we go home, the girls are tackling the late-night feeding, and I'm doing the early mornings since I'm normally up before the sun anyway. Gotta get back to the gym too."

"You can take him with you downstairs while you jog on the treadmill," James suggested. "As long as he's fed and clean, I'm sure he wouldn't mind sitting in his carrier and watching you run."

"That's actually a great idea!" Zach clapped him on the back. "Thanks!" Then he put a plate of cookies together and a slice of apple pie. "You guys have a great night!"

"It's crazy what a good night of sleep can do," Casey said once Zach was out of earshot. "I think I'm still a little in shock over their whole situation." Shaking her head, she said, "I don't know if I'd be able to do it all again with a newborn."

"I think it depends on the situation," James responded after a moment. "Sometimes you don't know what you're capable of until you're faced with it. And Zach has yet to meet a challenge he hasn't conquered, so..."

Ryder laughed. "That's the truth."

Selena held up her glass again. "To Zach and Gabriella and their new addition. It's going to be exciting to watch!"

"Cheers!"

Meanwhile, on the downstairs deck, Megan and Alex were also sharing a toast in the hot tub. "Here's to finally having a little quiet time by ourselves," Alex said as he touched his glass to Megan's.

"Cheers," she said softly before taking a sip of her wine. "Mmm...that's good." Then she sank a little lower in the water before placing her glass carefully on the ledge. "And so is this. I wish we would have taken advantage of this earlier in the trip. It's so relaxing."

"Yeah, but we have one at home, so it's not like it's a big deal. But yeah, now that we're in it, I'm kind of annoyed that we didn't do it sooner."

They sat in companionable silence for several minutes, each lost in their own thoughts.

"This has been a good trip," Megan said softly. "Sometimes I forget how much I love being around the whole extended family and how much fun we always have."

"I've been a little in awe of this family since I first met Zach. I don't think I've ever met another family that gets along as well and just genuinely enjoys being around one another. Even all the kids got along this time!"

"I think there were plenty of distractions for them, so there was always something to do. Between the game room, pool, and movie theater, there was something for everyone. And that was just if we stayed home!"

"This house certainly had everything," he agreed. "And the scenery was spectacular. It reminds me of home."

"It's the only reason I was agreeable to coming out here in twenty-degree weather to get in the hot tub—because we do the same thing at home!" She laughed. "Plus, no one else wants to be out here at night. I've seen plenty of people take advantage of them during the day, but..."

"I heard Jason and Maggie came out here one night, but decided it was way too cold when you got out." That made him chuckle. "That's what the heat lamps are for and why you essentially have to run back into the house."

"Amateurs," she laughed, enjoying the jets that were aimed at her lower back. "I miss our bed, though. I mean... the one in our room here is fine, but..."

"It's definitely not the same. I thought so too. But in a couple of nights, we'll be back at home."

She nodded and waged a quiet war in her head about whether to bring up the topic that they'd both been avoiding. She hadn't mentioned it to anyone—other than her mother—but she'd heard plenty of conversations over the last twelve days that had been adding to her inner battle.

"So, um...I don't know if you've noticed it or not, but there seems to be a lot of discussion around here about everyone wanting to cut back on their work schedules," she began cautiously. Her head was thrown back and her eyes were closed, and it was the safest way for her to broach this subject.

"I heard Mac mention it the other day, and Christian sort of tossed it out there earlier. I was a little shocked when he said it and I thought it was because of his ankle, but apparently it's something he's been thinking about."

Megan nodded again. "I haven't talked to him about it, but I'm a little surprised by that news too."

"Who else other than those two?" Alex asked.

"I know Carter's trying to make some changes—especially after this whole debacle with almost missing Christmas—and...I don't know, it just felt like that was the topic of so many conversations."

"O-kay..."

"And that got me thinking," she blurted out, still

unwilling to look at him. "I love my job working with Zach, Summer, and Ethan, but...it won't be long until things start to change there too. With Zach and Gabriella adopting Cayden, you know he's going to be spending more time away from the office. Then his girls and then Summer and Ethan's kids will be heading off to college and they'll be around less..." She let out a long sigh.

The water splashed and she opened her eyes to see Alex moving to sit beside her. "What are you getting at, Megan?"

Straightening, she took a moment to calm her rapidly beating heart. "Okay, so...the last big leap of faith I took was moving from New York to Oregon, and that led me back to you. It was scary and intimidating, but ultimately, it was the best thing for me. Now I'd be doing something scary and intimidating again, but I'd be doing it with you." She let out a shaky breath. "I...I'm not saying that I'm suddenly super excited and giddy at the prospect of moving and helping our kids start over in new schools, but...I think this has the potential to be something amazing for you and our family. So if you want to take this position..."

She never got to finish. Alex cupped her face in his wet hands and silenced her with a kiss that literally stole her breath away. Before she knew it, she was straddling his lap and wishing they were in their hot tub at home so they could strip off their bathing suits and take this to the next level.

Alex was the one who broke the kiss, but held her head so they were barely a breath apart. "I don't know what I ever did to deserve you, but you have to know how much I love you and how much it means to me that you're willing to take this chance. There are no guarantees that..."

Megan silenced him, placing her finger over his lips. "Life holds no guarantees on anything. We're not even promised tomorrow. All I know is that playing it safe and staying where we are would be fine, but...what if this move brings us something so much better? We have to try."

And for a moment, she swore she saw his eyes shining brightly with unshed tears. "I love you," he whispered.

"I love you too." They stayed like that, wrapped around each other in the hot tub for several long minutes

"How about we climb out, grab our wine, and go warm up in our own room?"

He kissed her softly. "That sounds perfect. Let's go." They were maneuvering out of the hot tub when Summer and Ethan stepped outside.

"Hey! Great minds!" Ethan said cheerily. "Are you guys getting in or out?"

"Out," Alex said. "We've been out here for a little while and decided to take our wine back to our room."

"Then don't let us stop you," Summer said, hugging them both as they walked by. As soon as they were in the house, Summer peeled off her robe and gingerly climbed into the tub they'd just vacated.

"Nice bikini," Ethan said, climbing in beside her. "You haven't worn one of those in a while."

"We're normally in the pool with the kids so..." Sliding lower under the water, she hummed with pleasure. "Why didn't we put one of these in the yard at the new house?"

Mimicking her pose, he shook his head. "Because clearly I'm stupid," he teased. "I don't remember us using it a lot at the old place, but now that we're in here? I'm tempted to order one to be delivered as soon as we get home."

"I'm completely on board with that plan."

"Did you check on Autumn before we came out here?"

She nodded. "She was enjoying having the room to

herself tonight while everyone else is sleeping in the theater for their Harry Potter marathon." With a sigh, she added, "I asked her if she wanted to invite Daphne to come and join us for the last few days here, but she said no."

"Really? That's surprising."

"I know...I thought so too, but apparently Christmas wasn't as devastating as Daphne was predicting, and Autumn felt like it was okay to wait until we got home to see her."

"Wow. I'm impressed with her maturity," Ethan said. "She's an amazing kid."

"Oh, I completely agree. That's why I hate that this happened to her. She was really having a great time."

"I'm just thankful it wasn't worse. A broken arm we can deal with and it's a fairly easy recovery. Anything more and I think I would have freaked out."

"You were already freaking out," she reminded him.

"We were all freaking out, Summer. If I close my eyes, I can still see her falling." He shuddered. "By the time we're done with them, we're going to own that damn resort!"

Sliding closer to him, Summer rested a hand on his thigh. "I agree that they need to be held accountable for what happened, but we have to go about this with a level head and not one full of emotion. We already know they're covering all the medical expenses, but you have to trust the lawyers to work everything else out."

Even though there was a part of her that wanted to go back there and pretty much scream the place to the ground, she was just beyond grateful that her daughter walked away with minor injuries.

Still, she was trying to hold it together so Autumn wouldn't know just how freaked out she was. Ethan, however, wasn't as good at that sort of thing. And it was just one of the reasons she loved him so much.

"Anyway, she's resting up in her room and Lulu is with her," she told him.

"Great. Now we'll have two rooms to clean up accidents in," he mumbled.

"Oh, stop picking on her! She's really trying! It's not her fault it snowed for days!"

Groaning, Ethan leaned his head back. "This has been an exhausting vacation, that's all I'm saying. The next time, I'd like to go somewhere tropical, just the two of us."

She kind of liked that idea too. "Someplace tropical, huh?"

He nodded.

"A place where we have our own private pool or even a private beach so we can skip the bathing suits?"

Ethan slowly turned his head and opened one eye. "If I knew no one was going to come out here, I'd be peeling that bikini top off of you right now."

She blushed, nibbling her bottom lip and wondering if it was worth the risk.

"Don't even think about it, Summer," he said with a laugh. "There are too many people here—and pretty much all the kids are here on the lower level. Let's just...we'll look at the calendar when we go back upstairs and pick the earliest date we can find. My folks or yours can stay with the kids. I just really want us to be alone somewhere."

"I'd love that too." Leaning in, she kissed him before getting comfortable in the water again and making sure the jets were hitting her in all the right places.

"Bora Bora?" Ethan suggested from his relaxed position.

"Last time we were there, the bungalows were too close together."

"Fair enough. Hawaii?"

"You know how much Jensen loves it there. I'd feel guilty going without him."

"O-kay...Belize?"

"Maybe?"

He chuckled quietly. "If you're not into this..."

"I am! I'm just...I want to find something with the perfect balance of new and yet familiar. Does that make sense?"

"Um...not really." He sighed and took a minute to think some more. "Fiji? Maldives? Cancun?" He paused. "Martinique? St. Lucia?"

"Actually, Alex and Zach were talking about doing some fishing tournament in Costa Rica. Do you remember our honeymoon trip there?" she asked lazily, the warm water in jets deeply relaxing her.

His laugh was deep and throaty before he gruffly said, "I most certainly do. That teeny tiny white bikini you wore was the stuff of fantasies."

She was about twenty pounds thinner then, but she might be able to find one to wear again. "We always said we'd go back, but we never did."

Taking her hand in his, Ethan raised it to his lips, kissing it. "Then that's where we'll go."

Smiling, she hummed with approval. "Excellent. Maybe we can recreate some of those memories."

"Hey," he said softly and waited until she looked at him. "I'd much rather make new ones."

And just like that, she fell in love with him all over again.

# TWENTY-FOUR

# NEW YEAR'S EVE

"NO OFFENSE, BUT...YOU CAN BE A LITTLE
SMOTHERING SOMETIMES."

"WHY IS CARTER POUTING OVER THERE?" Eliza asked no one in particular.

"We made him leave the kitchen," Monica replied. "Everything is under control and he's not the chef tonight. I swear that boy is belligerent when he doesn't get his way."

"Tell me about it," Emery murmured as she walked by and grabbed a crab puff.

The entire main floor was decorated in silver and gold. There were flowers and balloons and enough food to feed three times as many people. Music was softly playing, champagne was flowing, and there was a feeling of happiness and festiveness in the air.

"I think we pulled together the perfect New Year's Eve party," Janice said as she came to stand with them near the kitchen. "The food is delicious and everyone is having a good time."

"Look," Eliza said, pointing toward the area by the Christmas tree. "Zach and Gabriella, Summer and Ethan, Jason and Maggie, and Megan and Alex are dancing!" She looked around. "Maybe we should find our beaus and ask them to do the same?"

"Sounds like a wonderful idea," Monica agreed. Glancing around the room, she spotted William speaking with Noah and began heading their way. "That poor boy probably wishes we never called him last week."

"There's my lovely wife," William said with his typical charming smile. He kissed her cheek as he wrapped an arm around her waist. "You outdid yourself tonight. Everything has been wonderful."

"Thank you, but it was a group effort." Then she smiled at Noah. "I hope you're enjoying yourself."

"I am," he said politely. "Thank you."

"I heard you got your car back today too!"

He nodded. "The damage was minor and there are a few spots that I'll need to take to a body shop to get repaired, but it's running perfectly and that's all that matters. I know I'll make it home safely."

"Always a good thing," William said, but then his attention was drawn to the hallway where the elevator was. "Uh-oh."

"What?" Monica asked. "What's the matter?"

"Lily looks upset. She just punched the button and winced. I should go talk to her," he said and started to take a step away when Noah stopped him.

"Why don't you and Mrs. Montgomery enjoy a dance and I'll go talk to her," he said, already moving away and not really waiting for an answer.

"Thank you, Noah," Monica said before leading William to where the others were already dancing. "I know you're concerned about Lily, William, but maybe talking to someone her own age—that she's not related to—is what she needs right now."

"Do you know why she's upset?"

"I think it has something to do with her boyfriend. Emma mentioned that he was delayed, but...it's kind of late now."

"And you think he isn't coming?"

"It would explain her mood," she reasoned. "Let's hope Noah can cheer her up."

That's what William was hoping for too.

Noah got to the elevator just as the doors opened. He held them as Lily stepped in. "What are you doing here?" she asked, and he could tell she was crying.

"Saw you punching that button and then wincing, and I wanted to make sure you were okay." It wasn't a total lie. The truth was that it was kind of a drag being the lone single guy in a room full of couples. If he wanted to feel this pathetic, he could have just stayed home by himself. But... when the boss asks you to stay and you're trying to impress him, you stay.

"Yeah, I forgot about my collarbone for about three seconds and then the pain flared up and reminded me," she said sarcastically as he stepped in beside her and the doors shut. "I'm fine. You didn't have to ride upstairs with me. I'd rather be alone."

"It's not like I can go anywhere right this second," he reminded her. But when the doors opened and she stepped out and headed down the hall, he followed.

"What?" she snapped as she spun around and faced him.

"What what?" he asked.

"I just said I'd rather be alone and you're following me!"

"I guess I was curious why you were crying, that's all. Jeez. I didn't realize it was a crime to be concerned." He shrugged, but he didn't move away either. "Your grandfather wanted to come and talk to you, but I thought that might be weird." Another shrug. "But I can go get him if you want."

"Oh my *God!* What part of I want to be alone is hard for you to understand?" she asked hotly as she stomped her foot.

Now he did move closer. "I may have only been here for a week with your family, but even I know if I go downstairs and your grandfather sees me coming back without you and not knowing what your problem is, he's going to come up here to check on you himself. So either tell me or you're going to tell him. The choice is yours."

She groaned loudly—practically growled—as she glared at him. "Why are you like this?"

He knew he was essentially throwing himself on the grenade, but...

"You want to know what my problem is, finance boy?" she sneered. "My boyfriend isn't coming. Actually, he's not even my boyfriend anymore because he took off to Key West with my roommate from the cruise. And he didn't even have the balls to call me and tell me. He did it in a text. So, um...yeah. I'm not feeling like celebrating with everyone." She took a step closer to him. "And if my grandfather wants to come up here and pretend like he understands how I'm feeling, then so be it."

He let her get almost to her door when he stopped her. "Are you upset because you really cared about this guy or are you upset because of how it all went down?"

For a moment Lily simply stared at him like he was insane—and maybe he was. After all, it was blatantly obvious that she didn't want to talk to him and yet here he was, still talking.

"It's both!" she snapped, hating the tears stinging her eyes.

Noah took a step toward her and then another before stopping. "For what it's worth, I'm sorry that this happened. His timing and his actions clearly suck. But in time, you're going to see that he did you a favor. Any man who pulls a stunt like this and disrespects you by taking the easy way out isn't the right man for you."

She swiped at her eyes and hated seeing the smeared mascara there.

"The last woman I dated sent her best friend to break up with me. She didn't have the decency to tell me to my face." He let out a long breath. "She claimed there wasn't another guy, but...when you won't sit down with the person you were in the relationship with, it's usually because you're ashamed of something you did."

"Or you were a total jerk and she just didn't want to have to deal with you anymore," she snapped and then instantly regretted her words. With her good arm, she reached up and covered her face before looking at him again. "God, Noah, that was...that was a shitty thing for me to say. I'm sorry. I'm just really not in the mood to be around people. Please tell my grandfather that I'm fine, but..."

"You'd rather be alone. Got it."

"Thanks." Turning toward her room again, she paused when he said her name. When she looked up, he was right there beside her. As much as she'd been annoyed with his presence all week, she had also been mildly intrigued by him. He was everything she genuinely disliked in a guy, but...he also seemed like a decent person.

And that was messing with her because, based on her own experience, most guys weren't nice or decent.

Her grandfather's words from earlier in the trip came

back to her: *Maybe it's the type of guy you're dating that's the problem, Lily.*

Maybe.

All she knew was that now was not the time to deeply examine that.

"Look, I get that you're upset, but...everyone's been dealing with stuff on this trip," he said, his voice soft and sincere. "I've heard stories of unexpected adoptions, marital crises, career crossroads...there were accidents, arguments, and a lot of injured pride." He paused and gave her a lopsided grin. "But what I learned while listening to all of this is that this family of yours is the best to be around when you're struggling. My entire life, I've never seen anything like it, and..."

His phone rang from his pocket, and he was going to ignore it when Lily motioned to it. "It could be important," she said, but he had a feeling she was going to use the distraction as a means to escape and lock herself in her room.

"Just...promise you'll let me finish," he said as he pulled his phone out. When he saw his brother Simon's name, he hung his head, muttering a curse.

"That good, huh?" she asked with a laugh, but when Noah held up the phone to her, she gasped excitedly. "Noah, you have to answer it! And you have to let me talk to him! Please! It will totally cheer me up!"

He glared at her, but he was also smirking as he did, so...

"Simon! Hey! This is a surprise! What's up?"

"Hey! I finally had a free minute to call you back. I've got a show in two hours, but I'm having something to eat and thought I'd call and wish you a Happy New Year! What are you up to tonight?"

He laughed softly. "I'm still up in the mountains with

my boss and his family. They invited me to stay and ring in the new year with them, so..."

"Ugh...hanging with the boss does *not* sound like a promising way to kick off the year, bro. We need to get you a proper social life again."

"Yeah, well..."

Lily was practically bouncing on her toes in front of him and holding out her free hand.

Hint taken.

"Listen, I'm standing here with a friend," he said, "and naturally, she's a fan. She's also a fan who fell off a ski lift the other day and broke her collarbone and could use some cheering up, so would you mind..."

"I know she's putting you on the spot because you normally hate this kind of crap, but sure. Put her on. What's her name?"

"Lily," he told him. "Hang on. Here she is."

"Oh my goodness! Hi!" she said excitedly when she had the phone. Then she walked a few steps away. "I cannot believe I'm actually on the phone with Simon Bennett! This is crazy!"

Noah walked to the end of the hall and leaned against the wall. He really didn't care to hear the conversation. His brother was right—he hated it when people used him to get to Simon. It was hard to know who was really a friend and who wasn't when you were related to someone famous. And unfortunately, he was related to *two* famous people.

*Living the dream...*

The only positive thing here was that this time, he did it for a good cause. It sucked that Lily's boyfriend dumped her via text—the douchebag—but maybe now she'd be open to rejoining the party.

If she ever stopped talking to Simon.

*Sigh...*

Five minutes later, she finally came walking toward him. "Okay, great! And thank you, Simon. Happy New Year!" Then she handed Noah his phone back. "Thanks. Wait here for me, okay? I just need to fix my face." And with a smile, she practically skipped into her room and shut the door.

"Wow, dude, you truly are magical," he teased when he got back on the call.

"Me? What did I do?"

"Lily was a bit of a mess before she talked to you, and now she's practically glowing," he said with a laugh. "Good job!"

"Yeah, well...she told me about the boyfriend and I just...you know...did what I could."

"Oh my God...did you sing? Did you sing to her?" he asked, still laughing.

"Maybe. She said her favorite song was Lost in You, so... I may have sung a few verses..."

He sighed dramatically. "Thanks, Simon. Seriously. I had no idea how to make her feel better, so..."

"No problem. But unfortunately, I really need to go. I promise to call next week. Happy New Year, Noah."

"Yeah, to you too, bro. Knock 'em dead tonight!" He hung up with a sigh, hating that they didn't have more time to talk, but...it was all for the greater good, he supposed.

Lily stepped out of the room a minute later with her makeup perfectly done and the best part, she was smiling. "I still would rather not have to hang out downstairs," she said, "but I believe you were telling me why that's going to be a good thing."

Was he?

Oh, right. He was.

"I don't come from a big family, and the family I have? Well...we're not that close. My brothers and I are, and we're close to our mom, but our extended family isn't very involved in our lives. So when I say I've never seen anything like your family, I mean it. No matter who was upset this week or who was struggling with something, there was always someone there to help them through it. So if all of them could be down there smiling and celebrating..."

"Then so can I," she finished for him with a curt nod. "I know you're right; I just needed a few minutes to have my own pity party."

"If you need more time..."

But she shook her head. "I'm going to put a smile on my face and go downstairs and hang out with some of the best people in the whole wide world."

Together, they walked to the elevator.

"You know we can take the stairs, right?" he said. "It's your shoulder that's hurt, not your legs."

"Ha, ha...maybe I'm just lazy." Then she looked up at him and winked. "How often do you get to stay in a house with an elevator? Come on!"

When they arrived back on the main floor, William spotted them and his smile was so wide it made his face hurt.

*I knew that boy was the one...*

But for now, he'd keep that to himself.

Lily walked right over to him and hugged him with her good arm. "Thanks, Grandpa."

He pulled back, still smiling. "For what?"

"For just always knowing what I need." All around them, people were laughing and smiling and dancing. "Shall we dance?"

He and Monica had just finished, and she'd gone to check on the next round of food, so...

"It would be my pleasure." And as he carefully spun her around, he caught Noah's eye and mouthed, "Thank you."

Noah gave him a nod and then blended into the crowd.

"This is ridiculous," Gina murmured, knocking on her mother's door for the third time. When Barb finally opened it, she was still in her robe. "Mom? What in the world? The party's been going on for well over an hour! What are you doing?"

"You know I don't stay up on New Year's anymore," Barb said as she stepped away from the door. "I grabbed some food before the party started and made myself a plate. I'm fine in here. It's not a big deal."

"It is to me!" Gina told her and knew it was finally time for them to have "the talk." Closing the door, she walked across the room and sat down on the futon. "Everyone is out there and they're all asking for you. It's rude for you to hide away in here."

Barb's eyes went wide. "It's rude of me? Are you seriously reprimanding me right now?"

She nodded. "I am! We have gone out of our way to include you in everything, and yes, I think it's rude that you just made yourself a plate and locked yourself in your room! When you come to live with us, you can't just do things like this!"

Now she frowned. "When I come to live with you?" Barb repeated. "Um...what are you talking about?"

Gina's shoulders sagged. "Mom, come on. We all know

this is what's coming. You told Monica, Janice, and Eliza that you wanted to move back to North Carolina. It's getting harder for you to live on your own, so...Mac and I talked about it and we're going to meet with an architect and build an addition on the house for you. I've been trying to talk to you for the last couple of days, but it felt like you were avoiding me."

"I was."

"What?! Why?"

"Well...I do want to move back here, but...not specifically with you, Mac, and the kids," Barb began.

"I...I don't understand."

Sighing, Barb sat down beside her. "For the last several years, whenever I came to stay for an extended visit, I met up with a lot of old friends."

"I know this, Mom. You've been going to the silver sneakers classes and on day trips with the seniors' group."

"Exactly. I really enjoy my time with them, and last year a few of the gals moved into an assisted living facility—which really felt like an all-inclusive apartment complex—and..." She paused and looked at Gina. "I really want to move in there. I've put in my application and they'll have an apartment for me in March."

Gina simply blinked at her for a moment. "Why didn't you tell me about this?"

Barb waved her off as she got to her feet again. "I didn't want to offend you." Turning, she looked down at her. "I love you and Mac and the kids, but...I'm not cut out to live with all of you. I enjoy my privacy and I enjoy knowing I can come and go as I please without having to report to anyone." She shrugged. "No offense, but...you can be a little smothering sometimes."

Now Gina jumped to her feet. "I can be smothering? *I*

*can be smothering?!*" she cried. "You spent years smothering me! And now..."

"And now I realize just how awful that was." She took Gina's hands in hers. "Sweetheart, I feel like we're finally in a good place with each other, and I don't want to ruin that. You and Mac will be empty nesters before you know it. Take that time to enjoy each other." Pausing again, she swallowed hard. "Not all of us get that chance. Trust me."

Tears stung Gina's eyes. "I don't even know what to say, Mom. Of course I'm happy that you have a plan and something in place. I just hate that you didn't think you could share that with me."

"I knew I would eventually. I just needed to find the time."

"Can I see this place when we get back to Charlotte? I swear I'm not going to try to talk you out of it; I'd just like to see where you chose to live."

"Of course you can! I was actually hoping you would want to see it. Mac too." Pulling Gina in for a hug, she said, "Now go out there and have some champagne and maybe dance with your husband."

"And what about you?" she asked as she stepped back. "I'd really love it if you joined us. You don't have to stay up until midnight, but..."

Barb nodded. "I'll be out in a little while. I'll need to get dressed."

"Thanks, Mom." She hugged her one more time before heading out of the room.

When she reached the living room, she stopped and looked around, trying to figure out where Mac was. When she spotted him, he was standing talking to Alex, Megan, Jason, and Maggie. She snagged a couple of glasses of champagne on her way across the room—it didn't look like her husband was holding one—and practically skipped up beside him.

Eyeing her warily, he said, "What? What's going on?"

Handing him a glass of champagne, she smiled before blurting out, "My mother doesn't want to move in with us! She's moving into an assisted living community in Charlotte! But not with us! Cheers!" She didn't even wait, she just took a long sip and then grinned at their group. "You guys have no idea how great this news is!"

Beside her, Mac drank all of his champagne before grinning down at her. "Now that is the best news to kick off the new year with!"

Jason, Maggie, Megan, and Alex all held up their glasses and toasted to them. "Good for you guys!" Maggie said. "Crisis averted!"

There were so many conversations going on around the room—so much laughter and maybe a few tears—but as Monica gave her nod of approval for the pizza bagels, mac and cheese bites, and cheeseburger sliders to head downstairs to the game room for the kids who were throwing their own New Year's Eve party, she decided that the entire trip had been a success. Sure, there had been more than a few hiccups, but overall, this had been a most memorable holiday in all the best ways.

"You're looking very pleased with yourself, Monica," Janice said as she grabbed a fresh glass of champagne and then a second for Monica.

"I am," she agreed. "I'm just looking around and thinking—all things concerned—it's been a lovely vacation."

"If you don't count all the broken bones..."

"It could have been worse. We were all very lucky that no one had anything more serious happen. And honestly, I think those of us who weren't hurt were more traumatized."

"I wouldn't say that...Christian's still rather upset and I don't think Lily's feeling that great."

"Her boyfriend broke up with her in a text message," she said with a snort. "Sadly, it's typical of the boys she dates."

"Mmm...I supposed. But I noticed she and Noah were spending a lot of time together and just came off the elevator together. Do you think there's anything...?"

Monica shook her head. "Absolutely not. Lily despises men in suits. It's sad, really. I had hoped she'd grow out of that rebellious phase, but so far, she hasn't."

"That's too bad. He's a nice-looking young man. It makes me wish Willow was a little older. I would set the two of them up in a heartbeat."

"Well...I'm sure by the time she's through with college, there will be some nice new executives at Montgomerys that you can try with."

"From your lips to God's ears."

They laughed and sipped their drinks before slowly making their way back into the living room with everyone.

When it was just five minutes to midnight, William loudly announced that he would like everyone's attention. When the room was quiet, he watched as the servers walked around and handed out champagne to anyone who needed it and then, as all the kids came up from downstairs, they were handed glasses of sparkling cider.

"I know I've given more than a few toasts and speeches this week, so I promise this one will be my last," he began. "I want to thank all of you again for coming and sharing the holidays with us. This has been better than we even imagined. Of course, it wasn't all sunshine and roses and yet we have a lot to be thankful for. Lucas, Christian, Autumn, and Lily, it breaks my heart that all of you were injured, but I am also incredibly relieved that your injuries weren't nearly as traumatic as they could have been and I'm thankful you're all here to celebrate with us tonight."

He took a moment to compose himself because just thinking of what could have happened threatened to overwhelm him.

He gently cleared his throat before continuing. "Our family has grown more than I thought it would, and I love that we're still growing. Having Cayden join us just made this holiday season extra special." He nodded toward Zach and Gabriella. "I feel like there was a reason we chose this year to finally get together like this, and I have a feeling the coming year is going to bring some big changes. Besides the business merger, I believe there are some wonderful changes coming all of your ways. I love you all more than you'll ever know, and it does my old heart good to stand here and see all of your beautiful, smiling faces. Here's to saying goodbye to this year and opening our hearts and arms to the year to come."

As he held up his glass, Jason yelled out, "Perfect timing, Dad! We're ready to count down! Ten!"

Everyone chimed in. "Nine! Eight! Seven! Six! Five! Four! Three! Two! One! Happy New Year!!"

Confetti was thrown, noise makers went off, and it was wonderfully chaotic.

It seemed oddly normal that Lily found herself standing next to Noah as the ball dropped. All around them couples were hugging and kissing and if her life didn't suck so much, she'd be kissing Ash right now. She'd always had someone to kiss at midnight ever since she was fifteen, and it felt weird to just be standing there doing nothing.

So she did what she had to do.

She reached up with her good arm and pulled Noah down and kissed him.

If he was surprised, he didn't let on, but he certainly kissed better than any guy she'd ever kissed before.

Dammit.

But rather than think too much about it, she simply held on and enjoyed the hell out of it.

# TWENTY-FIVE

# NEW YEAR'S EVE—PART TWO

## "IF THAT'S SOME SORT OF CODE WORD FOR SEX…"

ACROSS THE ROOM, Lucas and Emma were slowly swaying while *Auld Lang Syne* played over the sound system. "Happy New Year, beautiful girl," he said, resting his forehead against hers.

"Happy New Year, wonderful man." She hummed softly as she pressed closer. "How's your arm feeling?"

He shrugged. "Like it's broken," he joked. "But…I've had worse." Looking around, he spotted Becca laughing hysterically at whatever Willow and Skylar were telling her. Then he spotted Sloane singing happily with Autumn, Ariel, and Nora. "The girls all look like they're having a good time."

Emma followed the direction of his gaze and smiled. "They certainly do. And why shouldn't they? It's been a great night." She glanced around and froze.

"What? What's the matter?" Now it was his turn to follow her gaze and when it landed on Lily, he muttered a curse. "Son of a *bitch*."

"Lucas, do not go over there and…"

But he was already walking over there.

"And there go the warm fuzzies," she murmured.

Lucas wasn't going to make a scene, but he sure as hell was going to put the fear of God into Noah Wylder. Several people tried to stop him as he crossed the room, but he was a man on a mission. When he was close enough to touch them, he cleared his throat.

Loudly.

They broke apart and Lily looked up at him—all wide-eyed shock—and Noah looked like he was going to be sick. Lucas almost felt bad for him.

Almost.

"Noah? A word?" Lucas said through clenched teeth.

Lily moved in front of him. "Dad, stop. It's not what you think, okay?"

"Really? Because it looked like Noah was kissing you," he said, quietly and menacingly. Then he looked up at Noah. "Did my father put you up to this?"

"Excuse me?"

Nodding, Lucas gently moved his daughter aside and almost smiled as Noah stumbled back a step. "My father. I'm sure you caught on to the fact that he's big on playing matchmaker in this family. So did he ask you to spend time with Lily? Maybe he offered you some sort of advice on how to get on her good side considering she normally hates any guys that actually have a future?"

"*Dad!*" she cried. "That's unbelievably insulting!" Then she glared at Noah. "Wait...did he?"

His eyes went wide as he looked at her. "Seriously? You kissed me!"

"You did what?" Lucas roared.

"Okay, okay, okay...show's over," Emma said loudly as she began moving them all toward the back door and out onto the deck. "In case no one noticed, there is a party going on and you were making a scene!"

"And my father convinced Noah to hit on Lily!" Lucas told her.

"She kissed me!" Noah countered. "And for the record, no one told me to do anything!"

"You better hope not," Lucas warned as he moved in close, towering over him. "Because if I find out he did, your days at Montgomerys are numbered."

"What in the world is going on out here?" William asked, sliding the glass doors closed behind him.

"Your little pet project here was kissing Lily!" Lucas snapped.

"Um...I kissed him," Lily corrected as she leaned in between her father and grandfather. "But only because it felt lame to have no one to kiss at midnight! It's not like I *wanted* to kiss Noah. He was just there!"

"Hey!" Noah huffed. "Now that was insulting!"

"Oh, hush!" she hissed at him.

"Lucas, I don't know what you think is going on here, but I'm telling you, you're wrong," William said firmly. "It sounds to me like this is between Lily and Noah."

"Sure," Lucas sneered. "And you're going to stand here and tell me your little matchmaking bug hasn't been waiting for this moment? You've been bragging about how this is your thing for years! Now it's time for the next generation!"

"And believe me, when she's older, I just might look around for a man worthy of her," William fired back. "But that has nothing to do with why Noah's here! If you'll recall, he came here as a favor to us! His willingness to take time out of his personal vacation made it possible for us to finish our work sooner. Maybe instead of trying to intimidate him, you should be thanking him!"

"I am not going to *thank* him for kissing my daughter, Dad."

"No one said to thank him for kissing Lily…"

"I kissed him!" Lily shouted. "Can we please acknowledge that? I'm a grown woman and I'm allowed to kiss whoever I want, whenever I want!" When Lucas glared at her, she refused to be intimidated. "Face it, Dad, I'm not a kid anymore. It was midnight and it was one kiss. That's it, okay?"

He stared hard at Noah for a solid minute and felt a small sense of satisfaction that he squirmed a bit, but he finally said, "Okay."

"Excellent!" William said. "Now, can we all please go back inside? I don't care how many heat lamps are on out here, I'm freezing!" He walked to the doors and gave Lucas one last look. "Are we good?"

Lucas nodded.

William went back inside, and Emma took Lucas by the hand and pulled him inside with her, leaving Lily and Noah alone.

She huffed out a small breath. "I'm sorry. I guess I didn't think anyone would care if we just kissed quickly at midnight."

"Uh-huh…"

"I mean…I only meant for it to be a quick kiss. I didn't expect you to get all…you know…into it."

It was on the tip of his tongue—the one that only minutes ago was tangling with hers—to argue with her, but he decided against it. Right now, he was at risk of losing his job or at the very least losing all the progress he'd made with the Montgomery family this last week.

"You know what, Lily? It was nothing. Let's just forget about it." And with a tight smile, he walked back into the house. It would be easy to go upstairs and pack up his things and leave, but he'd had a couple of glasses of champagne and he wasn't stupid enough to drive. But first thing tomorrow morning, he was out of here.

Lily watched him go and for a moment, she really felt bad about how this had all played out. She'd wanted someone to kiss, and he was there.

It just sucked that he was such a good kisser.

Like...*really* sucked because normally a guy like Noah wasn't her type, but now that she might consider changing her mind, it was too late. She was pretty sure he hated her.

And she couldn't blame him one bit.

"Happy freaking New Year to me," she murmured before sliding back into the house and doing her best to simply blend into the crowd.

"Poor kid," Carter said as he and Emery sat near the fire. "That had to be embarrassing."

Emery nodded with a sigh. "Yeah. I don't think anything romantic or even sexual was going on between them. Lucas kind of overreacted."

Carter had to agree, but he wasn't going to dwell on it. He had something important to talk to his wife about. "Listen, I have a gift for you that I didn't want to give you for Christmas, but...I really wanted to give it to you tonight."

She eyed him warily. "If that's some sort of code word for sex..."

The bark of laughter was out before he could stop it. "No. I really do have something for you. How about we grab a plate of dessert and a bottle of champagne and head to our room?"

It didn't take long to gather all their things, and considering their room was literally right next to the living room, they were there almost instantly.

In their room, Carter poured them each a glass of champagne and then smiled as Emery kicked off her shoes and sat up on the bed with her legs tucked under her. She was just as beautiful now as she was when they first ran into each other again so many years ago. She still took his breath away.

Handing her one of the champagne flutes, he smiled. "I know I've apologized for all the delays in getting here, but...I wasn't completely honest with you about why it took so long."

Her smile faded. "Oh?"

"Yeah, um...I realized that I've been spreading myself too thin, and it took me so long to realize it because I've just always been that driven. The pace felt natural to me until... it didn't. I've been feeling a bit overwhelmed for a long time, but I didn't know what to do about it."

"O-kay..."

"So..." Pausing, he turned to his dresser, opened the top drawer, and pulled out a small gift box wrapped in silver paper. "Here. This is for you." Another pause. "Well...for us. Originally, I wasn't going to wrap it up, but..."

Emery put her drink down before taking the gift from his hands. After carefully unwrapping it, she took the lid off and found...papers.

Legal papers.

Her heart was practically pounding its way out of her chest. "Are you divorcing me? Is that how you think you'll make your life easier?" she cried hysterically. "Because let me tell you something, Carter Montgomery..."

"Em...Em..." he said hurriedly, crawling onto the bed beside her. "No one's divorcing anyone. Would you just look at these please?"

Swallowing hard, she unfolded the papers and started to read.

And then re-read the first paragraph multiple times.

"Wait...so...you sold the restaurants?"

He shook his head. "No," he said with a hint of amusement. "I sold half of three of the restaurants to Rocco. He's been wanting in for years, but I was too stubborn to share the responsibility. But honestly, he's been doing half the work for a long time, even though he was only supposed to assist me in the New Orleans place." Carefully, he reached over and picked up her glass and handed it back to her. "After we get home, we're going to have a meeting with all the management—via video, so no one has to travel—and discuss some changes. And...we're hiring two additional chefs per location to make sure we're never in a bind like we were last week."

"How is Max? Have you talked to him?"

"It's going to be a while before he'll be back in the kitchen and cooking, but he wants to come in and oversee things. Rocco and I agreed it would be a great way for him to train some new people."

"Carter, I...I don't know what to say," Emery said quietly. "Your restaurants have been your life for so long..."

"No, Em. You and the boys are my life and I'm sorry for all the times I didn't put the three of your first." He kissed her softly. "New year, new me. And I'm pretty sure you're all going to get tired of my face because I'm going to be around so much more."

"Never," she said, kissing him. "I'll never get tired of this face. Now feed me some cake and make love to me. I want to start the year off right."

"My pleasure."

～

The party went on until after two, and for the most part, everyone stayed awake.

Including Barb and Cayden.

Actually, Barb fed the baby his last bottle and got him down for the night so that Zach, Gabriella, and the girls could enjoy the rest of the party. But once he was asleep, she made her way to her own room and crawled into bed, relieved that she and Gina finally talked earlier.

Eliza and Phillip were the next to leave the party and once they were alone in their room, he laughed softly.

"What's so funny?"

"Your family is very entertaining," he told her. "I feel like this trip had a bit of everything, including one of the best parties I've attended in years." He walked over and kissed her. "Thank you for allowing me to come and be a part of this."

"I'm glad you were able to be here. I hated the thought of us not spending the holidays together, but..."

"Family comes first. I know that."

"And yet you didn't get to spend time with yours. I feel a little guilty about that."

But he shook his head. "This was the in-law year, so I was going to either be on my own or have to tag along a little like Barb did. It's not always a comfortable thing. So really, you saved me."

They each moved around the room getting ready for bed. It wasn't until they were both under the blankets that she turned to him and smiled. "I want to thank you."

"For...?"

"You said I saved you, but I want you to know that you saved me too," she quietly admitted. And when he looked at her curiously, she continued. "I've been alone for a long time and I thought it was always going to be that way. I have my kids and my grandkids, and—as you saw—the entire Montgomery family, but it's hard to be here with them when you're the odd one out."

He nodded.

"So, thank you for being gracious enough to come and not only be with my family, but with Joseph's. I'm sure it wasn't comfortable the whole time, but it meant a lot to me."

"You mean a lot to me, Eliza." He paused. "I've enjoyed all the time we've spent together and getting to know each other. Meeting your kids was a great honor." Leaning in, he kissed her again before saying, "I love you."

It was the first time he said it and Eliza felt her heart skip a beat. Swallowing hard, she whispered, "I love you too."

They held each other for a long time before finally giving in to sleep.

In the rest of the house, things were quieting down. Tomorrow was their last day in Asheville, and there was going to be one last massive meal together before having to pack everything up.

Upstairs, Noah was all packed and ready to go. He didn't think anyone would mind if he wasn't there for breakfast. He was eager to get on the road and put this whole thing behind him.

Across the hall, Lily wanted to toss and turn because she couldn't get comfortable, but her collarbone was killing her. Her sisters were still giggling at the fact that she got caught kissing Noah.

"Oh, yeah? Well, earlier tonight, I got to talk to his brother on the phone," she snapped, feeling slightly superior when they both stared at her in shock. "Now can you both just drop the whole kiss thing please?"

In Christian and Sophie's room, she was adjusting the pillows under his ankle while wearing nothing but her white bra and panties. Christian teased her that she was his sexy nurse and she was more than willing to play along.

He spotted an enormous box in the corner of the room. "What's that?"

Glancing over her shoulder, Sophie let out a small sigh. "That was supposed to be here a week ago. It was a surprise gift to you from Noelle. She'd like to open it with you tomorrow if that's okay."

Even though he was wildly curious, he nodded. "Done."

Downstairs, Ethan took Lulu out one last time for the night and when he got back up to his and Summer's room, she took the puppy from him and then warmed him up in the naughtiest of ways. If that was his reward for helping with the dog, he'd gladly do it every night!

Meanwhile, Emma was giving Lucas a bit of a cold shoulder because of his behavior earlier. She knew she'd get over it, but she wanted him to know just how unhappy she was with him. Unfortunately, he was in a black mood and seemed more than happy to be getting the silent treatment.

Several doors down, Willow and Skylar quietly discussed whether they were going to sneak downstairs and bring Cayden up to their room or if they should let him be.

And downstairs, Zach and Gabriella were asleep as soon as their heads hit the pillows, but the last thing they said was they hoped the girls would surprise them by getting Cayden's middle-of-the-night feeding.

In the living room, there was just a small group left—Jason, Maggie, Alex, Megan, Gina, Mac, James, Selena, Casey, and Ryder. The last of the parents had gone to bed, the catering crew was gone, and yet they were all still enjoying having one last drink before heading to their rooms.

"So," Jason said, his arm around Maggie's shoulder as they sat comfortably on one of the sofas. "You guys can go home without worrying about Barb." Then he looked at Selena and Casey. "And you guys have a plan for the business that doesn't include reality TV." He nodded in approval. "Those were some big issues."

"Definitely," they all agreed.

"Um...we have some news too," Megan quietly interrupted.

"Oh?"

She looked at Alex and he nodded. "We're moving to Colorado. Alex got a great job offer and...we're leaving Portland."

"Holy shit!" Ryder said. "When did all this happen?"

"On our way here," Alex said. "We left a few days early and spent a couple of days there to check out the area. I wanted Megan and the kids to be there with me and if they weren't interested, then it wasn't going to happen."

"But...what about your job, Megan?" Casey asked. "Have you told Zach?"

"No, but with everything going on, it didn't seem like the right time. Once we get home, I'll do it."

"Wow. This is all just...wild," James said. "Do you guys realize just how much is going on with everyone? I mean... when does life calm down? When do we just get to relax and maybe coast for a while?"

Jason laughed softly. "What would be the fun in that? I think it's fascinating to watch all these changes and it keeps us on our toes. And I think it's going to be even more fun watching what all our kids are doing in say...five years." He winked. "Don't you?"

"Ugh...I don't even want to think about that right now," Megan said as she got to her feet. "I'm beat." Alex stood with her. "We'll see you guys in the morning. Goodnight!"

"Goodnight!"

It didn't take long for everyone to follow suit, and before long, everyone was in their rooms and the big old house was dark and quiet. But they all knew it wouldn't stay that way for long.

# EPILOGUE

## JANUARY 2ND - DINNER

### "CARE TO MAKE IT INTERESTING?"

One long table was covered in Chinese takeout.

There was a fire roaring in the fireplace and there was some Frank Sinatra playing on the sound system. All the kids and grandkids were gone and it was pleasantly peaceful.

"I know I should say that it feels strange without everyone here, but...I'm just enjoying it too much!" Janice said as she reached for the dumplings.

"I have to agree," Monica said. "Although for us, they all live within fifteen minutes of us, so I'm sure we'll have a houseful this weekend whether we're ready for it or not."

"I wish all of mine lived closer," Eliza said as she helped herself to the wonton soup. "But it always gives me something to look forward to, whether I'm traveling to see them or someone's coming to see me." She shrugged. "But as of right now, no one's doing any of that until March. I should be recovered by then."

They all laughed.

"If you ask me, this is the way it's supposed to be," Robert said as he poured the wine. "You get together and have a wonderful visit, but then you get to go home and go back to your regular routine." Then he looked at his wife. "But I have a feeling we're going to be traveling back and forth to Portland more now that there's a new baby."

"Oh, absolutely!" Janice agreed. "I'm still in shock over the whole thing, but I know we need to give them some time to settle in at home with the baby. As much as I want to be there just like I was with all the other grandkids, I think after being together here for two weeks, they're eager for it to just be the five of them."

"And rightly so," William said. "You'll know when the time is right to go and visit." He smiled as he accepted the container of fried rice from Phillip. "Thank you." He paused. "So I hope we didn't overwhelm you, Phillip! We're a bit of a rowdy bunch and there was some more drama than usual."

Phillip waved him off. "Every family has drama. I just hope I didn't add to it too much." He laughed softly. "When Eliza and I talked about me joining her here for the holidays, we had no idea how everyone was going to react."

"You were a pleasant surprise," Robert told him with a smile. "And I hear you were a hit with everyone."

"Well…I tried to simply take my cues from everyone. Hopefully no one's going to call Eliza tomorrow and demand that she stop seeing me."

"That's not going to happen," Eliza told him, patting his hand. "I won't allow that to happen. They all have someone, and now I do too." She looked around at all the food. "Did we order any spring rolls?"

"I've got them over here by me," Barb said, passing the container down. "I want to thank you for asking me to stay. I would have been fine driving back to Charlotte with Gina and Mac, but it would have been so crowded in that car with all of us and the luggage." She shuddered dramatically.

Monica nodded. "I know it's only a two-hour drive, but it's still a lot when you're not fully comfortable. You can't relax!"

"Exactly!" she agreed. "Plus, I think after everything Gina and I discussed, I'm sure she and Mac wanted some time to think about all of it."

"So you're really set with this assisted living complex?" Janice asked. "I feel like you're almost too young for such a thing."

"I thought so too, but the reality is that I'm not," she said with a small laugh. "Just thinking about not having to worry about any kind of maintenance and how I won't have to cook for myself unless I want to...plus, there are all kinds of activities scheduled every day so I'm not alone."

"Well, I think it sounds fantastic," Eliza said. "It's important to stay active and to be around other people. Living alone is hard."

"I agree," Barb said. "And there are a lot of single men living there, so...you never know. Maybe next Christmas I'll be the one introducing a new beau!"

They all laughed and encouraged her.

"So William," Robert said, after taking a sip of his wine. "What are you going to do about Noah and Lucas?"

But William waved him off. "Lucas will cool down in time, and it's not like he and Noah work directly together."

"Still...I thought he was going to strangle the poor boy!"

"Oh, I'm sure he was, but I think Lily would have stopped that from happening. She was very adamant about telling us all that she was the one to kiss Noah."

"I was hoping that would happen," Monica said slyly. "She dates the worst boys. Always has. She has a rebellious streak a mile wide! And I don't know where she gets it because her sisters aren't like that, none of my boys were like that, and from everything I know about Emma from her parents, she wasn't either!"

"Lily's always been her own thinker," William commented. "She came out of the womb and was fiercely independent and did her own thing. Personally, I think it's great that she dates all the wrong guys."

All eyes turned and looked at him like he were insane, which made him laugh heartily.

"Because when the right man is introduced into her life...like at a family holiday event...maybe she'll realize she was wrong." Then, with a shrug, he took a bite of one of his spring rolls.

"William!" Janice said with pure amusement. "Are you saying you...?"

"At first, there was a genuine reason for Noah to be here. But then I got the idea and...I had to be creative in order to keep him here," he replied simply. "Granted, I didn't plan on him having to stay as long as he did—that was fate."

"But...how did you know he and Lily would connect?" Eliza asked.

He grinned. "As we all know, I'm no novice at this sort of thing. I genuinely like Noah. He's an excellent employee and a respectful young man. But now that I've had some time to get to know him outside of the office? I'm even more convinced that he's perfect for Lily."

"William," Monica chided. "You can't possibly know that. She spent half Noah's time here being annoyed with him. And the kiss last night was a fluke!"

"Or...do you think it's the start of something wonderful?" he suggested. "I guess only time will tell, but I see this as a beginning, not an end."

"I think you're ridiculous," Janice said with a tsk. "Not every couple you think belongs together ends up together. Haven't you ever made a misstep in this matchmaking thing of yours?"

He shook his head. "Sorry, but...no. I'm telling you, I just know." He took another bite of his dinner before continuing. "Do I think they're suddenly going to fall madly in love? Absolutely not. But I also know that Lily's going to be back home in Charlotte for the next few months, and whenever she's home, she tends to come to the office frequently to see me."

"Oh, good Lord..." Monica said with a sigh.

"So I plan on inviting her to lunch maybe...once a week. And maybe on those days that she meets me there, I'll be finishing up a meeting with Noah. I'm telling you, by this time next year, we'll be planning a wedding."

Everyone laughed and they ate in companionable silence for a few moments before his brother spoke up. "Care to make it interesting?"

William arched a brow at him. "How so?"

"I don't think your granddaughter is going to fall that soon. She's dealing with an injury and she has big plans for dance positions later in the spring." He looked around the table when everyone seemed to stare at him. "What? I spent some time talking with her and she told me about the different tryouts she had on her calendar!"

"You're so sweet," Janice said, leaning in and kissing him on the cheek.

"Anyway," he went on. "I'm thinking this should be a three-to-five-year plan. She shouldn't have to give up her dreams just because you've decided you found the right man for her."

"Noah Wylder is the right man!"

"Then he shouldn't mind waiting, should he," Robert stated.

William glared at his brother. "Okay, here's what I propose—if Lily and Noah aren't a serious item and getting engaged in two years..."

"You said by the end of the year," Robert reminded him.

"I've reconsidered based on you reminding me of Lily's upcoming schedule," he countered. "So if they're not engaged in two years, then I will give you...my boat."

"William!" Monica cried. "I love that boat! You can't just give it away!"

Robert chuckled, shaking his head. "I have my own boat. I was thinking more of..."

"No," Janice interrupted. "There is not going to be a wager, do you hear me? This isn't a game. You're dealing with people's lives. And if you're both trying to win something, you're going to push the odds in your favor."

"I agree," Monica said, admonishing both men. "Shame on you. We never resorted to wagers in the past. Let's just see where this one goes, okay?"

"Fine," both men grumbled.

"Excellent! Now, who has the shrimp lo mein?"

But William and Robert exchanged glances and knew they'd pick up this conversation as soon as they were alone, and personally, William couldn't wait. He'd done a hell of a job finding the perfect match for his sons, nieces, and nephews. It only seemed fair that he had the opportunity to do it for the next generation.

WHAT HAPPENS TO NOAH WYLDER
AFTER HIS CHRISTMAS WITH THE
MONTGOMERYS??

Find out in

# PROLOGUE

SWEAT WAS LITERALLY POURING off her body, and her hair was practically matted to her head. Her heart was racing, her throat was dry, but as the choreographer took his spot in the corner of the room, Lily Montgomery took her position and waited for the music to begin.

The bass beat started, and Tag loudly counted them down. "And five, six, seven, eight! Hold, two, three, four, right left, right left, pull...pull..." He clapped almost aggressively as he continued to count out the movements and Lily knew she was nailing every one of them. This particular piece was jazz infused with hip-hop, and when Tag smiled and winked at her as she strutted across the room, she knew he was pleased.

Catching her reflection in the mirror, she spun several times before leaping three times along with the fifteen other dancers currently on the floor. It wasn't until she landed and held her pose that she felt a twinge of pain in her hip that wasn't there before.

*Shake it off...*

The routine was new and challenging, and perhaps she over-extended on that last leap. Either way, when they took their water break, she'd do a little extra stretching just to play it safe.

"Take five!" Tag called out. "And when we start back, I'd like to see a little enthusiasm out of all of you, not just some of you!" He turned away without another word.

It wasn't the first time class went on past midnight this week, so that didn't throw her. But looking around at the full group–all thirty-six of them–it didn't look like everyone was feeling the same way. Tryouts for this year's squad was apparently going to be brutal, and as much as this had been a bucket list thing for her, she hadn't expected there to be so much competitive precision this long before auditions. She had come to Miami to get situated and settle in long before auditions–which were still almost six months away. Unfortunately, her chance to dance with the squad at the Dolphins' games wasn't guaranteed yet.

But it would be.

She'd danced for a year as a Rockette and she did another year performing with the national tour of Hairspray. Basically, she'd grown bored with New York and doing the Broadway thing and was ready to tackle the world of NFL cheerleading. When she'd seen some of the competition, she'd played up the fact that her father was a bit of a legend in the world of football. He'd been forced to retire because of an injury back before she was born, but his name still opened the door for her here.

And even though it stung a bit that she'd had to resort to dropping names, it just made her all that more determined to prove to everyone that she deserved to be here.

*I've got this...*

With a shrug, Lily went to the back corner where her

bag was and pulled out a bottle of water. Taking a long drink, she allowed herself a solid minute to let her mind go blank before getting down on the floor and stretching.

Her nose was touching the floor when her friend Drea sat down beside her, mimicking the pose. "I'm ready to shoot Tag with a tranquilizer dart," she murmured. "I don't know why he doesn't call out the specific people who are screwing up." Turning her head, she grinned at Lily. "Because I don't see why you and I have to be punished for other people not learning the damn routine."

Lily straightened for a moment before bending to touch her nose to her left knee and winced.

"You okay?"

She hesitated only for a second before forcing a smile. "Yeah. I guess I didn't stretch as well as I thought I had earlier."

"Oh, same," Drea said, mimicking all of Lily's moves.

They were new friends, but...like...dance friends. They rarely hung out together outside the studio or rehearsals. It wasn't intentional, but mostly because once they were done rehearsing each night, Lily went home and slept for almost twelve hours. She knew she needed a break, but she was making up for some lost time after breaking her collarbone three years ago in a freak accident.

*Still...it would be nice to go home and see everyone...*

"And we're back!" Tag called out. He was a fantastic choreographer, but she wished they could move on to some-thing new.

Both she and Drea got to their feet, finishing their waters. "I bet Tag picks me to be in his top five tonight," Drea said confidently. "He's been winking at me all night, so I know he sees how I'm nailing the choreography."

"Or maybe he's just got some sort of nervous tick," Lily muttered.

"*What?*" The friendly girl she'd been chatting with was gone judging by the sneer she was giving Lily.

"I'm just saying...he's winked at me too," she quickly explained.

Muttering something under her breath, Drea stormed off, leaving Lily standing there, shaking her head.

*Diva...*

"Let me get group one up first!" Tag ordered. "And I want you all to watch Lily! If I had to pick someone to make the team right now, she'd get my vote!"

While she wanted to gloat, she didn't.

She did, however, smile sweetly at Drea as she took her position.

"And five, six, seven, eight! Hold, two, three, four, right left, right left, pull...pull..." he commanded, as he clapped with each count throughout the short routine. "And turn! Turn! Leap! Higher! Three, four..."

The music was blaring, and Lily was in her element. Everything she wanted was within her reach.

"Keep it going!" Tag yelled as he paced along the mirrored wall until the music ended. "I want to see that one more time and want those leaps higher and more powerful!" He clicked the music on again from the beginning and counted them in once more.

Slightly winded, she immediately jumped right into it as if she'd had a break. She smiled, she preened, she mentally high-fived herself when Tag winked at her with a nod of approval. She had this—she knew she had this. There was a bit of a high that she got from dancing, and right now, she was experiencing it at a whole new level.

The big finish was coming up again. She nailed her

turns and swiveled her hips in a sexy little move before taking her three steps and...

"Leap! Leap! *Leap!*" he called out, but something in Lily's hip snapped as she crashed to the floor in excruciating pain.

*Well...shit...*

# CHAPTER ONE

THERE WERE dozens of butterflies in Lily Montgomery's belly threatening to take flight. Today was the day she was both looking forward to and dreading.

The day she found out if she was cleared to go back to dancing.

It had been three months since that fateful leap at dance rehearsals–three months since her dream pretty much crashed and died as she'd crumbled to the floor–but with any luck, her scans would show that she was good to go. With nothing else to do but wait, she pulled out her phone and figured she'd scroll through social media to kill time until the doctor finally came in to see her.

There were three missed calls and two texts from her mother.

Yeah...she'd been avoiding talking to her family because she knew they were worried about her and truth be known, she was worried about herself too. It was safer to keep her distance, otherwise she'd completely breakdown and wallow in self-pity. The missed calls had been on the phone for almost a week and she hadn't listened to the voicemails, but the texts were new.

**Mom: Lily, whatever it is I did to upset you, I'm sorry. I've left you multiple messages and your father said not to pester you, but I'm concerned.**

She laughed softly. Since her father had been a pro-athlete when he was younger, he understood how an injury could mess with your psychologically and the importance of people giving you space while you heal. Clearly he was running interference for her.

**Mom: We've got some stuff going on here and I know I've been a little distracted, but please call me. I miss you.**

Tears stung her eyes because...yeah...she missed her too.

She just didn't want the pity she'd been getting ever since her injury. It was almost as if her mother knew something she didn't–like this injury was going to end her career. Glancing around the office, she chose to take it as a good sign that she was sitting here rather than an exam room. Although...

The door opened and Dr. Mathis walked in. She was the orthopedist she'd been working with since her injury. She was in her forties, specialized in sports injuries, and came highly recommended. From the moment they'd met, she'd been nothing but kind and understanding, and always put Lily's mind at ease. But as she walked by on her way to her desk, she suddenly looked a bit imposing.

"Well?"

Dr. Mathis took a seat behind her desk and let out a soft breath. "I wish I had better news for you, Lily, but..."

Her heart sank.

"But I'm not healing," she said miserably. She'd been preparing herself for this day. After three months of physical therapy, she definitely felt better, but not healed. With her shoulders sagging, she braced herself for what came next. "So? What are my options?"

With a patient smile, Dr. Mathis replied, "That depends on what you're looking to do."

"Meaning?"

"Meaning, if you want to go back to dancing full-time, then surgery is really your only option."

"What if I don't do the cheering? I know that was way more aggressive and challenging than anything I'd ever done before. What if I go back to the Rockettes or...or... Broadway? Or..."

"I can tell by that response that surgery isn't an option for you."

It really wasn't. The thought of it terrified her because there were too many 'what if' things that could happen.

She shrugged. "Not that it's *not* an option, but...I want to make sure we exhaust every other option first. I know I've rested; I've done P/T, I've done the over the counter pain relievers..." She paused. "What about the shot? We haven't done the cortisone shot yet."

"We haven't," Dr. Mathis agreed. "But it's not a cure, Lily. I need you to understand that. Cortisone shots can provide relief for anywhere from two weeks to six months, but that's it."

"And will I be able to dance during that time?" She had already lost valuable prep time for the cheer squad and didn't have anything else lined up. Fortunately, there were normally auditions open year-round all over the world for all kinds of shows if she wasn't too picky.

The look Dr. Mathis gave her wasn't optimistic. "I think you can try, but you'll end up aggravating the injury more." Pausing, she got up and walked across her office and pulled a brochure off one of her bookshelves. "This is some litera- ture about the surgery. The recovery time is lengthy—three to six months—but I truly believe it's the best option for you."

She begrudgingly accepted the brochure. Surgery was the absolute last thing she wanted to do. Call her stubborn, but she truly believed she would heal on her own.

The thought made her laugh. How many times had she heard the stories about her father and his stubbornness regarding surgery for an injury he received while playing pro football?

*Like father, like daughter.*

Still...maybe she could talk to him about this and get his input. So far she'd downplayed her injury to her family and had even turned down multiple invites to go home for a visit because she didn't want anyone fussing over her. The last time they'd done that was after the ski lift accident three years ago. Her father and two of her cousins had been injured as well, but it felt like everyone hovered over her during her recovery until she thought she'd go mad.

Unfortunately, it didn't look like she had much choice. Her short-term rental lease was almost up, and it just made sense to go home to North Carolina and regroup.

"Okay, I promise to think about it," she told Dr. Mathis.

Nodding, she sat back down behind her desk. "I hope you don't just think about," she said carefully. "I think you should go for another opinion. Maybe two. Talking to more professionals may help you understand a bit more what an injury like this can look like in the long term, whether or not you do the surgery."

She hadn't thought of seeing another doctor; mainly because Dr. Mathis was the top in her field in this part of the country. But perhaps it was something she could also ask her father about, since he had to make a similar decision regarding his own surgery.

"I'll do that," she finally said. "I'm planning on heading back home to North Carolina and I'll look up some doctors there."

Smiling, Dr. Mathis asked, "Where in North Carolina?"

"Charlotte. That's where I'm from and my family is all still there."

"I actually have several colleagues that I can highly recommend in the area, plus several at Duke. I know that's a few hours from where you live, but…"

"I appreciate any recommendations. My dad played in the NFL back in the day and had to have multiple surgeries after an injury. I'm sure he'll have some names as well." Then she paused. "Although most of those doctors may have retired by now." Laughing softly, she shook her head. "That would be my luck."

"I know this isn't the news you were hoping for, but this isn't the end of your career. It's a small detour. You're young and healthy and you're obviously willing to do the work to get better."

She nodded. "Thanks. It's all just…it's a lot. This is the second injury in the last few years and…well…it's scary. Dance is all I know," she admitted quietly.

That's when she saw the sympathy on the doctor's face and it nearly made her cry. But rather than give in to that feeling, she forced herself to sit up straighter and forced herself to smile.

"But I'd really like the shot just to get me through until I decide. Is that okay?"

"Absolutely." Standing, Dr. Mathis walked around her desk and came to stand beside her. Giving Lily's shoulder a reassuring squeeze, she said, "Give me a minute and I'll get a nurse to set you up in one of the exam rooms."

"Thanks, Dr. Mathis."

An hour later, she was walking into her apartment with mild discomfort. The damn shot hurt almost as much as the injury. Tossing her purse on the sofa, she gently collapsed next to it with a groan. The smart thing to do was call her mother and let her know she was coming home, but...it could be fun to surprise her again. No one made her feel more loved or missed like her mom. Tears stung her eyes as she slowly nodded because...yeah. It was time to go home.

Glancing around the apartment, she knew there wasn't really a whole lot she needed to do. The place came furnished–including all the pots, pans, and dishes–so realistically, she could have all her personal stuff packed within the next day or two. Some things she'd ship home, but the rest she could toss in the car with her.

"I could realistically be home by Friday and get the whole weekend with everyone," she murmured. And just the thought of sitting down to dinner with all of them and then going to see her grandparents over the weekend was enough to spur her into action.

It was barely lunchtime, and she opted to throw a quick salad together before she began packing. But once she got started, she dove into it like she did everything else–with every ounce of energy and a determination to get it done.

First, she made a bag of clothes to donate. Next, she

went through her pantry and filled a box with unopened food to take to the local food pantry. Then she packed up all her non-essential things that she could ship first. Fortunately, she kept all the boxes she had moved in with, so it was just a matter of putting them back together and taping them for packing. Once she knew how many she was going to ship, she called her neighbor Robin to see if she could borrow her pickup truck so she could get them all to the UPS store. By four in the afternoon, she had called the leasing office to let them know she was moving out early, made arrangements to get the keys to them, and was loading everything into Robin's truck—with Robin's help—before driving all around town dropping them off.

After stopping to buy more tape, she was back home by dinnertime and made herself another salad before tackling laundry and more packing. The next thing she knew, it was midnight and, although she was exhausted, she was also done.

"I don't know if I'm pathetic for not having a lot of stuff or proud that I'm super-efficient," she said with a laugh. There were a handful of framed pictures on her dresser that were the last things she needed to pack. Looking at them always cheered her up when she was feeling down, and it was only natural that they'd be the final things she put away. She was carefully wrapping them to place in one of her suitcases when she picked up the one from Christmas three years ago. It was a silly picture, really. A group shot where no one was really posing, but they all knew the picture was being taken. With a smile, Lily gently ran her finger over the glass. She was standing with her cousins, Willow, Harry, and Tanner.

And Noah Wylder.

Ugh...Noah Wylder.

He was with them for Christmas due to work reasons, not because he was related. He'd shown up for what was supposed to be one night and ended up staying for over a week. Even after all these years, she still wished she could go back in time and stop herself from the humiliation of that trip and her behavior toward him.

And with him.

She groaned and quickly wrapped the picture up. If she stared at it any longer, she knew she'd still remember every moment of their kiss at midnight on New Year's. Her boyfriend had dumped her via text, she was lonely and hated the thought of being alone when the ball dropped, so...she'd kissed Noah.

And he'd kissed her back.

Spectacularly.

Yeah, he might be a numbers nerd like the rest of her family, but the man certainly knew how to kiss.

Sadly, she hadn't been kissed like that since.

Damn him.

"Okay, no more thinking about *that*," she quietly reprimanded herself. "You have a job to do here. Finish packing and you could potentially be on the road tomorrow."

It was an almost twelve-hour drive back to Charlotte and while that normally wouldn't bother her, she needed to be logical. She had some things to take care of before she just hopped in her car and drove home, but...if she did the drive in two days...

Yawning, she gave herself a full body stretch and decided to call it a day. She'd take the two days to get home, arrive there on Thursday–earlier than she originally planned even with the extra day of driving–and could settle in and relax.

Stripping out of her sweaty clothes, she contemplated a

shower, but ultimately decided against it. She'd wash the sheets and take a shower in the morning before she left. And as she crawled into bed, she couldn't help but smile. In forty-eight hours, she'd be home with the people she loved most in this world.

And hopefully closer to figuring out what was next for her.

Getting called into his boss's office wasn't anything new and it certainly wasn't cause for alarm.

It was the other people in the office with him that still made him quake in his shoes a bit.

Three years.

Three damn years and he was still getting the stink eye from Lucas Montgomery over a stunt his daughter pulled. A stunt that she admitted to being responsible for, and yet Lucas was still holding a grudge toward him.

Noah Wylder was used to dealing with stubborn people. Hell, he was related to the most stubborn man in the world. But with the way his boss's son was still trying to intimidate him, he'd have to say he was the second most stubborn man in the world.

And he was tired of it.

Noah was an excellent employee and got along well with William Montgomery and his three sons until he went to Asheville three years ago. He was invited to their family holiday retreat to finalize important contract work for their merger because they trusted him. Unfortunately, the weather had turned and Noah had essentially gotten snowed in with them. He had been making great strides in securing the fast track to making it to the executive level, and the time he gained with them out of the office had been invaluable.

And then Lily Montgomery–Lucas' daughter–had derailed everything for him.

Okay, maybe not *everything*, but it had taken months to get everyone to see him as the same model employee he'd been before the holidays and not the guy who kissed the Montgomery princess on New Year's Eve. A kiss that she loudly announced she'd initiated. And yet...it felt a little like he was still being punished.

At least it was only one Montgomery still holding a grudge and not the rest, but...geez.

Knocking on William Montgomery's door, he forced himself to smile as he stepped in. "You wanted to see me, Sir?"

"Noah!" William said jovially. "Good to see you! Have a seat!"

Naturally, the only seat available was next to Lucas.

*Great.*

He nodded t both Mac and Jason and then did his best to avoid eye contact completely with Lucas as he sat. Then he waited to hear why he was there.

"Noah," William began, "My sons are going to be away for the next month. They're leaving Thursday morning and taking their wives on a Mediterranean cruise that was a gift from Monica and myself."

"O-kay..."

"We've been talking," he went on. "And we'd like you to step in and oversee their top clients while they're gone."

Noah was fairly certain his eyes were comically large. "Really? You *all* want me to do this?"

Everyone clearly caught what he was really asking, and luckily, they all laughed.

Even Lucas.

"We've all taken time away from our clients for holidays and vacations," Mac explained. "But this is the first time we're going to be away for this long. You're the strongest guy we have and while we'll be sharing our clients within our own teams, we each have a few that require a little more attention."

"You excel at that," Jason chimed in. "I don't want to say they're difficult, because they're not. These are the clients that prefer to call in at least once a week so they know exactly what their money is doing."

"I can handle that," he told them.

"Going through our lists, we each had two to three clients that we felt you'd be a better fit with rather than anyone else," Lucas added, and Noah wondered if it physically hurt him to have to give him even that tiny bit of praise. "However, we weren't sure what your current list of clients is like or if you even have the time to take on more—even if it's temporary."

"How many exactly would I be responsible for?"

"Seven," Mac said. "Possibly eight. I'm still working some things out."

Nodding, he worked out in his head what that would look like for him. Realistically, it could be as simple as an additional ten hours a week. His schedule wasn't jam-packed so it wouldn't require any overtime—and even if it did, it would be minimal.

"You'd also have all our assistants available to help you with anything you needed," Jason said after a moment. "We realize we're putting a rather hefty workload on you, so if you need someone to take on a few of the smaller tasks, Andrew, Kylie, and Joanne can handle it."

"And the same goes for Sara," William added. "Rose is

now officially retired and this will be her first week completely going solo, but I think she'd be just fine if you needed her for something, Noah. Don't be afraid to ask."

The mirthless laugh was out before he could stop it. "Um...I think I should be more than okay with three assistants. If I need to get Sara involved, then maybe I'm not the right guy to help with this."

"No one's saying you're not the right guy or that you're even going to need the help. We're just letting you know that help is available if you need it," Mac corrected. "I know I'd be a little hesitant if someone told me I'd be managing eight extra accounts for a month."

"I thought you said seven?" Jason reminded him.

He shrugged. "Changed my mind. I think Noah can handle them all."

All four Montgomerys were looking at him expectantly and it was the first time in...well...three years that he felt like he had finally earned their respect.

Even Lucas'.

"This really means a lot," he said, his voice gruffer than he intended. "I appreciate your confidence in me, and I don't want any of you to worry about your clients. I'll take good care of them."

"Excellent!" William said as he shifted slightly in his seat. "Now, why don't we go over all the accounts you're entrusting Noah with, so if there are any questions, he can ask you directly." He shifted again in his chair and seemed to grimace.

"Dad?" Lucas asked. "Are you okay?"

"What? Oh...I'm fine. I slept the wrong way and my back's a little sensitive today." He laughed softly. "It's not easy getting old."

After that, they spent the rest of the day discussing

clients and making sure Noah felt comfortable with everyone's accounts. It was a little overwhelming, but he also knew there were plenty of people available to help if he needed it.

It was a little after five when he walked out of the office, and as he walked to his car, he contemplated whether to pick up a pizza or shopping for groceries.

With a weary sigh, he climbed into his car and knew he was going to do the practical thing and shop for groceries. With the extra work he was going to be doing for the next month, it would just be smarter for him to stock up on things he could easily pack up and take to the office for lunch.

"Probably going to be spending a lot of time at my desk rather than going out on my lunch break," he murmured, but he wasn't particularly upset about that prospect. Instead, he was thrilled to have this opportunity. He had a plan for his life and this was the first time in a long time that he felt like everything could work out. If things went well over this next month, maybe by the time everyone was back from vacation, they'd see he was someone who was a prime candidate for a promotion, and possibly a good choice to head up his own office. Just a small one; he wouldn't be opposed to branching out somewhere outside of Charlotte. He wasn't particularly tied to the area.

Hell, he wasn't particularly tied to any area.

If they suggested wanting to open an office in the northern-most tip of Alaska, he'd say yes to it. If it meant securing his future? He'd go wherever they asked him to.

His mother was still here in North Carolina, but she was about five hours northeast of Charlotte in the same small town he'd grown up in. He went home to visit occasionally, but it wasn't a place that held any good memories for him. In the last ten years, whenever he and his brothers got together with their mom, it was a neutral location. But that was mainly because his middle brother was a pop star who was seemingly always on tour, and his baby brother was playing football in Wichita. They all led very busy lives and spent more time on Zoom calls with one another than actually sitting in the same room.

Unlike the Montgomerys.

It didn't matter that he'd been working for them for almost four years, it still boggled his mind a bit at just how close they all were. And not just the four that he worked with–although how they could all want to go on vacation with one another after working together every damn day was a mystery to him–but the entire extended family. The Christmas he had gotten snowed in with them in Asheville, there had been over fifty of them in the house! And all they talked about were all the things they enjoyed doing together. Shuddering, Noah pulled into the Wegman's parking lot while mentally making a shopping list.

It took a little over an hour for him to walk through the door of his condo with his arms loaded with bags. He was somehow both energized and exhausted, but more than anything, he was starving. Placing the bags down on the granite countertop, he kicked off his shoes and strode into his bedroom to change into a pair of shorts and a t-shirt. The place was a little on the small side–only one bedroom and one bathroom plus an office–but he didn't need a lot of space. The location was fantastic, and it offered a concierge, fitness center, clubhouse and next day dry cleaning services.

It was a single guy's dream, even if it was a little too quiet for him sometimes.

Six months ago, the girl he'd been dating for almost a

year broke up with him. She said he worked too much, was never around, and basically was a huge bore.

Noah shrugged it off. He hadn't been in love with her and even though he'd cared about her, if she didn't understand what he was trying to accomplish, then it wasn't meant to be. Some day he hoped to get married, but not until he was financially secure and firmly settled in his career. Only then would he feel confident that he could put the time into a relationship that was needed.

"So maybe I'm a little rigid," he mumbled as he walked back out to the kitchen and began putting groceries away. "There's nothing wrong with that. I would never tell anyone I was involved with that they had to work less just so they could hang out with me. A good work ethic is important."

And apparently...boring.

Okay, that one stung, but it was just bad timing. Plus, he was still trying to prove himself at Montgomerys. In a month from now, he knew he'd be able to breathe easier.

"And it's gonna feel great."

Once everything was away and the countertops wiped down, he grabbed the steak he'd purchased as a bit of a celebratory thing, and placed it under the broiler. Next, he grabbed the ready-made side of mashed potatoes and green beans and heated them up. Looking across the room, he spotted a bottle of merlot that would really go great with the meal and decided he deserved that too. Only one glass since he had to work in the morning, and he was going to savor it.

When the food was ready, he carried his plate and glass into the living room and put them down on the coffee table before going back for silverware and the salt. When he finally sat down on the sofa, he turned on the TV to CNN and got caught up on the day's news.

Another hour later, he was pleasantly full and utterly

bored. It was only eight o'clock and he was sitting alone with nothing to do.

"I should probably see if there's anything going on downtown this weekend," he said as he cleaned up the dinner mess. Maybe he'd call a few friends and see about going out for drinks or something. For the next month, he was going to be busy with work and doing everything he could to make a great impression on his bosses.

And maybe after that, he'd look into getting out a little more and perhaps finding a hobby.

Not that it was helping him right now.

For now, he sat back down on the sofa with his iPad and scrolled aimlessly until it was time to go to bed.

It definitely was a solitary life, and he was okay with it.

At least...that's what he kept telling himself.

He liked things neat and orderly; quiet and uncomplicated. He'd grown up in an extremely chaotic environment, and always swore that as soon as he was old enough to move out, he'd embrace the peace and simplicity of a normal life.

And he'd found it.

He was living it.

But as he climbed into bed and turned out the light, a strange thought hit him.

*Am I really even living?*

Get IRRESISTIBLE LOVE here:
https://www.chasing-romance.com/irresistible-love

And check out the entire MONTGOMERY series here:
https://www.chasing-romance.com/the-montgomery-brothers-series

## ALSO BY SAMANTHA CHASE

**The Donovans Series (Laurel Bay):**

Call Me

Dare Me

Tempt Me

Save Me

Charm Me

Kiss Me

**The Donovans Series (Sweetbriar Ridge):**

Loving You

Teasing You

**The Magnolia Sound Series:**

Sunkissed Days

Remind Me

A Girl Like You

In Case You Didn't Know

All the Befores

And Then One Day

Can't Help Falling in Love

Last Beautiful Girl

The Way the Story Goes

Since You've Been Gone

Nobody Does It Better

Wedding Wonderland

Always on my Mind

Kiss the Girl


**Meet Me at the Altar:**

The Engagement Embargo

With this Cake

You May Kiss the Groomsman

The Proposal Playbook

Groomed to Perfection

The I Do Over


**The Enchanted Bridal Series:**

The Wedding Season

Friday Night Brides

The Bridal Squad

Glam Squad & Groomsmen

Bride & Seek

## The RoadTripping Series

Drive Me Crazy

Wrong Turn

Test Drive

Head Over Wheels

## The Montgomery Brothers Series:

Wait for Me

Trust in Me

Stay with Me

More of Me

Return to You

Meant for You

I'll Be There

Until There Was Us

Suddenly Mine

A Dash of Christmas

A Merry Montgomery Christmas

## The Wylder Love Series:

Irresistible Love

Indescribable Love

Undeniable Love

Christmas Inn Love

The Christmas Plan

**Life, Love & Babies Series:**

The Baby Arrangement

Baby, Be Mine

Baby, I'm Yours

**Preston's Mill Series:**

Roommating

Speed Dating

Complicating

**The Protectors Series:**

Protecting His Best Friend's Sister

Protecting the Enemy Protecting

the Girl Next Door Protecting the

Movie Star

**7 Brides for 7 Soldiers:**
Ford

**7 Brides for 7
Blackthornes:**

Logan

## Standalone Novels:

Jordan's Return Catering

to the CEO

In the Eye of the Storm A

Touch of Heaven

Exclusive

Moonlight in Winter Park

Waiting for Midnight

Mistletoe Between Friends

Snowflake Inn

His for the Holidays

# ABOUT SAMANTHA CHASE

Samantha Chase is a New York Times and USA Today bestseller of contemporary romance that's hotter than sweet, sweeter than hot. She released her debut novel in 2011 and currently has more than ninety titles under her belt – including THE CHRISTMAS COTTAGE which was a Hallmark Christmas movie in 2017 and WEDDING SEASON which was a Hallmark June Wedding movie in 2023! She's a Disney enthusiast who still happily listens to 80's rock. When she's not working on a new story, she spends her time reading romances, playing way too many games of Solitaire online, wearing a tiara while playing with her sassy pug Maylene...oh, and spending time with her husband of 34 years and their two sons in Wake Forest, North Carolina.

Sign up for my mailing list and get exclusive content and chances to win members-only prizes!
https://www.chasing-romance.com/newsletter

Start a fun new small town romance series:
https://www.chasing-romance.com/the-donovans-series

## Where to Find Me:

Website:
www.chasing-romance.com

-

Facebook:
www.facebook.com/
SamanthaChaseFanClub

<u>Instagram:</u>

https://www.instagram.com/samanthachaseromance/

Twitter:
https://twitter.com/SamanthaChase3

Reader Group:
https://www.facebook.com/groups/1034673493228089/

Made in the USA
Monee, IL
13 November 2023

46470998R00215